Where The Green Grass Grows

Where The Green Grass Grows

This is a work of fiction.
All characters and events portrayed in this book are fictional,
and any resemblance to real people is purely coincidental.

For information contact: Shalako Press
P.O. Box 371, Oakdale, CA 95361-0371
http://www.shalakopress.com

ISBN: 978-0-9846811-4-3

Cover photo of Seth Riley & Kelly McKinley by author
Cover design: Karen Borrelli
Editor: Judith Mitchell

PRINTED IN THE UNITED STATES OF AMERICA

Dedication

*To my father, Clarence, whose collection of Zane Gray
books gave me a love for the old west.*

Acknowledgments

This book is a combined effort of many people. I would like to thank Kelly Phillips and Lauren O'Brien for their input and helping to correct my mistakes.

A big thanks to Seth Riley and Kelly McKinley for allowing me to use their photograph on the cover.

And as always, hugs and kisses to my editor-in-chief and wife, Judy, who always turns my hieroglyphics into something readable. Thanks kid.

WHERE THE GREEN GRASS GROWS

The butcher knife in Ida Ollar's hand hissed as she pulled it repeatedly across the whetstone. She stopped and stared blankly at the dirty window pane as she checked the edge with her thumb. It was as sharp as any barber's razor in Kansas but she continued moving the blade back and forth, to pass time more than anything else. And time was something Ida had plenty of. It seemed to creep more slowly each day as the weeds outside the drafty one-room shack grew tall, like prison bars. But today, God willing, she would be set free, one way or the other.

Her dark brown eyes set into deep sockets had become large holes that refused to see any of the beauty of the grasslands beyond her window. She paused once again to brush back a strand of black hair that had been salted generously with gray. Her teeth felt loose inside her hollow cheeks and her once healthy body had taken on the appearance of a skeleton with skin stretched over the top. Her stomach used to ache, but she hadn't felt any hunger pains in quite awhile now. She was amazed that her skin still bruised, but her swollen and discolored cheek still bore the evidence of the last beating Lowell had given her. She had turned into an old woman at the age of twenty-eight and was looking forward to death.

"Lord, I ain't never asked you for much, simply because I don't know if you exist like most folks think. But in case you really are somewheres up there, just give me this one thing. Let me kill him, or cause him to kill me this time, because I can't take anymore." She put the whetstone on the table as she heard his horse trotting into the yard. Rising from the chair, she backed against the stone fireplace and held the knife in the folds of her skirt behind her.

"I want my baby, Lowell," she said as he banged the door open.

"What?" He steadied himself against the frame.

"I want my baby. She was all I had, and I want her back. Now!"

"Oh, will you shut the hell up about that baby? You're so skinny you couldn't feed or take care of her anyway." He staggered inside and slammed the door.

"And who's fault is that? You drank up all the money, then sold everything we had and drank that up too."

"Ain't nothing wrong with a man taking a little drink now and then."

"You won't work. You won't plow the ground. There's not even any seeds to plant a garden with." She continued as though she hadn't heard his argument. "There's nothing for me to eat in this house. You eat in town with your friends when you're drinking, don't you?"

"Hush your mouth, woman." He made a threatening motion with the back of his hand but she didn't flinch.

"You sold her to that couple in that big wagon with the fancy clothes, didn't you? While I was laying sick in bed from the last beating you gave me, you sold my baby just so you could go have another drink."

"I said, hush you mouth." He took one giant stride toward the fireplace and brought his huge hand downward toward her face. "Ahhh!" He jerked back to stare at the bloody gash across his palm as Ida waved the butcher knife back and forth.

"I ain't letting you hit me again, Lowell. Now, I want my baby. Where'd them folks go? Where'd they take her? I want her back."

"Damn bitch!" He flung the chair too quickly for her to duck and she lost her grip on the knife as she hit the floor. She made a frantic dive for the weapon but cried out in pain as the heel of Lowell's boot came crashing down on her fingers.

"Think you can cut me and get away with it?" Ida scooted backward trying desperately to get to the door. "See how you like it." The knife was so sharp she hardly felt the cut it left across her cheek. She kicked at him as he flashed the knife again and again, leaving cuts on her arm and legs.

"I ought to cut you heart out!" He grinned and waved the blade back and forth in front of her. Ida leaped from the floor in an attempt to claw at his eyes but ran directly into his fist. He laughed as she lay on the floor holding a trembling hand to her crushed nose.

"You stupid bitch," he said kicking her. "I should have left you here to starve long ago." He kicked her again. "You ain't nothing to look at any more, and you never was any damn good in bed." He tossed the knife into the fireplace and brought a boot down across her face. "I'll kill you if you ever try something like that again." He grabbed a fistful of hair and raised his hand again.

Chapter 2

"Well, why can't I wear it?" Vicky Blue clenched her teeth as her daughter Caroline stomped her foot and held the buckskin dress in front of her.

"Because I said you can't, and I'm the mother, remember? Hold still," she said, trying to button the white shirt on her four-year-old son.

"But I like it. It's comfortable. I don't like that old dress with all the stuff underneath."

"They are called petticoats and that dress is not old. Your Aunt Alice gave it to you only last month, and, you are going to wear it to church just like I said, so quit whining." She grabbed a brush and began working on her son's wobbly head.

"You wear that Indian outfit every day of the week but Sunday, so I don't see where you have a right to complain."

"Uh-uh." She snapped her head around to glare at her mother. "You won't let me wear it to school. I have to dress like a sissy."

"That's right. I'm the teacher, and my daughter is going to go to school dressed like a proper lady. And I never complain when you change into your other clothes when we get home, do I?" She picked her son up and set him on the edge of the bed. "Don't you dare move until your father comes in from hitching the team."

"There, isn't that better?" she said, tying the blue bow on the back of the gingham dress.

"No. I feel itchy all over."

"Well, you'll get used to it." She stood back to look at the defiant nine-year-old in front of her. "As a matter of fact, you should be proud. You look very pretty in that dress."

"I don't want to look pretty."

"Too late," Matthew said closing the door behind him. "You're already pretty, and there's nothing you can do about it."

"Daddy, Mama won't let me wear the dress I want to. Why do I gotta wear this old itchy thing?"

"You talk to her. I've got to get myself ready." Vicky's lips were set in a thin line as she turned away.

"Because we're going to church," Matthew said.

"But God doesn't care what you wear." Vicky glanced over her shoulder to see how her husband was going to handle this one. He shot a helpless look toward her before clearing his throat.

"No, but your mother and I do. Now, we're all going to church dressed up just like everyone else. You can take your favorite dress for the picnic afterward, but that's the best I can do. See?" he said smiling. "I'm wearing a tie, myself."

"Aw, alright." She grabbed the buckskin dress, leggings and moccasins before heading to the door.

"Don't forget your bonnet," Vicky said, receiving a cold glare in return. "Why do we have to go through this every Sunday? Why can't she just get dressed like any normal child and be done with it?" Vicky wrapped her shawl around her shoulders.

"Maybe she is normal. Come on Marcus," he said, picking up his son.

Vicky stopped in the middle of tying the bow on her bonnet to stare at him. "I'd hate to think so."

"Hate to think what?"

"That that type of behavior is normal. I don't ever remember giving my grandmother that much trouble. Or, my mother while she was still alive, for that matter." She gave the bow a final tug and picked up her Bible and picnic basket.

"You don't, huh?" His blue eyes twinkled as he grinned at her. "The last time we visited her, I distinctly remember your grandmother telling me you had a horrific temper."

"Ahhhh, she did not!"

"Did so. Ask Caroline. She was there," he said, helping her up into the buckboard.

"Ask me what?"

"Didn't you hear Grandma say that your mother had a bad temper when she was growing up?"

"Matthew Blue, don't you dare cause my daughter to lie," she said as Caroline covered her mouth to giggle. "Let's end this discussion right here and now, before...before...what are you laughing at?"

"You," he leaned over to kiss her, "are the most kind, generous and loving person I know."

"Stop that," she said, making her face a moving target.

"But you still have a bad temper." He finally caught up with her lips. They both broke into a giggle as their daughter made a gagging sound in the back of the wagon.

Chapter 3

"May I?" Caroline's eyes drifted up from the dust on her shoes to the lanky man standing in the aisle.

"Sure." She scooted over to bump Mark on the pew next to her and he immediately whined and gave her a push.

"Thank you. I'm afraid there isn't much room elsewhere."

She brushed the wrinkles out of her skirt with her palms and let her eyes drift in his direction again. Albert Meeks had only arrived in Leon a few days ago and was staying at the boarding house. *Dang,* she thought to herself. *He's so long he can't fit his legs between the pews.* This was the first time she could remember ever hearing him speak. But that wasn't unusual, seeing as her family lived six miles out of town on a horse ranch, and never came to town except to shop or go to church. *Well, that wasn't quite true either,* she thought. Her mother was the school teacher, so they were sort of here every day. But they seldom came on into town after school, unless it was to see Uncle Harvey and Aunt Alice. She dropped her gaze back to the dust on her shoes.

"Like to share?" He held the hymnal open for her to share as Mayor Joe Parker stepped to the pulpit to lead the Sunday singing. *Sing? I never sing where anyone can hear me.* He shoved the hymnal closer as Freda Wilson's fingers began torturing the keys. Caroline mouthed most of the words as the organ coughed and wheezed its way through ALL HAIL THE POWER OF JESUS' NAME. She listened as Mr. Meeks' soft tenor voice floated toward the rafters and by the end of the song she discovered she had been actually singing the words out loud.

"That was good. You have a beautiful voice," he said turning the pages with his long dainty fingers. They weren't like her father's, or even her mother's for that matter. They didn't have any scrapes or callouses, and he had a diamond ring on his right hand, opposite where a wedding ring should be. She snapped her mind back as the organ screeched and howled HOLY, HOLY, HOLY, then returned to analyzing the dust on her shoes during Pastor Herbert Billings' sermon.

"Mr. Meeks?" Her mother stretched her arm across Caroline's face after the closing prayer and shook the man's hand. "I'm Vicky Blue and this is my husband, Matthew." The men exchanged nods. "This is our son, Mark. And I think you've already met our daughter Caroline."

"Yes I have. She was kind enough to share her spot on the pew with me. You have a fine family, Mrs. Blue." He gave a slight smile and bowed gracefully. *He's got real sad eyes. I wonder what's wrong with him?*

"We were wondering if you would like to join us at the picnic? That is, unless you have other plans." Her mother smiled as she waited for an answer. He took time to study each and every one before nodding his dark brown head.

"Yes, thank you. I would enjoy it very much, but only if you'll allow me to provide dessert. Is there any place I can purchase a pie or cake in town?"

"The Ladies Auxiliary will be selling pies and cakes at the picnic to raise money for a new organ, so you can buy one right there."

"They need to buy someone who can play the thing." It just slipped out of her mouth. "Sorry." Caroline giggled as her mother frowned at her.

They said their goodbyes and stopped by Aunt Alice's house, where everyone changed into more comfortable clothes. She thought it was pretty neat that Uncle Harvey dressed nearly the same no matter where he went. Tan trousers, white shirt, brown vest with a silver star, and a brown hat. No one ever said he looked out of place anywhere he went.

She watched as her mother spread the blankets under an oak tree in view of the men pitching horseshoes. She helped her set out plates of fried chicken and corn on the cob. Her mother was still slim and fit-looking, even though Caroline knew she'd have a new brother or sister in a matter of five months from now. Aunt Alice arrived with hot biscuits, mashed potatoes and gravy. She was finishing the last braid in her hair when Albert Meeks arrived with an apple pie.

"Are you the same young lady I sat beside in church?" The small derby looked like it might fall as he tilted his head to one side.

"Yep." She jumped to her feet to dance in a circle. "Like it?"

"Well, yes I do. It's different, but I think it looks very becoming...on you, that is."

"Your clothes look different too, and you talk funny. Where're you from?"

"Caroline!" She shot a glance to her mother's crimson face.

"That's quite alright. I guess I do talk funny," he said handing her the pie. He had a friendly laugh, but Caroline had a feeling that his smile was not familiar with his own face. He squatted on his heels and tapped his lips with his index finger as he studied her.

"I'm originally from London. Know where that is?"

"Yep. My mama teaches school." She set her lips in a thin line and nodded her head.

"Oh, that's wonderful. Well, I came to America about five years ago and I've never bothered to change the way I dress. But you see, where I live most of the time, there are a lot of people who dress like I do."

"And where might that be, Mr. Meeks?" Aunt Alice said as she began filling their plates.

"Better dig in, or there won't be nothing left," Uncle Harvey said, handing him a plate.

"Oh yes, thank you. My first name is Albert, ma'am," he said as Alice placed a drumstick and a hot biscuit on his plate. "But I would appreciate it if you simply called me Al. I actually live in New York right now, where my father owns a shipping company. And, to answer a question you've been dying to ask me," he sat beside Caroline and leaned closer, "I make my living sitting behind a desk." Caroline dropped the corn she had been gnawing on and glanced toward her mother.

"No, it's alright. You see, I noticed you staring at my hands while we were sitting in church." He held them up in front of her. "And I'll admit, they are kind of soft, but I've never had to do more than keep track of how much money my father makes." He paused and picked up his chicken. "I work for him, you know. And don't tell anyone this," he leaned close to whisper, "but he's filthy rich."

"Shipping? You mean ships crossing the ocean?" Her mother dabbed her lips with a napkin.

"Yes," he paused to look off in the distance. "I believe he owns five...no...six ships now."

"Well, you're a long way from the ocean now, son. What brings you here to Kansas?" Uncle Harvey held out a cup for Alice to fill.

"Looking for someone, actually." He bit into the corn and wiped his fingers on a napkin.

"Oh? Well that's my line of work. Any particular reason?"

"Yes," he blushed as a grin crept across his face. "There's this girl I met...woman, actually. Ida Montgomery. Prettiest woman God ever created, present company excluded, of course." He tilted his head toward Caroline and winked. Everyone waited in silence while he continued chewing at the corncob. "Mmmm, this is good." He dabbed his lips with the napkin.

"Grew it myself in the field behind my house," Uncle Harvey said.

"Well? What happened to the girl?" Aunt Alice almost yelled.

"My father didn't approve of my keeping company with her, because she was from what he considered a lower social class than ours." He wiped his fingers before picking up the chicken which he waved around as he continued. "Well, to make a long story short, I had to take a trip to England on some business. When I got back, she was gone. It was my father's claim that she ran off with a drummer who happened by, which I wouldn't accept. So, against his protest, I started out to find her. That was a little over a year ago." The sadness returned to his eyes and he dropped the chicken back to the plate.

"You never found her?" Mama's voice cracked.

"No." He shook his head and sighed. "Last word I had was that she was somewhere around here, but it seems that no one's ever heard of her." He rolled the chicken over in his plate to study it. "A man in El Dorado said that a woman who matched Ida's description had passed through some time earlier heading this way. But she turned out to be that lady over there." He nodded toward a woman sitting with a group of people under the next tree.

"Lillian Hancock?" Aunt Alice said, reaching across Uncle Harvey for a biscuit.

"Christ Almighty, woman," he said as the rim of her bonnet jabbed him in the eye.

"I'm sorry." She reached for him, but he leaned away, holding a hand over his wounded eye.

"Guess that's why they call them 'poke bonnets'," her father said. "They're always poking the person next to whoever is wearing one."

"Why didn't you tell me about this woman before? Just maybe one of us could have helped you," Uncle Harvey said with a growl, rubbing his eye. Al shrugged.

"I've actually given up, I guess. I'm thinking seriously of returning home to face my father's wrath."

"Well, before you do, let me put out a few feelers first. I'll ask around a bit, and Matthew here's the best damn tracker in the territory. Give us a few days before you high-tail it. Never know what we might turn up."

"Thank you. Thank you very much."

"Well, I think I'm gonna save my pie for later. You ready to get whupped again, boy?" Harvey stood to his feet to tower over her father.

"Huh, not likely," her father said and laid his plate aside. They paused as an argument broke out among a group of people under the next tree. Mr. Hancock was standing and brushing at his trousers as he yelled at his wife.

"How could you be so stupid? Look at this. They're ruined. Come on, let's go." He grabbed her by the arm as she was trying to pick up their baby, and gave it a jerk. Alice clucked her tongue and shook her head as Al Meeks leaned over to look Caroline in the face.

"Let that be a lesson to you lass. One that's more important than the message your pastor preached this morning. Not that it was a bad one, mind you. But you can learn a lot about a man by the way he treats his wife. That fellow thinks of no one but himself. Be careful to never let that happen to you. That poor woman is in for a lifetime of pain."

"You can say that again. A lot of folks think he's the cat's meow because he's planning on having the railroad build some kind of spur down here from El Dorado. But I've never really taken a shine to him myself," Harvey said stuffing in his shirttail. "I've wanted to slap his face more'n once for that same reason. Stupidest damn thing I've ever heard of anyway. We've already got a railroad that goes all the way to Wichita. Come on, Al. You can play the winner."

"You know, that woman with the bloody-poor husband does look a lot like my Ida," he said laying his plate aside.

"Ya don't say? Hope she got herself hooked up with someone better than Lillian did," Harvey said as they headed toward the horseshoe pit.

Caroline sat picking at her plate. *Poor Mr. Meeks. It'd be horrible to love someone like that, then lose them and not be able to find them again at all. You'd be wondering how they were and if they were happy.* She had a vision of an old man with long gray hair standing on the bow of a ship with a telescope, looking, searching for his lost and lonely love somewhere on the horizon.

She jumped to her feet and dusted herself off. *Glad I'm not like that. I ain't never gonna fall in love with no one unless they're like Daddy. He loves Mama more'n the whole world, and he'd never let me get out of his sight.* She spied Bobby Sorenson and Jack Caldwell, two boys from school, at the far end of the church yard with a small bay-colored mare. She smiled as she laced up her moccasins.

"Mama?"

"Mmmmm?"

"I'm gonna go teach them boys how to ride. Okay?"

"Caroline," he mother rolled her eyes, "you are going to go teach *those* boys how to ride."

"That's what I said. Is it okay?"

Chapter 4

Lillian Hancock blinked her eyes several times and held the blanket tightly under her chin. Douglas' embarrassing her in front of the people at the church picnic that afternoon was nothing new to her. They had only arrived in Leon two months ago, and he had been successful in belittling her in front of every person she could think of. And yet, for some reason, everyone still seemed to love him. Douglas was that way. Give him five minutes in front of a crowd of people and he would have them eating out of his hand. He probably would obtain his dream of being elected to the State Senate some day, she mused. Given time, he might even make it to the White House.

The room was quiet except for Douglas' snoring in the twin bed on the opposite side of the room. She hated the arrangement, but twin beds were something he had insisted upon. She remembered standing in the bedroom of their Virginia mansion on their wedding night and staring at the tiny beds. "That one's yours, and this one's mine," he had said, and that's the way it had been ever since. He had never come to her during the night, unless it was for his personal gratification, and those visits had grown further apart. Lillian had always been afraid to be alone in the dark, and her fear grew worse on nights like this. She wanted desperately to snuggle close and feel safe as the storm moved closer. But

Douglas had never really made her feel safe. She rolled her head to stare at his darkened form lying against the opposite wall. *God, I wish I could make you understand.*

Another flash of lightning followed by a clap of thunder made her catch her breath. Her nightgown clung to her damp body and beads of sweat stood out on her brow. The air hung thickly like a musty, damp quilt. She found herself gasping as she tried to fill her lungs. *I don't know why you insisted on moving to Kansas.* She brushed her bangs back with a sweaty palm. Alice Blankenship told her to enjoy the heat, because they would freeze when winter came. It was true that they had similar weather in Virginia, but at least she would have been close to Ma'amaw. She started to kick the blanket off her but another clap of thunder in the distance caused her to pull it back tightly with white knuckles.

Ma'amaw was the black nurse who had taken care of her after her mother died. Her real name was Clara, but Lillian had started calling her Ma'amaw when she was a baby and the name stuck. She missed her desperately. Ma'amaw understood that storms frightened her. She'd let Lillian scoot under her blankets and bury herself against her own soft body when lightening danced across the sky. Lillian felt safe as the old woman smoothed her long raven hair with a gnarled hand and cooed softly. It was Ma'amaw who helped comfort her after her father had been killed in that freak accident. Ma'amaw had actually taken over the running of the plantation for her father, and was proving herself almost as knowledgeable as the Colonel himself. But Douglas took charge after the accident and things never seemed quite the same. He fired several of the servants who had been part of her family as long as she could remember.

But Douglas had made quite a striking figure when she met him for the first time. He rode into the yard on a black mare, dressed in some of the finest tailor-made clothes she'd ever laid eyes on. "Miss Farthington?" He had smiled at her warmly.

"Yes?" She felt her cheeks burn.

"You wouldn't be the pretty Charlotte Farthington that Corporal Bodard was always bragging about?"

"No, I'm her younger sister. Charlotte got married last year and moved away." Lillian paused to study the grass at her feet.

"Then you must be Miss Lillian."

"Why, yes I am. May I help you." It had suddenly become warm, and difficult to breath under the bodice pressing against her breast.

"I was wondering if I may water my horse at your fine plantation before I continue my journey?"

"Why, certainly." She told one of the black children to take care of the horse before asking him to sit beside her on the bench in the shade. "You say you knew my cousin Samuel?"

"Yes, I did. We were close friends. In fact, I happened to be with him the night he died."

"How awful!" Lillian's hand fluttered to her lips. "Could you tell me about it?" She dabbed her eyes as he told her how Sam had died in his arms, and showed her the picture and letter from Charlotte that Sam had given him to take care of. He also told her that his family owned a large plantation just a few miles from Clarksburg and he was anxious to get home.

"I haven't seen my mother since I left to go to war."

"Oh, and where have you been so long, sir?" She fluttered her eyes and looked away.

"I was wounded in the war and spent some time in a Yankee hospital. Then, I guess I simply lost track of time and stayed up north longer than anticipated. I know my mother and father will be glad to see me, and I'm anxious to see my brother Timothy. I heard he made quite a name for himself fighting Yanks." The boy returned with the horse and Lillian rubbed the mare's neck as she listened.

"I'm sure they will all be very happy to see you." She was afraid that he might disappear if she took her eyes off him.

"Well, thank you for your hospitality, but I must be going. I have enjoyed your company immensely." He bowed gallantly before climbing back onto the horse.

"I do hope you will come to call again."

"You may rest assured, Miss Farthington, I will call again very soon."

That evening Lillian ignored Ma'amaw's comment that the man was dressed right smartly for a rebel that had just been released from a Yankee hospital. "Especially," she said, waiting on the dinner table, "seeing as the South is in such a terrible state from that Yankee aggression." Her father agreed with the maid.

Douglas returned a few days later looking sad and dejected. She remembered crying as he told her of finding out that his mother and father had both died while he was away. He also told her he was stunned to learn that his brother had been killed at Fredricksburg. He seemed so alone at the time. He asked if he could continue to come visiting, and she gave her consent.

"No, by God. You're only fifteen, and that man's pushing forty if he's a day old," Colonel Farthington had said.

"He's only thirty-three, father. And he needs me." They were married a few short months later.

She was scared stiff at first, being the wife of such an important man as Douglas Hancock. She saw less and less of him as the days went by. The duties of taking care of both plantations seem to overwhelm him. Men dropped by all times of the day and night to conduct business in the study. Some of them were friendly and would smile, but there were others who were downright mean, like that Mr. Durkson who tried to force himself on her once when he caught her alone in the darkened hallway. And sometimes they brought women who were all painted up and wore clothes the likes of which Lillian had never seen before. She told Douglas that she didn't really like his friends stopping by without being invited, but that only made him angry. She discovered that it was easier to become a proper wife if she simply sat quietly and smiled and made herself available when he needed her.

He always carried large sums of money stuffed inside his wallet and spent it on foolish things, like it was free. But she had never questioned anything her husband did or said until overhearing several servants discussing him when they thought she was out of the house. One of them called Douglas a traitor and said that no one but the carpetbaggers would have anything to do with him. When she asked him about it later, he hit her. That was the first time. There had been several other beatings since, so she had become expert at sitting quietly and smiling. But smiling didn't help the pain and fear, especially when the storms came. And smiling didn't hide the fact that their son Bobby was lying in a cold dark grave back in Virginia. The thought made her shiver.

A flash of lighting, followed quickly by a loud clap of thunder, caused her to jump and catch her breath. She glanced toward her husband, who simply rolled to one side and continued snoring. *He more than likely slept through that entire war of Yankee aggression.* The curtains began a ghostly dance as the wind seeped through the partially open window. It's finally here. She clenched her jaw tightly and closed her eyes with the next crackle of lighting. A baby's cry from the next room caused her to open them again widely.

Lottie! She kicked the blanket off and pattered down the hall in her bare feet. Lillian opened the door and started toward the crib. A gust of wind caused the curtains to flap wildly, so she turned to close the window instead. Her hands were poised ready to give the open pane a pull when a long crack of lighting lit up the sky. A large black man dressed in a buckskin shirt and bead necklace was standing on the opposite side of the window staring back at her. He was holding her daughter in his arms. The thunder rolled through the open window, drowning her scream. Rain pelted her face and soaked through her thin nightgown as she leaned through the window.

"What the hell's the matter with you?" Lillian turned toward her husband who stood in the open doorway.

"He...he...he...Lot..." she said with her eyes darting between the window and Douglas.

"Close that window, you're letting the rain in."

She leaned back out the window. The only sign that anyone had ever been there were two footprints in the mud, and they were quickly filling with water.

"Dammit Lillian, are you crazy? Close the window."

She stared at Douglas, trying to make her mouth work. The strange man was gone, and he'd taken Lottie with him.

Chapter 5

Otto Mauerman took three steps before turning on his heel to stare back at the empty cage. How could something like this happen? He had taken great care, as always, in making sure all the cages were shut tightly and locked after last night's feeding, but Cleopatra's cage was standing wide open and she was gone. The lock had been tampered with, that much he was sure of. One could plainly see the marks left by a crowbar where it had been pried away. But why would someone want to steal an African lion? None of the other cages had been tampered with.

He glanced toward the large wagon as he trudged slowly, picking his way through and around the puddles. There was a big glob of mud on the red, white and blue sign that read, *Whiteman and Whiteman's All American Circus*. That wasn't really true. There was only one Mr. Whiteman, and he was going to be very angry. And as a matter of fact, most of the performers were from Europe. But none of that mattered at the moment.

The small circus had been inching its way across Kansas, playing the smaller towns, and hoping to get back on its financial feet. Mr. Whiteman had been saving money by having some of the animals pull the wagons through the last few towns instead of taking the rail. Things were going to be different when they reached El Dorado, he assured them.

From there, they would take the railroad on into Wichita, and then they would only play the larger cities where the real money was. Things were sure going to be different, alright. They would play El Dorado without Cleopatra, unless someone could find her. The only good that Otto Mauerman could find was that they were out in the middle of nowhere right that minute, instead of the Wichita fairgrounds.

Chapter 6

Jim Larkin stood ready to close the gate as Matthew and Caroline drove the last of the mustangs into the corral. "Hey, now! Whoa!" he said, trying to slam the gate shut as a pesky two-year old dun, who didn't like the looks of the pen, bolted for open spaces. Matthew's pinto quickly side-stepped out of the path causing him to block Jim's effort. "Dammit." He ran around Matthew's horse waving his hat as the rest of the animals tried to follow the dun through the gate. "Yaaaa! Get back in there!" Matthew reached the ground in one bound and swatted the nose of a horse that was pawing the air. The animals raced to the far corner of the corral with whistles and snorts of protest.

"Eeeyaaa!" The shrill yell caused him to turn in time to see the nine year old girl cut across the dun's path.

"Better get out there and help her, Matt."

"No need. She can handle it just as well as you and I can."

The pony she was riding bare-back made Jim's heart race as it shot back and forth, keeping in front of the angry horse and urging him ever closer toward the corral. Caroline's blond pigtails flapped wildly in the wind as she yelled and waved a coiled rope. *They're beautiful.* He stood transfixed as the horse and girl worked as a team. The angry dun finally gave up and darted into the corral, allowing the men to close and latch the gate.

"Turned her into a damned Comanche like yourself, didn't you?" he said as Matthew helped the girl down. She was dressed in buckskin from head to foot, including beaded headband and leggings. He caught a glimpse of the bone-handle knife strapped to her right thigh when she swung her leg over the back of the horse. "Look a lot like your mother," he said patting the blond head. Her freckled nose crinkled as she smiled.

Matthew handed Caroline the reins and leaned against the gate as she led their horses toward the watering trough.

"Not afraid of work, is she?" Jim said, turning to study the horses he'd just bought.

"Never has been. Like her mother that way too." Matthew stepped up on the lower rail and leaned over the top to watch the milling animals inside. "Some of the finest stock in Kansas. They're sired from the mustangs you gave Vicky for catching Slim."

"Yeah, I know. That's why I'm buying them." He blinked hard and looked off in the distance. *That's funny*, he thought. *One wouldn't have thought there would be any dust left in Kansas after the way it had rained the night before, but his eyes burned like the dickens.* He had always loved horses, but this bunch was special to him. They seemed to connect him somehow to his daughter Karen even though she had been dead almost five years now. He could still hear her laughter echo down the hall of their large ranch home. There were times when he was working alone in his office that the familiar scent of the lilac perfume she wore would fill the room. He closed his eyes and gripped the top rail tightly before turning away to blow his nose and wipe his eyes. Seventeen was just too damned young for anyone to die, let alone the way she did. All cut up with Slim's knife.

He studied Caroline as she watered the horses. That was the only good thing that happened to come out of that ordeal. He had gotten to know this girl and her mother, Vicky. Caroline's father, Harold Jamison, had also been killed at that time. Then her mother up and married Matthew a few years later. *Boy, that caused a ruckus*, he thought. A pretty blond-headed, blue-eyed white woman marrying an Indian. It didn't matter none to the folks around Leon that Matthew was half white either. The Comanche was a fierce fighter and most white folks had tangled with them at one time or the other, or at least knew of someone who had, and they didn't normally cotton to the white man either. Seeing Matthew and Vicky together when they came to town took a little getting used to. He liked them both personally, after he got to know them. Besides, he owed them a lot too. Matthew almost died trying to catch Karen's killer.

"But now I got me a little problem," he said as Caroline headed their way.

"What's that?" Matthew glanced over his shoulder.

"I don't believe any of these horses are near as good as that pony your girl's been riding."

"Sugar?" Caroline's blue eyes sparkled in sunlight as she stared up at him.

"Yeah," he nodded. "I've never seen any horse work another like that before, and raising horses is all I've ever done. It was like watching a dog herd sheep. Who trained that little mare, anyhow?"

"Caroline." Matthew nodded toward the girl while he rolled a cigarette. "I broke her for riding, but she's Caroline's horse. She taught her everything else."

"Well, I'd like to buy her, if you'd let me. I'll give top dollar."

"No, you can't have Sugar. She's my horse! Tell him, Daddy." The color seemed to drain from the already pale face as she took a couple of backward steps.

Jim was instantly sorry for making the offer, but he couldn't help himself. He loved horses just as much as humans - more in some cases, and he had just witnessed the most extraordinary display of intelligence and ability he had ever seen in an animal. *Besides*, he thought, *they needed the money.* Matthew raised some of the finest stock around, but it had always been a struggle at best for them on that little place of theirs.

"I'm afraid she's right. Sugar's hers, and you'll have to deal with Caroline if you want to buy her."

"See? She's mine, and she's not for sale." She held her head high and her lips became a thin line as she spoke.

"Are you sure? Think of all the pretty dresses you could buy with the money."

"No. I don't want your money or dresses. My clothes are just fine."

"I'll take good care of her, and you could come ride her any time you want. Besides, what kind of name is Sugar for a horse anyway? I'll give her a new name much more fitting. How about North Star, to match the patch on her rump?"

"Noooo! Daddy...?" Her chin trembled as she clenched her fists.

"I don't want your horse. I was just joshin' you some. Come here." Jim held out his arms and gave the girl a bear-hug. "Well, I would like to have Sugar, but not if it'd break your heart. You keep her." She laid her head against his chest and hugged back.

"Besides, you'd have to take her too if you ever wanted the horse to work like that again." Matthew struck a match and lit his smoke. "I can ride her, but it's Caroline that makes her do that stuff. And I'll bet you she'll make most horses do the same, if you give her a little time."

"That right?" He took her by the shoulders and looked her in the face.

"I don't know. I never tried it with any other horse." She tilted her head to one side and grinned.

"Well, it doesn't matter. You've got a job with me anytime you want. I've got grown wranglers who couldn't herd a turtle near as well as you just handled that cayuse. You and your father both can work for me anytime, if he wants." He glanced toward Matthew who stood stone-like, smoking his cigarette.

"I can't. My mama says I've got to go to school. And when I finish, she says she's going to send me away somewhere to another school called a college or something." She whined as she spoke.

"Well, that's just fine. You go to school and learn how to cipher all you can, then come and see me, because running a big spread like this takes more than just being able to ride a horse. You have to know how to count and run figures. And you should also know how to read and write some too. Your mama's right. Most young girls can't think of nothing but getting married and having young'uns of their own. Then they're lost when something happens to their man."

"Looks like Cotton and Dave are coming to pay you a visit," Matthew said, shading his eyes against the sun.

"Wonder what they want?" Jim squinted and strained his eyes trying to make out who the riders were, but they only looked like ants topping the rise to the east.

"I know my eyes ain't near what they used to be, but I can't figure how you can tell who they are from this distance." He pulled a couple of cigars from his vest pocket and handed one of them to Matthew. "Here, get rid of that cheap tobacco and have a good smoke. They probably just want to swap howdies with us."

"Hardly." He accepted the light offered and puffed deeply. "Cotton wouldn't ride this far to say hello to the President, let alone a couple of drovers like us."

Jim grinned as Matthew draped an arm around the girl and gave her a squeeze. As the riders drew closer he could see the familiar white hair showing from beneath the brown hat the sheriff always wore. "You appear to be right again, Matt. But I still can't figure out how you do it."

"A Comanche's eyes are always better than a white man's."

"Don't give me that, you damnable sidewinder. You've got you mother's blue eyes yourself."

The Indian laughed as he gave him a friendly shove on the arm. "See how easy Cotton rides? He sits in the saddle like a true soldier. Someone who's spent years on the back of a horse. Dave, on the other hand, isn't part of the horse. He is a good rider, but he will be tired by the end of the day. Cotton will still be rested and ready for more work, even though he is getting old."

Jim was still watching intently when the two men reigned their mounts to a halt, trying to make out the subtle differences between them. He had always known Cotton to be an excellent horseman. He had seen him ride into places where most men would have gotten down and led their mount. But for the life of him he still couldn't see any distinction between the two men's ability to ride.

"Hello Sheriff...Dave." Jim nodded as he spoke. "What brings you two out here?"

"Howdy, Jim. We're looking for this renegade Injun. Vicky said we'd find you out here, Matt." Cotton sat in the saddle while Dave dismounted with a grunt.

"Been out to my place? That's a long ride. You must have gotten an early start. How's Vicky and Mark?"

"We got started before sunup. Rode out to your place before coming here. Your wife and boy are just fine." He slid out of the saddle and handed the reins to Caroline. "Here, honey. Can you see this buzzard-bait gets a drink? But not too much, now. I pushed him a little hard getting here."

"Sure thing, uncle Harvey." The old sheriff grinned as he watched the girl lead the animal toward the watering trough. They weren't really kin, but Harvey Blankenship was just about as close to Matthew's family as any real uncle could be.

"We've got trouble, Matt," Dave Price said as Caroline took the reins from his hand and led his horse toward the trough. "Someone stole the Hancock baby last night. Took her right out of the crib through an open window. We think it was Black Shadow."

"Stole their baby?" Caroline's shrill voice came from where the horses were drinking.

Jim felt a chill sweep through his body. Another girl, someone else's daughter. Only this one was a baby. He'd heard the tales about the son of the runaway slave from Georgia, but had discounted most of them as just fabrication. People always made things up about folks who did great things, both good and bad. You couldn't even believe most of the things you heard about the death of his own daughter, and that happened right here in Butler County only five years earlier. Folks he'd known all his life were saying downright stupid things and making Slim out to be some sort of hero, even though he'd butchered Karen and Carl Jenkins with that damn knife of his.

"What makes you think it was Shadow?" Matthew rolled the cigar back and forth in his fingers as he spoke.

"Lillian Hancock saw the man and gave us a description, after we got her calmed down that is. She said it was a black man dressed in Indian garb. Know anyone else like that, Matthew?" Cotton asked, wiping the sweatband inside his hat with a handkerchief.

"Sure, I met a lot of black buffalo hunters out on the prairie. So did you. And most of them wore buckskin."

"Yeah, and I agree, but this person didn't leave any tracks. None at all. He was there, and now he's gone. And so is the baby. Look," he said after a long pause, "it's all we got to go on. The whole town is in an uproar."

"It doesn't take much to get them that way, Cotton. What's this all got to do with me?"

"We want you to help us find him, Matt," Dave said in earnest.

"Na." Matthew shook his head and frowned at the mud on his boots.

"Whatdaya mean no?" The young deputy grew red in the face.

"Exactly that, friend. I have a daughter and son of my own, and a wife who's going to have another baby. If someone's going around stealing children, why would I want to leave my house unguarded?"

"How in the hell can you argue with that?" Dave tossed his arms in the air and turned toward Cotton. "I've got a little boy and a pregnant wife myself."

"Besides, I'm not so sure it is Shadow. Why would he want to steal a baby? It would only slow him down." Matthew loosed the reins of his horse where Caroline had it tied to the fence. "And even if it was him, you'll never be able to find his tracks, especially after that rain." He climbed into the saddle and waited as Caroline scampered up the fence railings and jumped onto the back of her pony.

"Does that mean you're not going to help us?"

He only smiled at the deputy.

"Hold on, Matt. You ain't got paid yet. Follow me up to the house," Jim said.

"Bring it to church Sunday." He touched the brim of his hat and dug his heels into the pinto's flanks. Caroline let out an ear-piercing peal as she gave chase.

"Pretty damned set in his ways, ain't he?" Jim tossed his cigar in the mud. He had a horrible taste in his mouth.

"Yeah, and I didn't hear you arguing with him much." Dave pushed his hat back and glared at Cotton.

"No need to argue. Nothing you could have said was going to change his mind right now. Besides, he'll be joining us in a day or two anyway."

"What makes you say that?"

"You don't know Manhunter as well as you think, do you?" Cotton glanced up from under the brim of his hat as he packed the bowl of his pipe. "Vicky will make sure he comes. He loves that wife of his more'n life itself, and he'll do most anything she says. Of course, she'd never ask him to do nothing stupid. She's a real lady that way. But she'll send him out to find that baby. Mark my words." He shoved the pipestem between his teeth and struck a match.

"What makes you so sure?" Dave put his hands on his hips.

"She was packing his grip the whole time we was talking and drinking coffee. Or, didn't you notice?"

Chapter 7

Douglas Hancock glared at the women in the sitting room. They were hovering around Lillian like a flock of chattering crows, telling her how sorry they were about Lottie, while drinking his tea and eating his cake. It was true that the sheriff's wife, Alice Blankenship, had brought the cake when she came earlier that morning, but she had given it to him and now these magpies were eating it all. And he despised the way they were acting. It was as though they thought Lillian was something special. *Well, that was the image you wanted them to get.* He snickered and turned away. *But if they really knew you, how crazy you are, what would they think of you then? And I bet they wouldn't think you were so special if they knew you couldn't even remember how your own son died, would they my lovely wife?*

He had worked hard to build an image that people could respect. And it was no easy task, especially when people discovered the truth behind Lillian. The fact that her father had once been the wealthy owner of a plantation and a colonel in the Confederate Army didn't seem to matter to many of the southerners he had dealings with. All they could dwell on was the fact that Lillian was weak-minded and her family was on the verge of losing everything when he married her. The old Colonel had insisted on keeping most of his slaves as hired employees after the war and paying them salaries. There wasn't a plantation in the South that could afford such an extravagance.

"We owe them more than just turning them out to starve," he said when Douglas tried to reason with him.

"I don't see how. You bought and paid for them once. They shouldn't mean any more to you than a cow or a horse. Look," he said when the old man turned his back on him. "It's okay to treat them humanely if you want. But people are starting to talk. Do you realize that they are calling you a nigger-lover?"

"Let them. My military record alone should prove my loyalty to the South. Besides, I admittedly don't hate these people. They've done nothing to harm me or my family."

Douglas hadn't known this side of the Farthingtons when he married Lillian and it made him wish he had been a little slower in his decision. The blacks were as much a part of the Colonel's family as his daughter was. Lillian had even eaten and slept with former slaves from time to time. The thought made his skin crawl thinking about it. And it didn't set too well with his friends either. He had overheard more than one conversation when his friends thought he was out of ear-shot. "Well, if she slept with that nanny of hers, I wonder how many of them big bucks she went to bed with?" He clenched his fists and stared blankly out the study window as the words echoed in his ears.

The move to Kansas had been a brilliant one on his part. People in this little town didn't know who he was and didn't pry into anyone's past. They were friendly and likeable folk who accepted others at face value and kept themselves busy trying to scratch out a living. Besides, Kansas had always been a free state, so outside of a few snickers, no one would care much about Lillian's past if they found out. They would care about her mental state, though. And it would ruin him if they ever found out about their son and how he died. But what really bothered him was that right at this moment, Douglas had the mayor and other civic leaders eating out of his hand. There was too much at stake to lose because his wife happened to be crazy, or because some drifter they called Black Shadow decided to steal a white baby. *If he wanted to take someone, why couldn't he have taken you, Lillian? You're the one who likes darkies.*

He took a sip of coffee and stared at a young boy through his kitchen window who was trying to catch a dog that had chased a cat up the tree in his front yard. The cat waited until the boy had drug the dog a safe distance down the street before bounding down the tree to disappear in the bushes beyond his picket fence. That was good. Douglas hated cats. Now, if he could only get rid of those women in the next room. He shot a glance over his shoulder before turning back to the window. *Yes you too, my dear. Marrying you was another mistake I'm eternally sorry for.*

Chapter 8

Matthew's pinto snorted and stamped angrily as the dog danced in circles and barked his greeting. Caroline slid to the ground and let the animal lick her repeatedly as she talked like a baby to him.

"Yes, Tippy, I'm glad to see you too. Did you miss me?"

"My guess is that he missed you terribly. Can't you tell? And don't ask me to kiss your cheek until you've washed it real good."

"He's clean, Daddy. Look how sweet he is." She held the dark snout between her hands and pointed it toward him.

"He's still a dog and you don't have any idea what he's been licking or eating. Wash your face."

"Don't listen to him, Tippy. He really doesn't mean to hurt your feelings," she said, holding her hands over the dog's ears. The dog broke free with a happy bark and knocked her to the ground with a chest-high bound. Matthew flung his right leg over the pommel and dropped gracefully to the ground as she rolled across the grass giggling, with the dog grabbing and nipping at her clothes.

He led the horses in a wide arc around the playful melee and toward the pond. He had never encouraged her to start calling him Daddy, but he hadn't tried to stop her either. He loved her as much as any natural father could love a child.

There were times when he wanted to pick her up and squeeze her as tight as possible and kiss her freckled cheeks repeatedly, but she was starting to get a little old to be treated that way. He paused and shook his head. *Na, not if he could help it. She'd never get too old to hold on his lap and hug.*

He stopped beside the picket fence that enclosed the graves of his first wife and son. *You would have loved her just as much, Prairie Flower, wouldn't you? Caroline and Vicky would have loved you too.* He smiled broadly, gazing at the neatly weeded area with fresh flowers planted on the small mounds of earth. *She does now.* He loved and respected the memory of Prairie Flower and Pita, but the thought of pulling weeds from around their graves or planting flowers had never entered his mind, not once in the sixteen years since their deaths at the hands of a drifter. It was Vicky who did these things. "I feel that I know them, Matthew," she told him on several occasions. *Funny*, he thought, *she probably does know you in some way.*

He removed the bridle and saddle from the paint and turned it loose before taking the bridle off Caroline's pony. She had a saddle but preferred to ride bareback. "I like to feel her when I ride. Don't make me put all that leather on her back." That was nothing new to Matthew. Being Comanche, he knew a lot of fine horsemen who loved the feel of horseflesh against their skin when they rode. He swatted Sugar on the rump and sent her galloping after the pinto.

"Daddy, Daddy!" He turned to watch his four year old son run toward him. "Daddy!" The boy threw his arms around his neck as Matthew hoisted him up in his arms and kissed his cheek.

"Missed you."

"Really?"

"Uh-huh." He nodded his shaggy head. The boy had his mother's violet eyes and Matthew's dark hair.

"Your sister and I weren't gone for a whole day and you still missed us?"

"Uh-huh."

"Well, I missed you too, Mark." He squeezed him tightly before hoisting him to his shoulders. Caroline ran past them toward the house, giggling, with Tippy nipping at her heels. She threw her arms around her mother who stood waiting on the porch.

"I missed your mama too. Think she missed me?"

"Uh-huh."

"You're a man of many words, Marcus." Vicky waved and Matthew lengthened his stride toward her. She had on her faded blue gingham dress and white apron. Even from this distance he could see a smudge of flour on her cheek. The small pooch of her stomach told of another son or daughter that would be born to them in a matter of months. She never looked more beautiful. He paused a few feet from the steps as the breeze made her golden hair dance in the sunlight.

"What's the matter, honey?" The smile fell from her lips.

"Nothing. Just looking at you standing there like that...you're a real angel, you know that?"

Vicky's hand automatically brushed a rebel strand of hair back behind her ear as she broke into giggles. "What did Jim give you to drink after you delivered the horses?"

"Just water." He put his son on the porch before folding her in his strong arms and kissing her slightly open mouth. "You're the one who makes me drunk."

"Yes, I can see that," she said, kissing him back. "Later, okay? Supper's almost ready."

"Yuck! Come on, Mark. I hope I never have to do that." Caroline pulled her brother toward the door by his arm.

Chapter 9

"Oh no, you got me," Matthew said, sprawling across the floor as Mark pounced on his back. Vicky grinned as she scrubbed the frying pan and watched them from the corner of her eye. This had become a nightly ritual. After clearing the table and feeding the dog, Matthew would wrestle and play with the children until it was time to read before going to bed. They would take turns. One night he would read, then Caroline, and the following night it would be Vicky herself. It might be poetry one night, or Shakespeare, or one of the classics, but they always finished with a chapter or two from the Bible. She was able to get hold of a history book from the last teacher at the school before one of the larger towns hired him away. Now Vicky taught the students, but with the baby coming in five months, and the long drive, she didn't know what was going to happen.

"Okay, Mark, you sit over here. It's you sister's turn now."

Vicky dunked the frying pan in a tub of clean water and leaned against the counter to dry it as she watched. This was the part she hated. Although he had never voiced it out loud, she knew Matthew was actually teaching Caroline how to defend herself against an attacker. *Dear God, never let that happen,* she prayed as he pounced at the girl. She winced as Caroline slipped the hold and gave him a quick kick to the ribs.

"Good! Now try this one." She flung her arms upward as he made a motion for her hair, but he kicked her feet out from under her instead. They squirmed across the floor like a pile of worms before Caroline latched onto his wrist with her teeth and broke free. The girl circled her father slowly in a crouched position holding her left hand chest high ready to ward off another attack. Matthew made a feinting motion and backed away as Caroline's right hand dropped to her thigh. The cast iron pan slipped from her grasp and hit the floor with a bang as her daughter whipped out the small bone-handle knife. Vicky covered her mouth and smothered a cry as the two combatants stared at her. Mark let out a wail as he ran to his father's arms.

"What happened? Did you hurt yourself? Where?" Matthew was holding his son in one arm and trying to examine her at the same time.

"No, I'm sorry." She choked back a sob. "It's just that when I saw the knife, it reminded me of the day Frank Barnes broke through the door and..."

"I'm sorry, Mama." Caroline put the knife back into it's sheath as Matthew folded her in his arms.

"It's okay." He kissed her forehead. "I'll make a play knife out of wood she can use."

"But why? Why must the two of you have to do that at all?" Her body shook all over.

"It's the way I am, the way I was taught." He kissed her on the ear before handing Mark to his sister.

"Here, it's getting late. You two get ready for bed. Who's turn is it to read anyway?"

"Mine," Caroline said, pulling her whining brother toward the cot in the corner of the room. Vicky's eyes drifted toward the loft where her daughter slept. She and Matthew had the only semi-private sleeping quarters in the house, a bed in the opposite corner, sectioned off by a heavy curtain.

The house was simply getting too small, especially with another baby on the way.

"Drink this. It will make you feel better." Matthew handed her a cup of hot tea and pulled a chair out for her to be seated at the table. She sipped the steaming liquid and smiled weakly as he took the Bible from the shelf and laid it on the table.

"Where're we at?"

"Luke Chapter One. We just finished Mark." She set the cup on the table to study his blue eyes. "That's the name of our next son, you know." She leaned back and patted her stomach.

"What is?"

"Luke. You're Matthew, and we already have Mark. So, the most logical thing is to have Luke."

"Huh. Are we going to have all twelve disciples?"

"Perhaps, but Luke wasn't one of the twelve disciples."

"Oh, yeah," he nodded.

"Would it bother you to have all twelve disciples?"

"Not in the least."

Caroline pulled the Bible from under his elbow as he leaned across the table to kiss her.

"Please, you two. We're going to read out of the Bible, you know."

Chapter 10

Vicky sat on the cold floor listening to Matthew's ragged breathing. The wound in his chest had started bleeding again, and he clung desperately between life and death with the smallest of threads. Caroline was three years old again and whimpered from where she was tucked under the heavy quilt in the bed. Vicky could hear the men in the next room through the curtain laughing and drinking. The body of Lieutenant Harold Jamison, her husband, was lying cold and stiff in the barn. He had been shot to death by Frank Barnes as he tried to defend his home and family. Her friend Otis Felts was dead also. Frank had plunged a knife into his chest as the wounded man lay on her kitchen floor bleeding. They would be coming for her any moment now. Frank had already told her what they were going to do to her and her daughter. After they were finished with her, they were going to kill Matthew. All because he had helped send Frank to prison a few years earlier.

She felt the cold steel of her husband's pistol in Matthew's hand against her trembling fingers. One of the men slammed a bottle on her kitchen table and scooted a chair against the rough plank floor. Matthew gave her a nod as he cocked the hammer back, and she quickly climbed on the bed to cover her daughter with her own body.

The curtain separating the two rooms was jerked aside and Frank stood there, glaring at her through bleary-eyes. He gasped as Matthew whipped the gun upward and squeezed the trigger. Part of Frank's temple disappeared as the weapon leaped in his hands. Vicky bolted upright gasping for air.

"Honey, what's wrong?" She could feel Matthew's hands against her back as he scooted closer.

"Nothing." She rubbed her palm vigorously against the quilt her grandmother had given her as a wedding present. Her ears were ringing and she could feel the weapon as she struggled to reload it that day.

"Don't lie to me." He wrapped her arms around her and kissed her between the shoulder blades. "They came back didn't they?"

She nodded.

"I know. It was a long time ago, but I still think about it myself sometimes. That's why I play that game with Caroline." He leaned his warm cheek against her. "I wish I could take it all away from you."

"I'm scared, Matthew." She threw her arms around his neck and kissed him as they fell against the pillow. "I feel safe when I'm with you, and I hadn't thought about it for such a long time. But when Cotton and Dave told me about someone stealing Lillian Hancock's baby...I don't know why, it just brought it all back."

"I was wondering when you were going to mention their visit." He took her face in his large hands and began kissing her eyes and nose before settling on her lips.

"You and Caroline seemed so happy when you got home I didn't want to spoil the evening. They did find you, didn't they? You know what happened, don't you?"

"As much as anyone else," he said, holding his index finger against her lips. "And I'm glad you chose not to spoil the evening. I'm jealous of every minute I get to spend with you and the children." He slipped an arm around her waist and pulled her body against him.

"Not now, Matthew. I'm too upset." She tried pushing him away but he rolled over on top of her and planted an elbow on each side of her head, cradling his chin in his palms. "You're squashing Luke," she said trying to squirm away.

"Victoria Blue, have you never read where lying is a sin?"

"I'm not lying. You're squashing me. Move!"

He rolled over to his back with a sigh. "Okay, I'll go join Cotton first thing in the morning."

"Is that what you think I want?"

"It's kind of hard to miss seeing my bedroll and pack sitting beside the door. When were you going to tell me?"

"I don't know." Her voice was no more than a whisper.

"I thought we both had agreed that I was going to give up chasing men. I thought I was going to stay close to home and love my wife and children. I'm supposed to raise horses, remember?"

"I know, and you've done more than that." She rolled over and touched his cheek with her palm. "It's just that Dave doesn't think they can find this man without your help. He stole a child, Matthew. Do you understand? A little baby."

"Alright." He sighed deeply. "I'll leave first thing in the morning, but I want you to keep the children and dog close to the house. And keep the shotgun loaded. Do you understand?"

She nodded and fell back to the pillow. She hated that thing. The sight of the huge gun made her stomach churn, and she didn't know how to use it properly in the first place. But she would keep it hanging near the door just in case. "Matthew?" she whispered, after a pregnant moment of listening to the crickets chirp outside the window.

"Mmmmm?"

"I'm sorry I'm asking you to do this. I just keep wondering how I would feel if it was Caroline or Mark that man took. And it just makes me sick to think how that poor woman must feel. It's just the way I am."

"Vicky," he rolled to his side and touched the tip of her nose with his finger, "I wouldn't change one little inch of you if I could. I even love your toenails."

"Oh, I'm so lucky to have you." She slipped her arms around his neck and kissed him deeply. He moaned as she straddled him and pulled her nightgown over her head. She took his hand and placed it on her stomach. "That's Luke."

"What if it's a girl?"

"Then we'll have to think of another name. Maybe Mary." She leaned over and kissed him again. She would make love to her husband tonight, for when the sun rose in the morning he would once again become Manhunter, and as always, there was a haunting feeling tucked away in the back of her mind that she might not see him again.

Chapter 11

"No! No more, please!" Ida flailed desperately at the air. Someone was trying to grab hold of her.

"Shhhhh, now no one's gonna hurt you. Just hold still, child."

Who's voice is that? It sounded familiar, but she couldn't remember. Her head hurt so bad. *Why didn't I die? I asked you to let me die. Why am I still here?* "Oh, God, no."

"Here, take hold of this arm. I gots to rub some of this here salve on it." Ida relaxed as the gentle hands massaged her arm. It felt good. "Quit yer crying, girl and bring me that water. This here woman don't need to hear you blubbering none."

God must hate me. Alvin's father had always said I was no good, and maybe he was right. Why else would Alvin have gone back to England after asking me to marry him?

"No, he didn't leave you any letter," Jonas Meeks had said with a laugh. "You are too simple to understand, aren't you? You're nothing to my son. You were just a little fling...someone to pass the time with. Now he's gone back home to find himself a wife. So, be gone with you. Go away and don't bother either of us again."

No good. Yes, that had to be it. She had cried for several days but then, in a fit of rage, had settled for Lowell Ollar, the first good-looking man to show her any attention after Alvin had abandoned her. That must have been another one of God's little jokes. Lowell seemed nice enough at first, and Ida had been able to put away a little money with her job at the boardinghouse. But it wasn't long until he drank it all away, and then hit her when she tried to explain that there wasn't any more. Then the owner of the boardinghouse caught Lowell taking some of the kitchen money and they had to leave town in a hurry. There were several jobs and towns in between while Lowell's drinking grew worse. Finally, after selling everything they had, he decided to sell her too.

Ida felt something close to relief the first time. She actually thought the old fat man was really buying her and she'd be rid of Lowell for good. It wouldn't have been so bad, she had reasoned. He had a lovely home and he did seem sort of nice. He was gentle and didn't try to hurt her in any way. But Lowell showed up the following morning ready to take her away. That was the first time. She couldn't remember how many other times he sold her, but it wasn't long until she was so weak and sick that no one wanted to buy her anymore. That's when Lowell brought her here and dumped her in this little shack.

"Lordy, Jessie, I just don't know where that brother of yours has gone. But just when we need his help, he ups and disappears on us." Something cool and soothing was draped over her eyes and Ida stopped rolling her head.

"It was Ben who found her like this Mama, then he come and told us."

"I don't care none. He's supposed to be plowing the field with his brother, not nosing 'round some white trash's house. And besides that, he ain't nowheres to be found. I'm shore gonna tan his hide when he gets home. Speaking of which," someone took the towel away and patted her on the shoulder, "we'd best be getting back ourselves."

"What about Ida, Mama? We just gonna leave her here like this?"

"Can't do nothing else, child. We can't take her with us. That devil would come looking for her and might hurt one of you young-uns." One of the shadows moved toward the door. "Shore wish the good Lord would send one of his angels to strike him down and let that poor woman have some peace. Well, come on. Let's get back to minding our own business and let her be." The smaller shadow floated away.

"No." Ida's hand groped at the air, but they were gone.

Chapter 12

Matthew sat on his heels rolling a cigarette while his horse munched the tall grass. It was a beautiful day. A breeze made the Kansas prairie dance with a soft rustle as butterflies and bees took turns skipping from flower to flower. It would have been a great day to sit with Caroline and Mark on the bank of the pond, with a cane pole stuck in their hands. The perch would have made a tasty meal. But tonight he would feast on a camp meal of beans, bacon and hard biscuits. And instead of sleeping in his warm bed with the feel of Vicky's body against his, he would be sleeping on the cold, hard ground listening to a bunch of men snore. He smiled as he struck a match against the bone handle of his .44 and lit the smoke. Either he was getting soft, or being a married man with children agreed with him. The latter, he thought. Regardless of the cause, he would rather have been home caring for his horses than chasing a fugitive across Kansas, especially when the crime didn't fit the accused. There was no reason for Shadow to steal a baby, especially a white one. Matthew inhaled deeply and blew a large cloud of smoke as he watched Dave Price approach with the posse in tow. There were ten of them counting Dave himself.

"Enjoying the scenery?" The deputy brought his horse to a halt in front of Matthew and arched his back before sliding out of the saddle.

"Nothing else to do except wait for you to show up."

"Now, how in the hell did you know we would be coming this way?" Dave said as he limped over and plopped to the ground beside Matthew.

"I've hung around you and Cotton enough to learn how a white man thinks." Matthew took the canteen from his saddle horn and tossed it to him. "That old hunk of rawhide's thinking that our man is headed east toward White Cloud's camp."

"Cotton? Well, ain't he?" Dave capped the canteen and handed it back to Matthew.

"Hardly. White Cloud might be old, but he isn't stupid. He'd know there would be a lot of people following a kidnapper, and White Cloud doesn't like a lot of company, especially white company."

"I was under the impression that the Indians had been confined to the reservation." Al Meeks looked up from adjusting his saddle cinches.

"Not all of them," Dave said with a chuckle. "I don't think you'd get White Cloud to stay on a reservation any more than Matthew."

"I didn't mean you." Al nodded toward Matthew. "After seeing you with your family, I've never really thought of you as an Indian."

"No offense taken." He hung the canteen back on his saddle. "I don't think of you as being white either. You're just a man, same as me." This brought a round of chuckles from the posse.

"Touché." Al held up a silver flask of brandy in salute before taking a nip.

"Hope you weren't planning on riding into White Cloud's camp with this bunch. Were you?" Matthew turned back to Dave.

"Well, not really. That's where you were supposed to come in. But what if I did? I've met the man and know him. I've sat in his teepee and eaten with him. You were with me."

"Yes, but that was just you and me. You didn't ride into his camp with a small regiment of armed men like you have here. Besides," he removed his hat and wiped the sweatband with his scarf, "the word is that Three Horns has joined him."

"Damn! That's all we need."

"I take it he is someone I'd rather not meet up with," Al Meeks said as several of the men mumbled and looked over their shoulders.

"I know you're new around here, but don't tell me you've never heard of Three Horns?" Dave said, biting down on a piece of jerky.

"No, I haven't."

"Well, he's a Comanche renegade who ain't never forgiven white folks for living." A crusty old man with a long beard looked up from packing his corncob pipe. "He don't even like Matthew here."

"Smokey's right with that one." Matthew laughed as he ran his fingers through his hair. "My mother was a white woman and I was a scout for the Army. My guess is that he's heard I've married a white woman who's given me a son. He probably hates me more than any white man."

"How did he ever get a name like 'Three Horns'?"

"Well, you see, it's like this." Smokey edged toward Al and got close to his face. "Injuns can change their names from time to time, and their names are usually tacked to something they do. Like Matt here. He's known as Manhunter, 'cause he chased down and caught the feller that kilt his first wife and their little boy. Then he went on for several years, doing nothing but chasing no good varmints that broke the law.

"Now, Three Horns," he paused to spit, "kilt hisself a buffalo that had three horns sticking out his head. One over here," he held up one finger on the left side of his head, "and two on the other side," he stuck up two fingers on the right. "He made a headdress outa that critter's skull and wears it everywhere. Most Comanches don't wear nothing on their heads unless they're going to war. But Three Horns wears his all the time, 'cause he thinks it gives him good magic."

"Sounds like the poor devil was just deformed." Al shook his head. "I don't know how such a thing could give someone 'good magic'."

"So, Matt, what's it going to be?" Everyone grew quiet as Dave waited for an answer.

"You're the one calling the shots, but I don't think I'd be willing to take such a large number anywhere near White Cloud's camp. He might take it as a threat."

"Then what do you suggest? Three or four of us go with you?"

"Just you and me." Matthew shook his head as the posse began to protest. "You'd be lucky to find him there anyway. Besides, what are ten of you going to do against twenty or thirty angry warriors if it turns into a fight? You'd only get yourself killed."

"I'm afraid Mr. Blue's right," Al said, pulling the silver flask back out of his coat pocket. He removed the cork and held it up as he spoke. "I for one detest violence, especially when it might involve my own pain." He took a nip and popped the cork back with the palm of his hand. "Do you think this White Cloud and Three Horns will let you arrest the kidnapper if he's there?"

"White Cloud's a just man like you and me. He might, but not Three Horns. I've known him most of my life. In fact, we were close friends growing up together. But something changed him. Now, I think he'd fight just for the sake of fighting. We'll let you know when we get back."

"If you get back." Al tossed the flask to Matthew. "Use it as a bartering tool."

"How far is it to White Cloud's camp?" Dave asked, as Matthew stuffed the flask into his saddlebag.

"Don't know." He paused to stare at the prairie. "It might be a day or two's ride just getting there. He moves around a lot, so no one knows for sure where they are located." He tossed the stirrup over the saddle horn and began adjusting the cinch. "One thing's for sure. When we get close enough, they'll find us."

"What are we supposed to be doing in the mean time?" Smokey said.

"Scout around a bit," Dave said, climbing back into the saddle. "Never know what you might turn up. If you don't hear from us in two or three days, head back to town."

"If you're not back, what are we supposed to tell Cotton? What about yer wife?"

"Oh, I don't know." Dave leaned in the saddle and grinned. "You'll think of something, Smokey. You always do."

Chapter 13

"Well, that was easier than I thought." It was late in the afternoon when Matthew brought his horse to a halt. Six Comanche warriors appear as if by magic as they approached the wash.

"That's what I hate about this country. You get thinking you can see everything from here to eternity, but there's a million places for someone to hide. I'll bet we're not even four or five miles from the posse. What do we do now?" Dave pushed his hat back on his head and leaned both hands on the pommel.

"Just wait and see."

"Who's that one?" Dave jestured toward a brave with one half of his face painted black and the other half red.

"Well, judging from the headdress, I'd say it's Three Horns. Doesn't look like he's in too good a mood, does it?"

The Indian raised his lance skyward and all six braves charged their ponies toward the two men.

Chapter 14

Benjamin Polk kicked the chair which was lying askew. He was stupid. Real stupid.

"Shut up!" he said as the baby started crying again. What possessed him to think it was a good idea in the first place? All he wanted to do was give this baby back to its rightful mother.

"Oh, please be quiet. I knows you're hungry, child. So am I." He knelt beside the cot in the corner of the dirty shack to caress the little head with a huge calloused hand. "Can't say as I blame you none. You ain't had nothing to eat for a whole day. Has you?"

The Ollar farm was deserted with the door to the shack standing wide open when he arrived. The blood stains on the floor made him fear the worst. He laid the baby on the cot and ran frantically from house to barn to woodshed and around the yard finding no signs of Ida. Then, trying to grab hold of himself, he began a careful search for signs of a grave, but with relief found none. He sat on the dirty floor and searched the room with his eyes, trying to think of what to do next.

"Shoulda killed that devil long ago myself. He ain't done nothing but cause good folks trouble." He wiped his palm across his tired eyes and sighed deeply. He was in big trouble. It didn't make any difference if they were supposed to be free. Kansas had been a free state all along, but he was still a black man, and he had stolen a white baby. If they caught him, they'd hang him for sure without asking any questions.

"Well, maybe you can tell me what to do." He let the small bundle suck on his knuckle while he talked. "If I was smart, I'd just leave you here and go my own way, but you knows I can't do that, now don't you? Guess I just has to take you home with me and give you to Mama to take care of, 'cause I shore don't know nothing 'bout taking care of no baby." He picked her up and walked to the door where he stopped to look around before continuing toward the mule.

"Boy, ain't she gonna be mad," he said with a laugh as he started the mule toward his small farm. "That woman's liable to skin us both when I shows up with you."

Chapter 15

Cotton sat at the kitchen table half-listening to Alice as he packed his pipe with fresh tobacco. The coffee in his cup had turned lukewarm.

"Harvey Blankenship." The tone in her voice caused him to jerk. "You haven't heard a word I've said. Have you?"

"Yes I have."

"Really?" She put her hand on her hip and pointed at him with the knife she'd been using to cut the potatoes. "Tell me. What did I just say?"

"Well, you were talking about... No, to tell you the truth, I wasn't." He stuck the pipestem between his teeth and struck a match. "What were you saying?"

"No, I want to know what it was that you were thinking about. What ever it is, it seems to be more important than listening to your wife."

"Well, a moment ago, I was worrying about Dave and the posse. We should have heard from them by now. But right now," he leaned an elbow on the table and smiled as he drew a puff, "I'm thinking that you're the most beautiful woman alive. Come here." He laid the pipe aside and patted his lap.

"Oh, Harvey," she said with a laugh, and turned back to her potatoes. "We're too old for that. What's got into you?"

"Old? Hush your mouth woman. I'm not a day over sixty, and you're not a day over forty-four." He rose from the table to fold his arms around her from the back and nuzzle her neck. "They say Abraham was a hundred and Sara was something like ninety when they had Isaac." He felt her body stiffen as her head fell forward.

"I'm sorry I could never give you children, Harvey."

"Alice," he said, taking the knife from her hand and tossing it in the bowl. He held her face in his palms and stared into her blue eyes. "I didn't mean it that way, and you know it. I've enjoyed every minute of being married to you these past twenty-four years. I wouldn't trade one second of that time to be with someone who could have given me a hundred sons."

"Well, I hope not. You couldn't support a hundred children on what you make between farming and being the sheriff." She wrapped her arms around him and laid her head against his chest as they both laughed.

"Now, come here." He pulled her by the hand and forced her to sit in his lap. "Okay, my beautiful wife, what was it you were trying to tell me?"

"I was just saying that there's something wrong with Lillian Hancock." She placed her hands on his shoulders and studied him intently.

"Go on."

"I've been over to their house several times since she lost her daughter. So have most of the women of the church, and they all think the same as I do."

"Well, what is it that's inside that head of yours? I might not like the man, but I haven't noticed anything unusual going on over there."

"It's just that," she paused to look away and purse her lips, "she doesn't act normal."

"Honey, she just had someone steal her daughter right out the bedroom window. How do you think she should act?" He gave her a quick kiss on the nose.

"It's not like that." She gave him a playful shove on the shoulder before growing serious. "There really is something wrong. I feel it in here," she said, placing her palm over her breast. "And you know I'm seldom wrong about these things." He had to nod his agreement. Alice's intuition about people was something he had learned never to question.

"Tell me about it."

"She just sits there staring at the wall. No, its not even that. It's hard to explain, but when she does talk, she doesn't make much sense. It's like everything in her mind is all jumbled up. Did you know they had a son who died in Virginia?" Cotton shook his head. "Well, according to her they did. And when she started telling me about him, that husband of hers ran us all out of the house, saying his wife was tired and needed her rest."

"Well, she might have been."

"That's true, but it's not like she doesn't have time to rest. She never leaves the house. She has a housekeeper. She doesn't even cook."

"Aha, do I detect a little jealousy here?"

"Not in the least." She swatted his arm. "It's more like she's a prisoner. The housekeeper won't let anyone in to see her unless her husband is around, and he's never very far away when we're there. He listens to our every word, and seems to think its his responsibility to interrupt everything she says. Now I know for certain that Lillian Hancock speaks perfectly good English. I just don't like the man. I don't trust him, Harvey. He's hiding something."

"More intuition?"

She nodded.

"Well, what do you want me to do about it? They haven't committed any crimes I know of."

"I didn't say they were criminals. Well, he might be...we really don't know. He certainly doesn't want anyone talking to his wife. That I can swear to in a court of law. I just want you to nose around a little."

"I am. We're looking for her daughter right this minute."

"I know you are, but that's not what I mean. I believe the woman is sick, Harvey."

"There's no crime in a person being unstable, unless they're hurting someone else. Now, if what you say is true, and her husband doesn't want folks to know, there's not much either one of us can do but mind our own business."

"No, but she might need help. You can at least find out, can't you?"

"Maybe, but it might be better to keep it a secret. How do you think folks around town are going to treat her if they think she's crazy?"

"I didn't say she was crazy." She set her lips in a thin line and glared at him. "And even if she was, I certainly wouldn't tell anyone, except maybe Vicky. I simply want to help her. Can't you see that?"

"Sure, okay," he said with a sigh. "I'll root around a little and see what turns up. I might even send a wire or two to Virginia and see if someone there can't shed a little light on something we don't already know. But if there isn't a body or two lying dead somewhere, or if he didn't empty any bank vaults, I don't want you bothering them. Is that understood?"

"Well, I would hope that you would do something if he's killed someone or robbed a bank. I simply want to know how to help his wife. I feel real sorry for her."

"And if she is sick and he still doesn't want anyone trying to help her, that's his business. Is that understood?"

"I know, but I've got to try."

"I know you do, and I love you all the more because of it." He slipped both arms around her as his lips lingered against hers.

"Harvey Blankenship," she said pulling away, "how can you think of such a thing after what we've been talking about?"

"I was thinking of it before you brought the subject up. Why should I change my mind because of something Douglas Hancock does or doesn't do?" He kissed her again.

"I've got to finish dinner." She tried pulling away, but he pulled her back to his lap.

"Okay, but let's have dessert first."

Chapter 16

"It won't be long now, Ida, until you get to see that squalling brat that's so important to you." Lowell laughed as he glanced toward his wife. Her body flopped liked a rag doll with every bump the wagon made on the rough road. He thought it downright comical the way her head rolled back and forth as if it wasn't connected to her skinny neck.

"Highya!" he yelled and slapped the reins. Lowell hated the wagon and seldom used it. He could have already been in Leon if it'd just been him and the horse. But he only had one horse and he thought it would be funny to see the look on that rich man's face when Ida told him she wanted her baby back. What was his name again? Douglas Hickcock? Naw, that's that marshal's name. It did have something to do with chickens though, didn't it? Well, no matter. Someone in Leon had to know who he was and how to find him.

"You ain't never been worth the powder to blow you away with, Ida, but you know something? You was sure right about one thing. We didn't get enough money for that kid. Fifty dollars? Hell, what was I thinking? They used to pay ten or twenty times that for a nigger slave where he came from. Of course they was all grown up and able to get right to work, mind you. But we certainly shoulda got more'n fifty dollars. And when we show up at his door, I'll bet he'll be willing to dig back into those pockets of his.

'Cause he sure won't want anyone knowing that baby ain't really his. He might even let you hold her for awhile." He slapped the reins again and laughed.

He grabbed the bottle stuck inside the top of his boot and pulled the cork with his teeth. After a long swallow, he jammed the cork back down with a grimy paw and returned it to his boot.

"You listening, woman? Aw, hell!" He brought the wagon to a halt as Ida relieved herself in the seat beside him. "Dammit!" He jumped to his feet as yellow urine dripped to the floorboards. "Why didn't you say something? Can't you control yourself? I ain't putting up with this any more." He gave her a shove with his heavy boot and watched as she toppled to the ground and rolled to a stop against a pile of rocks. "You never was any damn good nohow."

Lowell gave the horse a slap with the reins, and the wagon jerked forward. He turned in the seat to stare at a young Indian girl on a pony who appeared off to his left.

"Hell, that's all the better. Let the Injuns have you."

He pulled the bottle from his boot as he leaned back and laughed. He glanced over his shoulder for one last look, as the Indian walked her pony toward Ida's crumpled form. *Funny thing about Injuns*, he thought. *You can't never tell about 'em. That one's got yeller hair.*

Chapter 17

"Have you found anything yet?" Richard Whiteman sat atop one of the circus horses, watching the townspeople with rifles covering the countryside. The sight gave him a sick feeling in the pit of his stomach.

"Naw," Sheriff John Sattler said as he took a bite from a plug of tobacco. "Chew?" Richard shook his head. "Them folks out there's nearly stomped everything to death. They ain't gonna find no tracks even if there was some."

"So, what are you telling me? There's no possible way to find my lion?"

"No, didn't say that a'tall. I'm just saying we ain't gonna find her here. If she's like most cats, she's done lit out to where there ain't no people. That's why I got my best tracker, a feller named Carl Alls, some ways out," he pointed toward the southwest, "looking by hisself. He's got a couple of good hounds, and if that cat's out there, he'll find her for you."

"He's not going to shoot her, is he?"

"Not unless he has to. That lion really come all the way from Africa?"

"Yeah, and it'll be hard to replace her. If he finds anything, let me know and I'll take Otto out there to bring her in. He handles her like a kitten."

Chapter 18

This isn't good. Dave Price studied the scowling warriors gathered inside the lodge. Matthew sat cross-legged talking to White Cloud, who listened intently, but only gave a slight nod of his gray head now and then. The chief had seen more than sixty summers, yet, his powerful build and mannerisms gave Dave every indication that he had a say-so in everything that happened in the village. The smoke from the fire in the center of the tent stung Dave's eyes and tickled the inside of his nostrils. He was in the process of rubbing his eyes with the back of his knuckles when Three Horns jumped to his feet and started poking at him with his lance, as he addressed the chief in his native tongue. *No, this isn't good at all.* White Cloud raised his voice and Three Horns left the teepee in a huff, but not before giving him one more glare and a shake of his lance.

"White Cloud wants to know what's going to happen if he asks Shadow to come here," Matthew said, turning toward him.

"Tell him I only want to ask Black Shadow if he knows anything about the missing baby." Dave waited while Matthew interpreted. White Cloud regarded him with steel-cold eyes.

"He says Shadow knows nothing of the white baby. Be careful how you word your answer. Some of these braves speak pretty good English and they will tell him if you question his honesty." Dave glanced at the angry faces once more. "They're here to make sure I'm interpreting correctly."

"Okay." His voice sounded weak, so Dave cleared his throat. "Tell White Cloud I believe him. Tell him I would never question the honesty of such a great Chief or one of his braves. Tell him we don't believe Black Shadow had anything to do with the baby either, but there are some who do think he did, because of the description given by the mother. We must see him and ask him for ourselves, so we can stop those white people from coming to White Cloud's camp and causing him trouble."

"Good answer." Matthew smiled before turning to pass the message. White Cloud nodded and said something to one of the braves, who promptly left and returned a few minutes later with a giant black man dressed in buckskin.

"This is Shadow," Matthew said as the man glared at Dave. His hair, which was turning gray, hung in two long braids down his back, and a jagged scar ran across the bridge of his nose to his right cheekbone. White Cloud was speaking but the man gave no indication that he was even listening. He sat against the opposite wall and continued to glare.

"He's waiting for you to ask your questions," Matthew said.

"Oh," Dave said, drying his palms on his pant legs. "We hate to bother you, sir, but we have to ask you a few questions." He paused for Matthew to interpret and after a pregnant moment of silence, glared at his partner and gritted his teeth.

"I spoke English long before I learned Comanche. Ask your questions and be done with it." Dave's chin dropped.

"You heard the man. Ask your questions," Matthew said with a grin as he began rolling a cigarette.

"I'm sorry if I insulted you."

"Your words didn't insult me, deputy, but your presence does. Now, what is it you want?" Dave watched Matthew pass the cigarette to White Cloud while he tried to gather himself back together.

"Several days ago in Leon, someone broke into Douglas Hancock's house and stole his baby daughter. We were wondering if you knew anything about it?"

"Why would I know anything about a white man in Leon? I've never been there."

"His wife Lillian saw the man and described him as being a large black man dressed much like you are right now."

"Are you accusing me of taking her baby?" He knitted his forehead and leaned forward.

"No, no, nothing like that," Dave said, holding out his palms.

"Then what are you saying?"

"A lot of townspeople think it was you. They wanted to come here, but Manhunter and I stopped them. We thought it would be better if just the two of us came and asked you personally. That way we can go back and tell them what you said."

"A lot of people?" He laughed. "How many are there really? Nine besides you and Manhunter? And he isn't really part of your posse, is he?" Dave shook his head. "Tell them to come here and try to take me if they will. It's been a long time since I've killed a white man. And Three Horns would like nothing better than to meet them."

Dave glanced toward Matthew, who sat calmly rolling another cigarette.

"We've known about your little posse ever since you got within five or six miles of our camp."

"Yes, I thought you might. But I still had to ask my questions."

"Well, you asked, and you have my answer." He stood to his feet.

"One more question, if I may?"

"What is it?" He held the tent flap back with a huge hand and glared at him over his shoulder.

"Do you know who might be trying to impersonate you and make other folks think you would steal the baby?"

"No, but I'll kill him if I find out." He took a step outside then paused to look back. "One other thing, deputy. It will be easy for you to know it is me if I ever decide to take a white baby. I will kill it and leave it for everyone to see." He was gone and Dave couldn't help but shudder.

"So, now we know," Matthew said, striking a match against his gun.

~ ~ ~

"You weren't much help inside there," Dave said as they walked toward their horses.

"It was your job to ask the questions. It was my job to keep you alive, just like I hope I can right now." He held out his left arm to hold Dave back as Three Horns and several warriors appeared from behind a teepee. They stood between Dave and Matthew and their horses.

"Manhunter's mother was a white woman with white blood in her veins." Three Horns spoke loud as his gaze followed the crowd that had started to gather. "He has chosen to leave his people and go live with the white-eyes. It is said that he has married a white woman and has made white children. He must think he is white, for he comes now to accuse one of us of trying to steal a white baby."

"He speaks pretty damn good English," Dave said as the brave glared smugly.

"Told you. A lot of them do." The smile left the Indian's face as Matthew stepped forward to meet him. "What is it you want, Three Horns? I don't have much time." A pretty young woman with fearful eyes appeared from inside the tent. She had three small children with her.

"I think we should see if Manhunter's blood is red like a Comanche's, or white." He poked at Matthew with his lance but instead of backing away, Matthew grabbed the end of the weapon and gave it a jerk. The move caught Three Horns off guard and caused him to lunge forward, where he was met by Matthew's boot to his groin. He let go of the lance and grabbed his wounded part with both hands as Matthew placed a hard left hand to the base of his jaw. The brave fell in a heap with a groan. Matthew rolled him to his back with the toe of his boot and drove the lance into the ground beside his head. He then stepped back and placed his hands on his hips.

"When he wakes, tell him Manhunter has decided to let him live today, but if he ever challenges me again, I will kill him and give his scalp to my son." He stepped over the body and leaped onto his horse in one bound. Dave's knees felt weak, and it took him three tries to climb into the saddle. Matthew gave the woman a nod as he joined him. They didn't speak until they were clear of the camp.

"Jesus, why'd they let us go like that?"

"Because it was a personal thing between me and Three Horns. He gave the challenge, not the rest of them."

"I thought you were going to kill him for a second or two."

"I started to, but then it would have been open for any of the others to jump in. One of them would have certainly challenged you, too."

"Well, its over now, and we're out of there," Dave said, glancing back over his shoulder.

"Not by a long shot."

"Huh?"

"I might have whipped him this once, but I didn't kill him. And I just happened to hand him the biggest insult you could think of." He shot a glance from under the brim of his hat. "Guess I was mad and wasn't thinking right. But when I said I'd give his scalp to my son, that meant I didn't think Three Horns was much of a warrior and that his scalp wouldn't be a worthy prize for me to tote on my belt. We'll meet again. I insulted him in front of the whole camp so he'll have to defend his honor, even if he has to come looking for me at my own house."

"Who was the woman I saw you staring at?"

"That was Laughing Brook, Three Horn's wife."

Dave felt a chill sweep over him. "His wife?"

Matthew nodded.

"Then, she came close to seeing you two kill each other?"

"Along with their children."

"Damn you, Matthew Blue. That means the same thing's gonna happen when he shows up at your house, ain't it? Vicky and the kids are gonna have to watch as you two try to scalp each other. Ain't that right?" Dave yelled at him.

"Something like that." Matthew spurred his horse into a run.

Chapter 19

"Is she alive, Mama?" Caroline's voice broke with a sob as Vicky laid her ear against the woman's chest. Vicky could feel her rib cage through the thin clothing against her cheek. She was nothing more than a skeleton with a little skin stretched over her bones.

"Yes, I think so. Help me get her in the back of the wagon. Careful, now," she said as Caroline grabbed the woman's feet. She was amazed at how little the woman weighed. Caroline could have put her in the back of the wagon by herself.

"Why'd he do that, Mama? I saw him kick her out of the wagon. How could he treat her that way?"

"I don't know Carol. Some people are just plain mean, I guess." She glanced toward her son, who sat wide-eyed in the seat. "Just be thankful that God has blessed us with mostly nice, loving people in our lives. Your papa in his worst days would have never considered treating anyone this badly. And Matthew?" She paused from tucking a blanket around the frail body to stare off into the distance. "I've never known a kinder man. Cotton, Dave, and even gruff old Jim Larkin all have good hearts, but Matthew beats them all. Come on, you ride in the back and keep an eye on her," she said tying the reins of Caroline's pony to the buckboard. "We need to get her home as soon as we can."

"But why is she so skinny? What's wrong with her?" Caroline couldn't hold back her tears, so Vicky pulled her close in a gentle hug before tilting her daughter's head back to look in her eyes.

"Someone, maybe that man you saw, has tried to starve her to death. And from the looks of her face and body, they also gave her a terrific beating. Now, we don't have time for you to fall apart, understand? You've got to be strong if we're going to save her. Are you okay?" She nodded. "Good. Now, climb in back and hold her head in you lap and I'll take it easy going home. A few more bumps on her head will probably do her in." Vicky hiked the hem of her skirt and used the spokes of the front wheel to climb in beside her son. "Yah! Get up there Charlie. Move it Sally." She started the wagon forward with a snap of the reins. Mark placed a small hand on her arm and stared at her with huge, watery eyes.

"It's going to be alright, honey. Your father will be home any day now. He'll find the man who hurt her. The devil himself and all his demons couldn't stop your daddy from bringing that man back. Yah! Get moving, you lazy good for nothing hay-burners. Earn your keep." She gritted her teeth as the team fell into a brisk trot.

Chapter 20

"Good God, child! What's I gonna do with a white baby?" Benjamin Polk shifted nervously under his mother's angry gaze. "What's gotten into you, boy? Why ain't you got no common horse-sense?" His twelve year old brother, Joshua, snickered and skipped out of the way as Ben lifted a threatening back-hand. His two sisters, ages four and five, covered their mouths and giggled. "Well, say something. Or, has you forgotten your tongue somewhere along the way?"

"Bu...but Mama, it's Ida's baby." He pointed toward the small bundle crying in his mother's arms.

"I knows whose child it is. What I's concerned with is what's gonna happen to us niggers. What you think them white folks gonna do when they come looking for a white baby that's been stolen, and finds it here? What is you gonna say then, boy? Just tell me that. Huh? What is you gonna say then?"

"I don't know what I'm gonna say. I guess I wasn't thinking right."

"You can shore say that again." She bounced the baby in her arms and turned away. "How long since this child's had anything to eat?"

"Don't know." His voice was little more than a whisper.

"Well, speak up. I can't hear you if you don't talk. How long since this child's ett?"

"I said, I don't know how long. I didn't think to ask that woman who was screaming when I took the baby."

"Are you telling me that white woman seen you taking this baby out of her house?" She spun on her heel to stare at him wide-eyed.

"Yes'm."

"Lord have mercy," she said, rolling her eyes back toward the ceiling of their one room shack. "It's a good thing your father ain't alive to see this day. He'd skin you alive and nail your hide to the barn."

"It's okay, Mama. 'Cause I done dressed up like a Comanche Indian. She'll tell everyone that the Black Shadow took her baby."

"Black Shadow indeed! There ain't no such a person, do you hear me? That's just a story folks tells because they ain't got nothing better to do. Your daddy worked hisself right to the grave trying to hang onto this little scrap of ground, and now you go and bring more troubles on this family. You ought to be ashamed of yourself. Jessie," she turned to the five year old, "run yourself across the field and bring miss Mira back. Don't tell her why, but tell her I needs her right away."

"Yes'm." Ben watched his sister's skinny legs and bare feet through the open door as they kicked up little dust clouds in the yard and disappeared around the corner of the shed.

"Mira's done lost her youngun," Mama Polk said, as she bounced the baby in her arms and paced around the room. "But by the way she looked yesterday, I'd say she still has some milk. And you's so hungry you won't care none if it comes from a black nanny. No," she shook her head and smiled. "Don't reckon you'd care none no how, would you?"

"Ida was our friend, Mama. And she loved that child. It was all she had. I was only tryin' to help her."

"I know you was son. But the only thing that's gonna help Ida is for someone to get shed of that devil she's married to. That no account white man's worser'n any slave owner me and your papa ever seen. No one should treat a dog the way he treats her. That's why it didn't surprise me none when you told me he sold this baby to them rich folks from town. But then his kind's been buying and selling us folks for years. Now that Mr. Lincoln's done put a stop to it, guess they's gonna start buying and selling themselves." She paused her pacing to give him a worried smile. "You best get to your plowing you was supposed to be doing while you was out stealing white babies."

"Yes'm." He grabbed his hat and started for the door.

"Ben?" He turned to look at her. "I loves you son. But you'd best be thinking how we're gonna get this child back to the folks that bought her."

Chapter 21

"Hello, Douglas. Had one hell of a time trying to find you." Douglas Hancock stood frozen in the doorway as Chris Hari held out his thick hand. "What? No hello? No 'welcome to my home?' Not even a handshake?" Douglas took hold of the outstretched hand and grimaced as Chris squeezed it in a bone-crunching grip.

"What are you doing here, Chris?" he said trying to rub the pain out of his knuckles.

"What am I doing here? Now, is that the way to talk to an old friend and business partner?" He smiled a toothy grin and pushed his way inside. "Nice place you've got here, Doug. Real nice." He took off his coat and hat and hung them on the rack by the door. "Not near as nice as the plantation, but still pleasant enough." His sunburnt face matched his red hair.

"It isn't a good time for you to be visiting." Douglas stepped quickly to close the parlor door as Lillian rose from her chair and started their way. "You probably haven't heard, but my wife and I just lost our baby."

"Hell, don't give me that." Chris chucked. "You buried that kid of yours four or five months ago back in Virginia."

"No, our little girl."

"You don't have a girl." Chris' face turned red as he laughed aloud. "You've got to do better than that, Doug."

"We adopted a baby girl two months ago," he said as Chris wiped his eyes on his shirt sleeve and chuckled. "Honest. Just before moving here to Leon."

"Now, why do I find that hard to believe. And even if it is true, what's that got to do with me?"

"It's just that now's not a good time. My wife's sick, and our baby girl's gone. The sheriff and his wife and half the town keep dropping by to see how she's doing." Douglas stuffed his hands in his pockets as the corners of his mouth drooped. "Things aren't going too well, Chris. Not well at all."

"Well, they're about to get a lot worse. Charlie Stewart, Larry Tyner and Mike Steel are over at the drugstore waiting to talk to you." Chris grinned as the blood drained from Douglas's face. "Don't go passing out on me now."

"Dammit! What do they want?"

"What the hell do you think they want? You ran off with twenty thousand Yankee dollars belonging to us."

"I didn't do it, Chris. I swear to you on my mother's grave. I don't know who has that money."

"Well, you can tell it to the boys yourself." He tossed Douglas his coat from the rack before grabbing his own. "And please don't swear on your mother's grave. I know how you felt about the poor woman. Remember? I was with you the night you got drunk and danced a jig around her headstone." He opened the parlor door and poked his head inside.

"Good afternoon, Lillian. Sorry to hear about your little girl. I'm taking Douglas over to the pharmacy for a drink. We'll be back shortly."

"Thank you Christopher." Lillian's voice drifted through the cracked door. Chris shut the door and shoved his hat down over his red hair.

"She sounds fine to me. Come on, let's go." He grabbed Douglas by the arm as he opened the front door.

Chapter 22

Vicky set the bowl of soup on the table before facing her daughter's questioning eyes. "I don't know if she'll make it. She's too weak. I could only shove a few spoonfuls down her throat."

"What are we going to do, Mama? We just can't let her die."

"We're going to do everything we can, honey. I'll keep trying to feed her every few minutes, but you take Sugar and go get Doc Stevenson as fast as you can. I know it's getting late, but I don't think it can wait until morning. Hurry!" Caroline nodded and bolted through the door. Vicky watched until the horse and girl disappeared beyond the trees at the bend in the road, before turning back to the stranger lying in her bed.

"Be careful, baby. Be real careful."

Chapter 23

"Lowell Ollar leaned lazily against the counter holding the glass with both hands. His mind was beginning to numb and he was having trouble focusing on exactly why he had come to Leon in the first place. The drinks in the back room of the pharmacy were too expensive. Plain old whiskey was ten cents a shot, simply because it carried a label saying it was cough medicine. Lowell only had eleven cents lying on the counter and knew he couldn't survive the rest of the afternoon and evening on just one more drink. He'd have to think of something. He tilted his shaggy head and downed the last drops in the glass as the doors swung open.

"Well, I'll be damned! It's a miracle. That's what it is. A goddamn miracle." He wiped his mouth with the back of his hand and picked up his change. "Yes sir, Lowell, this is your lucky day." He wove his way toward the table where the five men were seating themselves.

"Hey, friend. How's that little girl of mine doing?" he said slapping Douglas Hancock on the back.

"What do you want?" Douglas scooted his chair closer to the table and growled at him. Beads of sweat mapped their way down his cheek as he tried to pour himself a drink with a shaking hand.

"You know this man?" The one with red hair and a friendly smile asked Lowell, as he pointed his glass toward Douglas.

"Yeah, sure. We're old friends, ain't we?" Lowell slapped Douglas on the back again. "He and that woman of his are taking care of my little girl, aren't you?"

"Shut up!"

"What?" The redheaded man joined the others in a friendly laugh. The only one not laughing was Douglas, who gripped his glass tightly.

"Yeah, my woman's been real sick, so they're taking care of the girl for me."

"I told you..." the man on Douglas' right pulled him back as he started from his seat.

"Here, come sit down," the redheaded man said, sliding his chair over to make room. "Have yourself a drink. I want to hear more." Lowell grabbed an empty chair from the next table and slid in beside them.

"My name's Chris Hari," he said sliding a full glass toward Lowell. "What sort of handle do you go by?"

"Name's Lowell Ollar." He gave Chris a quick nod before downing his drink.

"Glad to meet you, Lowell." He refilled the glass. "This here is Charlie Stewart," he nodded toward the big man with sandy-brown hair on Douglas' right. "He hails from Texas. He's a real handy man to have around when you need a good friend. That one there," he nodded toward the short, heavy-set man with dark curly hair on Douglas' left, "is Larry Tyner. Now you got to watch him around your woman, 'cause he'll take her away from you. That right, Larry?"

"You got it. Quicker'n you can blink," he said striking a match on the bottom of the table to light his smoke.

"And that's Mike Steel." Lowell glanced toward the good-looking youth. "He's mighty polite to everyone, including the whores in Ruby's Palace back home in Fredricksburg. But don't let him fool you. He handles that forty-four better than Charlie can handle a branding iron, and that's pretty damn good." Lowell nodded toward the men and downed another drink.

"Now, tell me," Chris said refilling the glass. "Where'd you meet our friend here, and what's this I hear about your little girl? It couldn't be that baby he's been trying to tell me about, could it?" A man at the next table scraped his chair against the wood floor as he got up to leave.

"Yeah, that's the one. He paid me fifty dollars if I'd let him take her." Chris' laughter was starting to give Lowell a headache.

"Hell, Doug, don't you know it ain't legal to buy humans no more?" Charlie Stewart said with a snicker.

"It isn't like that," Douglas said through clenched teeth.

"How else can it be?" Mike Steel said quietly. "You gave the man fifty dollars and took his kid."

"Hell, why not? Everything else around here's crazy. These Jayhawks voted in prohibition and shut down all the saloons back in '80. But you can still walk into most any drugstore and drink all you want," Larry Tyner said.

"Why did you come here?" Douglas was shaking visibly as he leaned across the table. "More importantly, how did you find me. I wasn't supposed to see you again."

"It weren't hard to find you. I just asked around a little, and some folks said they'd seen you here in Leon. As to why I'm here, I just wanted to see how my little girl was doing." Lowell stuck out his bottom lip as he spoke and shrugged his shoulders. "And I was kind of thinking that maybe, if you had the mind to, you'd come up with some more money. Things have been kind of tight lately."

"That's what I thought. You miserable bastard! How much do you want this time?"

"Oh, I don't know. How does a hundred dollars sound to you?"

"You leech!" Douglas lunged across the table only to be pulled back by Charlie Stewart.

"Having a little trouble boys?"

Lowell blinked his bleary eyes at the large man with a silver star pinned on his vest.

"Na, they're just arguing over which game we're going to play," Chris said with a grin as he picked up the deck of cards and gave them a shuffle. "Oh, by the way, I'm Chris Hari." He stood to his feet and offered a hand which the sheriff took reluctantly.

"You know these yahoos, Doug?" The sheriff stepped back and put his hands on his hips to stare.

"Yeah...yeah, I know them," he said nodding his head.

"Okay, that's good enough for me. But I want to tell you boys that I run a nice quiet community here, and I aim to keep it that way. You don't cause no one any trouble and I won't come looking for you. But you go raising hell, and I'll sure lock you up quicker'n you can blink an eye."

"Oh, you won't have any trouble with us sheriff. We're model citizens. You can count on that," Chris said with a wide grin.

"That's fine by me. Go on with your game." He turned away, but paused to look over his shoulder. "Doug? You don't look so good. Maybe you should go home and let that wife take care of you." Douglas nodded as the sheriff left through the swinging doors.

"That one's gonna be trouble." Mike Steel said, taking the makings out of his shirt pocket.

"Him? Na, he's just an old man trying to hang on to his job," Chris said as he shuffled the cards again and again.

"No, I know the type. He might be old, but he's harder'n a prostitute's heart when it comes to law and order." Mike glanced over the cigarette he'd just rolled and licked the paper. "I'll bet I have to kill him before this is over."

"Well, okay, you got my permission." Chris chuckled. "Now, let's get back to business." He clamped an arm around Lowell's shoulder and gave him a squeeze. "Our new friend here says he wants a hundred bucks. Give it to him, Doug."

"I'm not giving him any more of my money."

"You don't get it, do you? It isn't your money anymore. It's all ours. You ran off with twenty thousand belonging to us. Now give him the hundred he asked for."

Twenty thousand dollars? Lowell watched Douglas count out the bills wishing he'd asked for more before picking up the pile with a shaking hand.

"Now that that little matter is settled, let's get down to some real business. We want to know how much money you've got left, and how much you can lay your hands on."

"I don't know."

"Well, you'd better find out real quick, because you know me, Doug. I'll kill you right here where we sit if I think you're trying to flimflam me. I want to know what kind of game you're trying to play here with these hicks. I know you too well to think you'd rub elbows with a bunch of farmers if you didn't have to."

"Honest, I just wanted to get away. I wanted a fresh start."

"Damn." Chris shook his head as he pulled out his forty-four. He cocked the hammer and laid the weapon on the table in front of him. "Now, you can have it one of three ways. You can simply give us twenty thousand dollars and we'll go away and take our friend here with us," he swatted Lowell on the back. "Or, you can give us some of the money, say enough to tide us over. Then let us in on whatever you're planning to do here, so we can make up our losses. Or, if you don't like any of those deals, I can splatter your brains all over this room. Now, you tell me, which is it going to be? You've only got one of three choices."

"Okay, okay, you're in," he said holding up his hands. "In fact, it might be good that you showed up. This is how it goes." They all leaned toward the center of the table.

Chapter 24

Alice Blankenship was in Walker's General Store buying some apples and sugar to make a pie when she happened to see Douglas Hancock through the window. He was entering the Adam's Pharmacy across the street with a square-built man she'd never seen before. "Could you please save this for me?" she said, handing her basket back over the counter to Fred Walker. "I have to do something first."

"Sure thing, Mrs. Blankenship," he said with a drawl. "I'll set it right here. You just come back and get it anytime you want. Is there something wrong?"

"No," she paused at the door. "I just remembered I have some things to take care of before I go home." She held the folds of her skirt as she crossed the street at a right-angle and walked briskly toward the end of town. Bounding up the steps, she took the brass knocker in hand and rapped it soundly three times, then took one step back and waited.

"May I help you?" Joan Cornwell, the housekeeper, poked her head out the door.

"I'm here to see Mrs. Hancock."

"I'm sorry, Mrs. Hancock isn't taking visitors today." She started to close the door but Alice gave it such a shove, that it almost knocked Joan off her feet.

"I don't have time for your nonsense today, Joan. I want to see Mrs. Hancock."

"But Mr. Hancock will get angry if he knows you are here."

"Mr. Hancock be hanged. He's over at the pharmacy right this moment. I want to know what's going on here inside this house."

"There's nothing going on. What ever gave you that idea?"

"Oh, yes there is."

The housekeeper shook her head.

"How long have you known me, Joan?"

"Most of my life, I guess."

"Yes, and have you ever known me to do anything like this before?" She shook her head again. "Well, there is something wrong isn't there?" The sixteen-year-old girl stood like a statue. "I feel it right here, just as sure as I'm born. Now, what is it?"

"I'm not supposed to tell anyone. He'll fire me and I need this job real bad." She knit her brow and bit her bottom lip.

"Well, don't tell me then. Just get out of my way and let me find out for myself." Alice stepped past her to glance around the room. "Where is Mrs. Hancock?"

"In the parlor, where she spends most of her time." Joan followed her and leaned close to whisper as Alice opened the door. "She just sits there looking at that picture in her locket and holding that rag doll all day long. I think she's crazy myself, but I ain't supposed to tell no one. He'll get real mad if I do."

"That's okay, Joan. You don't have to go inside with me," she said squeezing her arm. "And if Mr. Hancock comes home before I leave, tell him I forced my way inside."

"Thank you, ma'am," she said as she hurried away.

"Lillian?" She stepped inside and closed the door.

"Oh, hello Mrs. Blankenship." Lillian stood with a warm smile and held out both hands. "I didn't hear you come in. I must have been lost in my own little world." She kissed Alice on the cheek and led her to the sofa, where she continued to hold her hand. "I don't get a chance to visit with people by myself very often. It seems my husband has arranged it so he's present when folks come calling." She grinned and leaned closer to whisper. "I think he believes I'll say or do something that will embarrass him. But it's actually the other way around. He's so gruff that he's frightened nearly everyone away."

"I'm not like everyone else. Besides, I'm married to the sheriff."

"Yes, that is so," she said with a lilt of laughter. "I think he's the only person around here my husband is genuinely afraid of, unless it's that big Indian that comes to town once in a while."

"Matthew?" She nodded. "He's really a nice, gentle soul. I've know him for years. He and his family are close friends of ours." Alice picked up the locket lying beside her on the sofa. "Yours?" she said, holding up the baby picture.

"Mmmhmm," she nodded and took the locket from her hand. "That's our little Bobby."

"I remember you mentioning you had a son one time. I've never seen a picture of him before. How long ago was it when he passed away?"

"He died a few days before we left Virginia," she said solemnly.

"I'm so sorry for you. I didn't know it was so recent." She placed her palm on Lillian's arm.

"Thank you, but you couldn't have known. Douglas doesn't want to talk about it much. That's why it was so hard when that man took our daughter. First Bobby, then Lottie."

"That's terrible. My heart just breaks for you." Alice pulled her close and embraced her. "And to think that husband of yours won't let you have visitors unless he is around. You need someone to talk to, if nothing else."

"Thank you. It does feel good." She slipped her arms around Alice and sniffed.

"How old was he?"

"Bobby? Six months old. Just a baby."

"That's even worse. I could never have children, but I can imagine what it would be like. It would just kill me if I had to go through the same thing."

"It almost did. And when I lost Lottie...I thought I was going crazy."

Alice pulled away and held her by the shoulders. "I don't blame you. I probably would have." She wiped a tear from the woman's cheek with her thumb then paused. "Wait, I'm trying to get this straight in my head. How long has it been since your son died?"

Lillian glanced toward the ceiling and wrinkled her brow in thought. "Just four months ago. We buried him and came right here." She patted the sofa.

"But you said he was only six months old when he passed away."

"That's right," she nodded.

"Lottie, your daughter isn't much older than that herself. Were they twins?"

"Oh, goodness no," she said with a smile. "I was feeling so blue about Bobby, that Douglas got me Lottie on the way here."

Chapter 25

"Mayor Parker? I'd like you to meet a business associate of mine from Virginia. This is Chris Hari," Douglas said as the men shook hands. "Chris is one of the major stockholders of the Topeka Santa Fe Railroad, and he's promised to help expedite our plans for the spur."

"Pleased to meet you, Mr. Hari. Please, gentlemen," he motioned toward the empty chairs, "make yourselves comfortable."

"The pleasure is all mine," Chris said, leaning back and crossing his legs. "Doug has been telling me about this project of yours, and it's really got me interested. Now I understand that he's willing to put up quite a sizable amount of money himself, and there are several interested investors as well. But you do understand that I've got a board and the rest of the stockholders to be responsible to." The Mayor rubbed his chin. "We need to know what makes you think this is going to be profitable for the railroad. What can we expect in return for, let's say, ten or twenty years in the future? The long haul."

"Well, we do hope to grow. Right now, the railroad connects us with Wichita, but the folks back east buy from markets in Dodge City or El Dorado. So, James Larkin has to ship his cattle and horses all the way to Dodge City, or drive them overland to El Dorado in order to find a good market.

So does Matt Blue, and ol' Wilson has to ship his hogs the same way, or by wagon. I'm sure everyone of them would appreciate being able to ship direct right out of Leon."

"Is that all? Aren't there any others?"

"Sure, nearly everyone around here is a farmer or rancher of some sort. And they all have the same problem getting their produce to market. Besides, Mr. Hancock has assured me that, with his connections in the South, it won't be long until we will have established a mercantile trade with the southerners that will turn this town into a bustling city. Look," he said, shifting nervously, "they all believe in this project. Everyone does. Jim Larkin believes in it to the point that he's been willing to mortgage his entire ranch to see that it gets done."

"Fine. That's what I wanted to hear." A smile crept across Chris' face. "You see, Mayor, your town may be putting up a large sum of money to get this project started, but it's going to cost my railroad a ton of money to keep it maintained. We just need to know that it's going to continue to pay for itself once we start sending railcars down the tracks from El Dorado to Leon." He rose to his feet. "It was nice meeting you." Mayor Parker shook the extended hand.

"Oh, by the way." Chris paused at the door. "When can we expect the entire sum to be available?"

"Now, Chris, I told you that I don't want any pressure put on the Mayor or anyone else around here. They're all hard-working folks doing the best they can. Besides, I'm going to be living here long after you've gone back east," Douglas said with a scowl.

"And I told you that we have a schedule to meet. I've got to keep my crews busy. And if Leon doesn't want the railroad, Piedmont and Fall River do."

"Gentlemen, please, there's no need to argue. I'm sure the money will be here soon."

"Are you sure? Because I have to let them know within the next few days so they can start making plans. You do understand, don't you?"

"Sure, sure, I understand. I'll see what I can do to hurry it up and let you know by tomorrow."

"Thank you, Mayor, and I hope you have a great afternoon." Chris smiled and closed the door behind him.

"Damn you, Winton Dahlstrom," Joe Parker said, hurrying to his desk. He grabbed his pen and started scribbling on a piece of paper. "Trying to steal our railroad, are you? I don't care if you are the mayor of Piedmont and related to my wife. I'll pull every string I've got and have that money here within the week."

Chapter 26

"What the hell did you let her in for?" Douglas was standing in the middle of the sitting room, yelling at Joan Cornwell. Tears streamed down the girl's cheeks as she trembled. "Well, I want an answer."

"I...I've been trying to tell you, Mr. Hancock. She just forced her way inside, like she does every time."

"She does? We'll just see about that. I don't care if she is married to the sheriff; forced entry is still against the law. If he won't put a stop to his wife going where she isn't wanted, then I'll go to the mayor. I have friends in this town. That woman should be behind bars." He grabbed his coat and hat.

"And next time I tell you not to let someone in this house, I expect you to carry out my orders. Is that understood?"

"Yes sir. Bu...but if she pushes..."

"Then shoot her. You know where I keep my gun, don't you?"

"Shoot her? Mr. Hancock, I can't do that."

"You want to keep your job?" He was so close to her that spittle spattered against her face. "Well do you?" She nodded. "Then do what I say."

"You're wrong, Douglas." He snapped his head toward the hallway where Lillian stood in her lavender sitting-gown.

"What? What the hell do you mean I'm wrong?"

"Simply that I invited Alice Blankenship to come visit anytime she wishes. And I asked her to bring some friends with her next time she comes."

"You had no right to do that." His voice dropped to a hoarse whisper.

"You seem to forget that this is my house too. I didn't complain when you brought Chris Hari and his friends here for dinner. And I don't know why it should bother you if I choose to have a few of my friends over for afternoon tea."

"I gave you strict orders that there was to be no one here unless I'm present." Joan let out a horrified gasp as he grabbed Lillian by the shoulders and flung her back against the wall. "Shut up." The maid cowered away as he raised his hand above her.

"Don't you lay a hand on that girl." Lillian stepped between them and Douglas raised his hand even higher. "Go ahead." She turned her cheek toward him. "It wouldn't be the first time." He lowered his hand and took a step backward. "So, you don't want Joan to see how you hit your wife, do you?"

"You...go to your room." He pointed a shaking finger toward the stairway.

"No, Douglas. I won't go to my room. I'm sick and tired of being a prisoner in my own house. I want to be able to have friends come and visit, and I want to go visit them when the occasion arises."

"Alright, Lillian. If that's what you want." He ran a shaking hand across his face and straightened the front of his jacket. "You may invite your friends over if you wish. I was just trying to protect you. I understand now, that you don't care if people know how sick you've been. I was doing it for you."

"That may be," she said, "but strange as it may sound, Alice Blankenship knows all about my sickness and still happens to like me."

"And just how much have you told her?"

"Only as much as I can remember. That we have a son who died, and that our daughter was adopted."

"Damn." He looked away.

"Why? What's the matter with her knowing that?"

"Nothing...nothing at all. Go ahead and visit your friends if you want. You're free," he said with a wave of his hand. "In the meantime I'm going to go have myself a drink." He grabbed his hat and coat.

"Oh, by the way. Joan? I'm sorry I lost my temper. Will you forgive me? I won't let it happen again."

"Yes, Mr. Hancock."

He closed the door and slipped into his coat as he walked briskly toward the heart of town. *Just like your damn father, aren't you Lillian? Well, I got rid of him when he got in my way, and I can get rid of you too.*

Chapter 27

"Now, what do you suppose went on while we were gone?" Dave asked as they surveyed the posse. The entire group seemed to be arguing.

"Hard to tell, but Smokey's giving Carl Evans the what-for. Better get ourselves over there before he decides to skin him."

"I'm certainly glad to see you're back. I was sure we were going to have to tie these two up to keep them from hurting each other," Al said as they dismounted.

"Yeah, what's going on, Smokey," asked Dave, facing the two men.

"This young whipper-snapper was suppose to be watching the packhorse and now it's gone."

"Gone? What about the supplies?"

"They's gone too. We packed up 'cause we was gonna go nosing around like you said. Now, the whole kit-n-kaboodle's gone. Horse and all."

"And no one saw it leave?" Dave pushed his hat back on his head.

"Everyone else was busy getting their horses ready to ride. We didn't see a thing," Al said. Dave turned to glare at the young man.

"I had to go behind the bushes for a minute. And when I come back she was gone."

"Na, ya didn't have to go behind no bush. Ya could've pee'd right where you was standing like everyone else. That mare wouldn't have cared none." Smokey spit and wiped his mouth with the back of his hand.

"I done told you. It weren't like that."

"Okay, okay, you two. Fighting amongst ourselves ain't gonna solve nothing," Dave said, holding up his hands.

"It weren't gonna be much of a fight." Smokey scowled at the boy before cocking his head sideways and squinting at Dave. "Say, how come you're back so soon. You didn't find them Injuns already, did you?"

"They're only four or five miles over that way," Dave said, pointing toward the southeast.

"And what about Black Shadow and the little girl?"

"He was there, but he doesn't know anything about the Hancock baby. He'd have no use for her."

"That's where our packhorse and supplies went." Matthew sat on his haunches pointing at the ground where the horse had been tied. Al Meeks craned his neck to look over Matthew's shoulder. "One brave came and took the horse when your backs were turned, while a second waited behind that clump of trees."

"He just walked off with the horse?" Al glanced around him.

"Yes, something like that."

"That's scary. Why didn't we see them leaving?"

"'Cause yer not supposed to. Them Injuns are brought up to be sneakier than any critter you can imagine. They'll take yer hair right off yer head while you's asleepin' and you won't know 'til the morning." Smokey's eyes grew large as he drew close to Al's face.

"What about Mr. Blue? Is he a sneaky critter too?"

Smokey fixed his gaze on Matthew before spitting and wiping his mouth on his sleeve. "He's worser'n any of 'em you ever seen. He's half white, so he gets you to forgetting the other half's Injun." Matthew tossed a stick at the man as both of them laughed.

"Well, at least White Cloud will be eating good tonight." Dave plucked at a tall blade of dried grass and poked it between his teeth.

"The children and women will eat. White Cloud and the braves will go without." Matthew glanced toward the others as he dug some jerked beef out of his saddlebags. "They're starving. This land's been hunted out and they need to move on, but there's no place to go except the reservation. Here." He handed each man a piece of meat. "It isn't much, but it's all I have."

"What do you mean, 'hunted out'? I saw an antelope not over an hour ago. And I've seen several rabbits and birds right here," Al said, trying to bite through the tough meat.

"Yes, but it's not enough to feed his people. There's thirty men, not counting all the women and children. No," Matthew shook his head, "they need the buffalo to live the old way, and there aren't any. They will have to go to the reservation where there are cattle to feed them, or starve."

"If they're so hungry, why do they keep wandering around here? Why don't they just join the others and get it over?" Carl Evans said.

"They are a proud people, Carl. This used to be their land," Matthew said with a sweep of his arm, "all they way to the Mexican border. Two-hundred-twenty-thousand square miles. The Comanche were a mighty nation of people and came and went as they pleased. They used to hunt buffalo right here where you're standing. Now they're told they can't live here anymore. They're supposed to share a small patch of ground with the Kiowa and eat cattle given to them by the government, and hunger has made most of them do just that. But a few, like White Cloud and Three Horns, are still holding out, hoping for the old days, but they will never come again."

"Damn!" Al stared at the piece of meat in his hand. "I feel guilty eating this hunk of leather."

"Well, don't. It might be all you'll get until we get back to town. We'd better hole up for the night and get an early start back home in the morning." Dave shaded his eyes against the setting sun.

"Know of a little hunting shack 'bout a mile or so off over there near Dry Creek," Smokey said, pointing toward the south. "Ain't much, but at least we'd have a roof over our heads."

"Okay, let's go."

Chapter 27

"Build up that fire, boys. I found me a sack of flour and a couple of cans of milk down in the root cellar. I'm gonna whip us up some lumpy dick," Smokey said, dropping the flour sack on the dusty table.

"You're going to do what?" Al said with a laugh.

"Make us some lumpy dick."

"And what, may I ask, is that?"

"Oh, I almost forgot. You're one of them ferners and they probably never had such good eatin's where you come from." He grabbed the three-legged pot sitting near the fireplace and handed it to Jim Larkin. "Here, give this thing a wiping out while I get things ready." Jim took the pot to the creek where a small trickle of water still remained in the sandy bed.

"Gather round, boys. I'm gonna teach you how to make some of the best eating you ever sank your teeth into, when you ain't got much to work with." Smokey took a bowl from the shelf, gave it a swipe with a rag and dumped some of the flour inside.

"Aren't those black spots bugs?" Al screwed up his face in disgust.

"They're weevils, boy. But don't worry, they ain't gonna mind none." Smokey opened the lid on one of the cans of milk.

"How old is that milk? Think it's any good?"

"Well, now ain't you just full of questions? I bet you never had to scratch around for anything to eat in your life, the way you're acting."

"Did the best I could," Jim Larkin said setting the heavy pot by the fire. "How do you make this here lumpy dick anyway?"

"Well, it's real simple. You get some milk real hot," he said, dumping most of the milk into the huge pot. "Then, you start making little lumps with the remaining milk and some flour, like this." He spooned some milk into the bowl of flour and made a dough-ball. "Normally, you'd add some salt and pepper, but we ain't got none. Learned this from one of them Mormon gals who come down the trail heading west awhile back. She claims her man and children like it real good. It's almost as good as grits an' grease. Bet you ain't never had none of that either, have you boy?"

"No." Al shook his head. "I don't even know what it is."

"Well, you ought to try it sometime, 'cause it goes down pretty easy. Ya take a bowl of grits and mix in some of yesterday's lean grease. Mmm-mmm," Smokey's head wobbled back and forth as he mixed the flour and milk into little balls. "Tell you what. You can spread it on biscuits and it's 'most as good as butter, if you ain't never had butter before. Now, a man can live on eatin' like that." He glanced up. "Is that milk hot yet?"

"Starting to scorch," Jim said, staring into the pot.

"Good. That makes it taste even better." He took the bowl of dough-balls over and started spooning them into the boiling milk. "Actually, this ain't half-bad. It kinda grows on you. Not too many folks 'round here who's heard about it though."

"Vicky makes it all the time," Matthew said peering over his shoulder. "Only she doesn't call it lumpy dick."

"Really? What's she call it?" Smokey glanced up with a grin.

"She just calls it paste. The kids use it to stick things together in school."

"Well, ya'all can poke fun all you want, but I didn't see none of you bringing anything in here to eat." He shook the spoon at Matthew's nose.

"Hey, I'm not complaining," he said holding his palms out. "Is it ready yet?"

"Yeah, come and get it."

They filled their tin coffee cups with the steaming mixture and all but Al Meeks began gulping it down. "You don't actually expect me to eat this, do you?" he said, staring at the cup.

"No, but if you don't want it, save it for someone else," Smokey said over a mouthful. "Ya oughta try it son. It'll stick to your ribs," Jim Larkin said.

"That's what I'm afraid of. Besides, it's got bugs in it."

"Them little flour weevils ain't gonna hurt you none." Some white dribble danced in Smokey's beard as they spoke.

"Not near as big as some of those hoppers folks were eating a few years back," Carl Evans said.

"Hoppers?"

"Yeah, back in '74." Dave paused to swallow. "Never seen anything like it, and hope I never do again. Grasshoppers everywhere. They got inside your house, your cupboards...even your bed. Billions of them. I was outside when they first came in from the northwest and I got covered from head to foot. The ground was covered," he made a sweeping motion with his hand, "in some spots three or four inches deep. Some of the trees along Walnut Creek were so loaded with hoppers that limbs broke off."

"They were so thick, they actually drove some horses and cattle crazy," Jim said. "Ate every blade of grass in sight. Weren't nothing for the animals to eat. Even started eating folks clothes right off their backs."

"What'd you do?"

"Well, I drove what cattle and horses I could down south, where I could feed them. Reckon other folks did the best they could. Some of them packed up and went back east."

"I thought I heard Carl say people were eating the bugs." Al glanced at the boy.

"Guess some of them did." Jim stirred the mixture in his cup. "They kind of figured since the hoppers ate their crops, there wouldn't be any real harm in eating the hoppers."

"Eeewww."

"It was do that, or starve. That's the way I look at it." Smokey wiped at the dribble with his sleeve. "Go ahead and eat son. Them weevils just add a little meat to the mix. Hell, I've ett lots worser things than a weevil in my life. How about you Matt?"

"I can remember sprinkling gunpowder over rotting horsemeat to kill the taste."

"Gaw, now you're lying to me." Al set the cup down in disgust as everyone laughed.

"No, honest to God." He held up his hand. "It happened when I was an Army scout. Roman Nose had us pinned down at the Pawnee River for several days. His braves caught us trying to cross and opened fire while we were in midstream. We had to take shelter on a little rock of island. They killed every horse we had and we couldn't even move without getting shot at. The only thing we had to eat was our dead horses. Some of them started to smell pretty ripe after laying in the sun for a couple of days while we waited for help to arrive. Had a hell of a time keeping the buzzards away from the one I was eating on."

"Oh," Al covered his mouth and bolted from the room.

"Yeah, them were the good ol' days," Smokey said, picking up Al's cup and offering it around the room to any takers. "I can remember running from Roman Nose a time or two myself. One damn good soldier, that half-breed was.

Too bad we was on opposite sides. I would've liked to of rode with him. But that would've meant he'd been fighting again' his own kinda folks, now wouldn't it?"

"Yeah, sort of like me," Matthew said, leaning back and covering his eyes with his hat.

"Hey, I'm sorry, Matt. I never meant it like that." The Indian remained silent.

Chapter 28

"Is she gonna live, Doctor?" Caroline asked as he dropped his stethoscope into his bag and snapped it shut.

"I don't know, child. As it looks now, I'd bet against it." He shuffled over to the table and plopped into a chair. Vicky set a mug of coffee in front of him and put an arm around her daughter. "It's her heart, you know." He squinted as he removed his glasses to clean them on the edge of her white table cloth.

"I was afraid of that. She seems so weak. I tried to get some soup down her, but she wouldn't eat hardly anything at all." Vicky watched Susan Price try to spoon some of the lukewarm liquid in the woman's mouth.

"No, her body might be weak from starvation, but I don't think it's gone so far that she couldn't pull through, given the chance. That's not what's bothering her at all. And you've done everything medically possible for her."

"Then what's wrong with her? Did that man hit her so hard she's gonna die?" Caroline said.

"No, that's not it either. Come here." He slid back from the table and held out his arms until the girl was standing beside him. He wrapped an arm around her and talked slowly. "It might be hard to understand, but that woman's seen and felt enough pain that she just doesn't want to live anymore. She wants to die, and that's why I don't know if we can help her or not."

"Thank you for trying to help her anyway, Roy. I know it's hard on you coming all the way out here," Vicky said.

"Oh, think nothing of it. I always enjoy seeing you and the kids." He paused to stare out the window at the blackness. "Tell you what, though. If you don't mind, I'd like to spend the night here before heading back in the morning. That way I can get a good cup of coffee and a home-cooked meal to start my day."

"We'd be more than pleased if you and Susan both did. You can have Caroline's bed and she can sleep with me in front of the fireplace. That way, we can all take turns watching our patient."

"I'll take the first watch," Susan said with a smile. "That means you get to watch Joshua."

Caroline walked over to her mother's bed and stared down at the pale creature with sunken eyes. "Don't die. Please get well. I don't want you to die."

Chapter 29

"How would you like to go riding this afternoon?" Douglas purposely kept his eyes on the front page of The Leon Vindicator as he asked the question.

"Go riding?" Lillian dropped her fork in her breakfast dish.

"Yeah, you know, horses? We used to do it all the time. You do remember how to ride don't you?"

"Yes, I remember how to ride very well. But you haven't suggested that we go riding together in over a year. What's gotten into you, Douglas?"

"Oh, I just thought it might be fun if we started doing some of the things we used to do." He folded the week-old newspaper and laid it on the table. "We've grown apart, Lillian. All we seem to do is fight and argue. I didn't like what happened yesterday any more than you or Joan did. I want things to change. Will you go with me?"

"Well, yes, but not today. I can't."

"And why not?"

"Some of the ladies are meeting at Alice's and they're going to start teaching me how to quilt."

"Quilt? You don't need to learn how to quilt. We can buy a damn quilt if you need one."

"Yes, but this is something I want to do. Don't you understand?" She blinked her hazel eyes at him and smiled. "We'll go riding some other time, okay?"

"Yeah, sure. I just thought you didn't want to go riding because of your father's accident."

"No, although that does bother me when I stop and think of it." Her smile vanished. "He was such an excellent rider. I don't know how he could have fallen off that horse and broken his neck."

"I've explained that a hundred times. He tried jumping that rail fence and the horse stumbled with him. It was a quirk of fate. It could have happened to anyone." He reached across the table and took her hand. "You're still not blaming me for what happened to your father, are you? I just happened to be there, Lillian. I didn't cause him to fall."

"No, I never did blame you, Douglas. His dying broke my heart, that's all. My father and I were so close."

"I know. It bothers me too." He rubbed her knuckles with his thumb. "So you will go riding with me then...sometime?"

"Yes, I'd love to. Just not today."

"Good." He got up from the table and kissed her forehead. "I've got things to do now. I'll see you later."

No, Lillian my dear, I didn't cause your father to fall from the horse. He grabbed his coat and hat and peered around the corner to smile at her. *The old bastard was actually bent over checking his horse's left front leg when I hit him with the rock. I don't believe he even felt it when I snapped his neck.*

Chapter 30

Matthew spurred his horse into a dead run, leaving the posse behind. The sight of Doc Stevenson's buggy parked at his front door only meant that something was drastically wrong. The old man was pushing eighty and didn't make house calls unless it was an emergency. The Doc's mare whinnied and backed away as he brought the pinto to a sliding halt. He was bounding toward the front door when Caroline met him and buried her face against his chest.

"What's wrong, baby?" he said, trying to peer through the door while she clung to him like a burr.

"He says she's dying, Daddy!"

"Oh, please God, no!" He gripped the door post to steady himself.

"What's wrong, Matt?" Dave said as he dismounted and scrambled up the steps to meet him.

Vicky came to the door wiping her hands on her apron and Matthew engulfed her in his arms, pinning Caroline between them.

"Daddy, you're squashing me."

"I've seen some men who've been anxious to get home, but this is ridiculous," Dave said as Matthew kissed Vicky over and over again.

"Well, she *is* rather pretty," Al Meeks said, removing his hat.

"You could learn something from him, David, if you had a mind to." Susan Price stuck her red head out the door and quickly disappeared back inside.

"Susan? What's going on here?" Dave said, squeezing past to catch his wife.

"Yes, what is going on here?" Matthew released his hold on Vicky.

"Wheew! Now I can breath." Caroline wormed out from between.

"You'd better come inside and see for yourself," Vicky said, pulling him toward the door. "Caroline happened to see a man push this woman out of a wagon yesterday while she was riding Sugar. He left her beside the road to die, so we brought her here. I sent Caroline to get Doc Stevenson, and he brought Susan along to help nurse. We've done everything we can, Matthew. I just don't know." Her chin quivered as she shook her head.

"I know this is going to sound bad, but when Carol grabbed me, saying someone was going to die, I thought...well, I'm just glad it isn't you." He leaned over to look at the woman on the bed and winced.

"My God, Roy, what the hell happened to her?" Dave was pale and leaned heavily against his pregnant wife.

"What does it look like? Someone's tried killing this poor creature little by little. Torture is more like it. I haven't seen anything like this in a long time." He got to his feet and went to the sink-board to wash his face and hands. "Actually, I don't know if I've ever seen anything exactly like this."

"Dear God in heaven," Al Meeks said, as he and several others of the posse crowded closer for a look.

"Hey, you varmints. Back outta here and give that woman some room to breath," Doc Stevenson said with a growl. They started to shuffle out when the woman rolled her head toward them.

"Albert?" Her voice was no more than a croak. Al spun on his heel as Vicky dropped the spoon she was using to dip broth with. "Albert? It's Ida, Albert."

"Ida? Ida Montgomery?" He fell to his knees beside the bed and took her hand. "Is that really you?" She gave a slight nod. "I'm sorry. I didn't recognize you."

"I don't wonder. I don't look much like the Ida you knew." She closed her eyes and grimaced with a catch of her breath.

"What happened, Ida? Dear God. I've been looking for you for over a year now. I can't believe it's really you. Who did this to you?" He kissed her hand time and time again.

"My husband, Lowell. I got married while you was gone. Now I know I shoulda waited."

"Oh God, I'm so sorry, Ida." A tear fell on her face as he leaned closer. "I love you."

"I know you do. I didn't think so back then." Her smile made her look more skeletal-like. "Don't worry, it don't hurt much any more, Albert. It used to, but not anymore. You get where you don't feel the pain after a while." She rolled her head toward the wall. "Besides, I been listening to them talk before you got here. They thought I was sleeping, but I was just too tired to open my eyes. I reckon I won't be around much longer." She closed her eyes as her words seemed to fade.

"Ida?" he said grabbing her by the shoulders. She rolled her head back to smile at him.

"Better let her get some rest, son," Doc said placing a hand on his back. Al got up and walked slowly out to the steps where he sat and hung his head between his knees.

"That's the first words she's said since Carol and I brought her here," Vicky was saying as Matthew sat on the edge of the bed and took the woman's hand.

"Ida? My name's Matthew. I'm Vicky's husband, and this is my house your in. I need to ask you one question before I let you go back to sleep." She opened her eyes with a flutter. "Do you know where your husband was going after he left you?"

"Leon, I think."

"Leon?" Matthew glanced up at Dave. "Do you know why?"

"To see the man who took my baby. He sold my baby." She closed her eyes and rolled her head back and forth. Dave let out a string of curses and stomped toward the door.

"I'm sorry, Matt, but you've got to let her rest," Doc said. Matthew went to the door to get some air just as Dave untied his horse and led it to the center of the yard.

"No you don't. Just hold on there." He grabbed the deputy by the shirt collar and pulled him back as he tried to climb into the saddle.

"I'm gonna get that son of a bitch and..."

"And what? It's getting late and we don't even know what he looks like."

"But we got a name."

"Yes, and it can wait until morning when we're rested and thinking straight. Then we'll all go to town and find him. Cotton can handle it from there on." The deputy stood with hands on hips glaring at him.

"You're too angry and you'll do something stupid. Just calm down. Here." He turned away and waved toward Smokey and the others. "You men unsaddle the horses and turn them loose out by the pond. And keep an eye on our friend here. He's too hot-headed to go into town right now." He paused at the doorstep as Al Meeks checked the loads in his revolver.

"Him too."

Chapter 31

It was close to midnight when Vicky finally lay on the pallet next to her husband and closed her eyes in exhaustion. She and Caroline had done their best to see that the men were fed and the house cleaned, as well as caring for Ida. Doc Stevenson had gone back to town much later than planned, taking Susan Price and her baby with him. Most of the posse had either bedded down on the porch with Smokey or out in the barn, with the exception of Al Meeks, who insisted on sleeping on her floor so he could be closer to Ida.

~   ~   ~

"I fell in love with that girl the first time I saw her," he said staring misty-eyed into his coffee mug earlier that evening. "But I was educated and from a wealthy English family. She, on the other hand, had no family and was dirt poor. So you can imagine how my father looked down on our relationship. Anyway, I'd already asked her to marry me in spite of his wishes, and had planned on doing just that as soon as I got back from England. But," he wiped his eyes on his sleeve, "she was gone when I returned home. I should have married her before I left. She was an orphan, you know. Anyway, my father was happy. He reminded me that he'd warned me she was no good. He said her husband was a drunken thief, and they had been run out of town. Naturally, I didn't believe him. So, I decided to go after her. God, I was livid." He smiled bitterly and set the empty cup on the table with a thud.

"What did you expect to find when you caught up with them?" Matthew asked, bouncing Mark on his knee.

"I don't really know. An explanation, maybe. Certainly not this." He shook his head as his eyes drifted toward the bed. "I don't know."

~   ~   ~

Vicky kicked the blankets back off as a deep moan escaped Ida's throat. She had to step over a snoring Al Meeks in order to reach the edge of the bed. "Its okay. Shhhhhh, it's alright," she said wiping the woman's brow as the head tossed back and forth. The eyes popped open wide to stare at her.

"Is there something I can get you? A drink of water?" She nodded and Vicky held the glass to her lips as she gulped.

"You're an angel, you know?" Her voice was a whisper.

"Well, not really, but thank you just the same. I'm just glad you're here so we can take care of you."

"I heard you reading the Bible and praying with your children earlier. Do you really think there is a God?"

"Oh, I'm sure of it," she said, wiping Ida's wet brow and cheeks with a damp cloth.

"I never knew if he existed or if it was all just a story, you know? I prayed a few times, but never really got an answer that I know of. Maybe he just didn't listen to me."

"I'll bet he did. What did you pray for, Ida?"

"Last time I remember, I asked him to help me kill my husband, 'cause he's so mean. Or, if he didn't want to do that, I asked him to just let me die. He never answered either one."

Vicky put the cloth back into the bowl and bowed her head for a second before taking the woman's hands and kissing them. "He couldn't answer that prayer, Ida."

"Why not? I meant every word."

"I know you did, and I'm sorry you've had to go through so much pain. But He couldn't help you murder someone, no matter what that person's done. Punishment belongs to God and the law, not us. And as far as you wanting to die, you weren't ready to meet Him. You didn't even believe He existed."

"Oh, I never thought about that." She let her eyes roll around in the sockets. "How can I get ready when I don't know for sure. If he's really there like you say, why'd I have so much trouble? Why'd I have to suffer like this?"

"Well, I believe we cause some of that ourselves." She paused to wring out the cloth and start wiping the bruised face again. "I understand Mr. Meeks wanted to marry you himself. And from what little I know about him, I don't believe that he would have treated you like your husband has been doing. He loves you terribly. Why did you run off with Lowell?"

"I had a hard time believing that Albert really loved me like he said. Him being so pretty and right like he is, and me being what I am, you know? And he was gone so long, I got to thinking that he might not even come back home, let alone marry the likes of me. I guess I listened to his daddy too much. He kept telling me that Albert went back to England to marry someone else. So, when Lowell came along and said he wanted me...I don't know. Guess I was desperate."

"You can't really blame that on God now, can you?"

"Guess not." She let her head roll toward the wall. "There ain't no hope for me now, is there?"

"Sure there is." She leaned close to kiss her cheek. "Just ask Him to forgive you."

"Who? God or Albert?" The dark brown eyes darted back toward her.

"Well, if it was me, I'd ask them both. And I know they will forgive you, because they both love you very much." She paused to brush back the matted hair. "Tell God you're sorry, and trust Him, Ida. He won't let you down."

"Think so?"

"I know so. Want me to pray with you?"

"Yeah." The voice was getting weaker, so Vicky placed her cheek next to Ida's and prayed for all she was worth. When she finished, she kissed the woman's cheek and Ida mouthed a tearful thank you. Vicky returned to the pallet and fell asleep. The next morning, Ida Ollar was dead.

Chapter 32

"Hear that cat last night?" Smokey leaned against the front wheel of the buckboard as Matthew hitched the team.

"Couldn't help it. Caroline's dog kept growling and barking. Got my gun and opened the door, but I saw you sneaking across the yard, so I went back to bed." He paused to study the old man. "Did you find anything while you were out nosing around?"

"Yep. Cat tracks, sure as yer born. Right over there." He pointed past the pond with the pipe stem. "Big feller, too. Kinda bunged up and lame, is my guess. But he didn't sound like no mountain lion I ever heard. Most of 'em cry kinda like a woman who's hurting real bad. But this one just growled like a bar."

"I haven't seen a cougar around here since I was a little boy, and that one was closer to the foothills. I wonder what he's up to?"

"Probably too old ta go hunting with the younger cats, so he's come outta the hills looking fer easy pickings. Like your horses."

"Did he get any?"

"Not that I could see. But he will sooner or later, when he gets one cornered in a pen like yer daughter's horse." Matthew shot a glance toward the small corral where Sugar stood watching them. "He probably smelled all us human folks sleeping round here last night and heered yer dog and decided he didn't want no part of this mess. But I'd keep that gate open so that filly can run free, or else she might get et."

"I'll tell Caroline." He gave one of the straps a final tug. "But I also think it's a good idea to go cougar hunting when this thing with Mrs. Ollar is over."

"I agree. But it might not wait that long. Ain't nothing meaner'n a hungry cat, and you got some mighty tasty lookin' horses around here." He gave Matthew a nod of finality, then walked away talking to himself. "Yep, ain't seen no cougars 'round here since the buffaler got kilt off."

Chapter 33

The children inside the one-room schoolhouse did their best to act sad when Matthew explained why classes were being canceled for the day. Several boys immediately dashed outside and tried climbing onto the wagon to view the body wrapped in blankets.

"No! Go away!" Al Meeks cried as he covered Ida with his own body.

"Hey now, y'all get away from there! Cornsarned kids." Smokey waved his hat in an effort to shoo them away.

Cheers escaped a couple of the boys as the wagon pulled away from the schoolyard and headed toward the sheriff's office.

"That was Bobby Sorenson and Jack Caldwell," Caroline said, staring back over her shoulder.

"Well, never mind them, darling. They just don't understand what's happened," Vicky said, urging the team on. Matthew rode close by while the posse filed in behind.

"Yeah, they understand. They just ain't got no brains."

"Caroline Jamison!" Vicky shot a glare toward her.

"Blue, Mama. I've been telling my friends that I changed my name to Blue."

Vicky turned toward Matthew, who raised his eyebrows and shrugged. "Alright, you can call yourself Blue if you want. But you still have to watch your mouth, young lady."

"Why? It's true."

"Even if it is true," she stopped the wagon in front of the sheriff's office and leaned close to glare at her. "I'm not only your mother, I'm also your schoolteacher. You should have said, they haven't any common sense. Not that 'they ain't got no brains.'"

"Yes, ma'am." Caroline smiled and climbed down as Cotton came out of the office to glance from the wagon bed toward Matthew and back again.

"That the woman Carol came bustin' into town yelling about?"

"Yeah, she died sometime last night," Matthew said as he helped Vicky down from the wagon.

"That's not actually true," Vicky said, stepping up onto the sidewalk and removing her gloves. She studied the questioning faces. "I was up with her in the middle of the night and we spent some time talking. I don't know for sure, but it was probably near twelve-thirty, pushing one o'clock when I got back to bed. She must have passed away some time in the early morning."

"Huh, and what did you two talk about?" Cotton pushed the brim of his hat back with his index finger.

"God and forgiveness, mostly. She wanted to die, Cotton. It was her time."

"She didn't happen to tell you who did this to her, did she?"

"Not last night," Vicky shook her head, "but she did earlier in the day."

"Just a name. And you'd better keep a handle on Al and that deputy of yours." Matthew shot a glance toward the two men. "They're madder'n a wet hen, and ready to skin that guy alive if they ever tie a face to that name. He was supposed to be heading to Leon, if you can believe what that woman was saying."

"That right? And do you believe her?"

"Oh, I believe here, alright. What reason would she have to lie? You seen this yet?" Dave said, jumping into the back of the wagon to pull the blanket back. Cotton grimaced and motioned for him to cover the body.

"And we do have a name. Lowell Ollar. I'm going to open every door and turn every barrel over until I find him." He grew red in the face as he jumped to the ground.

"And then what?" Cotton waited as Dave glared at him. "What you're gonna do is wait until I give the orders, then you're gonna do exactly like I tell you." He turned to point a finger toward Al Meeks. "And that goes for you too, understand? I don't want to have to lock either of you boys up, but I will, for God's sakes, if you go breaking the law." He waited for his warning to sink in.

"Now, here's what we're gonna do. First," he tapped Dave on the vest, "you're gonna take that poor creature to the undertaker's and then get right back up here for a confab. And I want the rest of you inside right now, so I can hear what went on while you was running around." He ran his fingers through his hair as he turned to enter the office. "God must be trying me. A whole posse goes out looking for a baby and returns with a full-grown woman...a dead one at that."

"You take your brother and head down to Aunt Alice's house," Vicky said, handing Caroline Mark's hand. "And stay there until one of us comes to get you."

"Make sure you tell Uncle Harvey about her baby."

"Don't worry, I will. And you mind her, and do your homework while you're waiting."

"Aw, Ma." She stomped her foot with a whine. Matthew leaned over his wife's shoulder and held up his index finger with a frown. "Okay, come on, Mark. They never let us have any fun."

"We never let them have any fun?" Vicky's eyes flashed anger as she tilted her head up toward him. "Seems to me that you take her with you nearly everywhere you go.

And you do real horrible-boring things like riding horses, fishing and hunting."

"Those are things we let her do. Now, if you told her she had to do them, they wouldn't be fun either. Come on," he said slipping an arm around her. "Cotton's waiting."

Chapter 34

Cotton leaned back in his chair and crossed his legs as he packed tobacco in his pipe. "Seems to me that none of you has shed much light on the situation. All you did was take a ride in the countryside and get some fresh air. All except for Dave and Matt. They do their best to start another Indian war. Nope." He struck a match and lit the pipe. Small clouds of smoke drifted toward the ceiling as he drummed his fingers on the desk and studied their faces. "It's getting more complicated by the minute. Guess I shoulda went by myself."

"You saying that we didn't do our job?" Dave jumped to his feet.

"No, but I probably could have sat and had a nice lunch with White Cloud without getting into a squabble with Three Horns. I'm surprised at you, Matt." He paused to draw deeply on the pipestem. "Sit down, Dave. You make me tired just looking at you."

"Just lost my temper," Matthew said, fumbling with the brim of his hat. "He was showing off in front of the whole camp."

"No doubt about it, but to save face, he's got to come looking for you. You know that better than I do. Then one of you is going to have to kill the other." Vicky turned pale and grabbed her husband's arm. "Didn't think to tell her about it, did you?" Matthew shook his head. "Didn't think so. Probably wasn't thinking about her or them kids when you got hot under the collar, was you?" He paused as Matthew's eyes dropped to the floor. "Sometimes, it's better to swallow an insult and walk away before doing something that you and a whole lot of people will regret later on. That goes for all of you." He let his gaze pause on each face before continuing.

"I purposely chose each one of you because you're leaders around here. Folks look up to you, and I want you acting in a way that they can admire and follow. You're better than that, Matt. You've got a double responsibility, being part Comanche. Both people, white and red, are watching you, trying to figure out what's right. You've got to show them that we can live together without killing each other. And you," he pointed his pipestem toward Dave, "represent the law around here. I'm not going to stand for one of my own threatening to lynch someone for any reason whatsoever. Understand that?"

"Yes but," Dave stammered, and pointed toward the door. "You saw what he did to her. You aren't going to let him get away with that, are you?"

"Hell no, I'm not! Begging your pardon." He shot a glance toward Vicky. "I'm telling you to catch him, bring him in here and lock him in one of those cells," the pipe shook as he pointed it toward the back room, "and let Judge Wilson try him. Then, when Silas Wilson says to hang him, I'll do it myself, 'cause that's the way the law says it's to be done. Anyone working for me is going to obey the law. Got that?" He stood and jammed the pipe between his teeth.

"That goes for all of you. And if you," he pulled the pipe from his teeth to point at Al Meeks, "find him first, you'd better bring him in here without a single scratch, or you'll be sleeping in the same cell beside him."

"But what if he don't want to be caught?" Smokey said, digging a chew out of his pouch.

"Then get some help or bop him over the head, but no one here had better shoot him unless you have a whole passel of witnesses, because I'll shore lock you up if you do. Is that understood?" He jammed the pipe back into his mouth to glare at them before sitting back down.

"Alright, now here's what we're going to do. Just so's you know I wasn't napping while you were gone. Smokey?" He squinted and pointed the pipe at him. "There's some new hombres hanging around town, mostly in the back of the drugstore, who're claiming to be friends of Douglas Hancock. One of 'em claims to be some sort of boss with the railroad. But I'm guessing none of 'em's really friendly toward Doug, let alone working for the railroad. First day they was in town, they got into a jawin' match with Doug while ol' Judge Wilson was sitting at the next table having hisself a drink of cough medicine. Now, seeing as Silas was dressed in his farming clothes, I'm sure they thought he was a no-account hog-farmer, and didn't pay him much mind. He came and told me they was claiming Douglas owed them a hunk of money and was going to send him home to his maker if he didn't pay up. I want you to nose around and see what you can turn up. Have yourself a drink and listen in on them while they're talking if you want, but be careful."

"Think they got something to do with the missing kid?" Smokey stood and jammed his hat over his grey hair. "Like maybe they got his girl and want him to buy her back?"

"The notion crossed my mind. Go see what you can find out." Smokey nodded and closed the door behind him.

"Dave, you take Al, seeing as you two are so hot to do something about poor Mrs. Ollar, and follow Smokey to the drugstore. There's another new feller that's been hanging around town. I'm sure you'll find him there, 'cause he's a fall-down-dead-in-the-mud drunk. He was acting pretty friendly with the men I sent Smokey to spy on, but I've got a feeling they were only playing the part. Seemed to me, what little time I spent talking to them, that our friend Douglas

Hancock has nothing but pure hatred for the man. Could be that he knows something we would be interested in finding out. Bring him here so we can get better acquainted."

"What are we supposed to bring him in on, seeing as you're so strict about obeying the law," Dave asked as he put his hat on.

"How about being drunk in public?"

"Thought that's what the back room at the drugstore was for."

"That's right, and he's drunk. Hell, arrest him for needing a bath, I don't care." Cotton glared at him. "If it'll make it any easier, Judge Wilson heard one of them call him 'Lowell Ollar' when he was having his drink."

"Yes, sir." Dave glanced toward Al and both men grinned at each other before leaving.

"The rest of you can go on about your business. I want to talk to Matt and Vicky for a minute. But hang close, because I've got a feeling all hell might break loose real soon." He waited until the last man closed the door before continuing.

"What are you going to do about Three Horns?"

"Let him come looking for me, I guess."

"Why didn't you tell me, Matthew?" Vicky's voice trembled as she knotted both fists in anger.

"I didn't want to worry you."

"Begging you pardon, but she's got a right to know. What if a dozen or so Comanche warriors showed up at your place looking for you? Don't you think that might worry her just a little?"

"Not unless she knew what they were after. I'm Comanche too, you know."

"Well, okay. But you can't take a chance of him meeting you at your place, Matt. You've got Vicky and the kids to think of."

"I know."

"Ohhhhh!" Vicky jumped to her feet and flung her bonnet at the door. "You make me so angry. The both of you.

You're acting like the children and I don't have any say in the matter."

"But I was thinking of you," Cotton said. "All I meant was, that I don't believe anything like this should happen in front of you or the kids."

"No, that's where you're wrong. Something like this should never happen at all. Two grown men threatening to kill one another over some stupid honor that they made up like...like...some silly game. What kind of honor would that be, Matthew Blue? To get yourself killed and leave me and the children all alone? And what about Three Horns, or whatever his name is? I'll bet he's married too. What about his wife and children? How would you think she'd feel if you killed her husband? I've a mind to ask her to come live with me, and let you two men go fight wherever. No, don't touch me!" She threw up her hands as Matthew reached for her. "I'm angry, and I've every right to say what I think. I think this whole thing is stupid, and you're stupid if you go along with it." She snatched her bonnet with white knuckles and opened the door.

"And you're just as bad, Harvey Blankenship." She shook an angry finger at the sheriff. "If you think them fighting to the death is the only way to resolve this situation, you have another think coming. I'll get the women of this town together and we'll show you." She slammed the door.

"Now, what the hell do you suppose she meant by that?" Cotton struck a match to relight his pipe before opening the door. Both men watched as Vicky brushed past Dave and Al in the middle of the street holding a drunken man erect by both arms.

"Don't rightly know. But I've learned one thing being married to her these six-odd years. She's apt to do anything, especially when she's angry. Right now, she's good and mad." He watched the swishing of her skirts as she bounded up the sidewalk and continued down the opposite side of the street. "Looks like you're gonna catch hell too. She's headed right toward your house."

        "Dammit! You ain't brought me nothing but trouble since the day I met you.

        "Dammit! You ain't brought me nothing but trouble since the day I met you.

Chapter 35

Douglas took a sip of coffee as he watched Lillian disappear inside the sheriff's house from his kitchen window. His own place was some hundred yards or so from the nearest residence, but that was still too damned close in his opinion. If he could have turned those yards into miles, that nosey woman would have never become friendly with his wife. He was positive that she was the main reason that things had started to unravel. All he needed was a little more time. If that witch and Lowell...yeah, Lowell Ollar was another one that needed special attention. He should have killed him and that skinny woman of his when he first laid eyes on them. Now, because Lowell showed up, the sheriff had called him in yesterday and started asking questions.

"Well, what about it, Doug? Does that baby girl we've been looking for actually belong to this man and his wife?" They had him cornered inside the jail, staring at Lowell slumped inside his cell. The sheriff and his deputy, Judge Silas Wilson and the Mayor, even that damned Indian were there.

"Might as well tell us, son. We'll find out soon enough. Did you buy that child from this man?" Judge Wilson said.

"It wasn't like it sounds. You see, our son passed away just a few months ago, just before we left Virginia, and it hurt us both deeply, so when we happened onto Mr. Ollar and his sick wife... You'd have to understand the conditions that poor child was being raised in." He suddenly became passionate. "Look at him. Do you actually think he'd make a good father? And his wife was half dead when I saw her. I'm surprised she lasted as long as she did." He paused to wipe his eyes.

"So, yeah. Yeah I gave him some money and took the baby as my own. Can you blame me? That child wouldn't have lived another six months under those conditions. So, if having compassion on a starving child is a crime, then lock me up." He held out both wrists toward the sheriff.

"Well, Harvey, I'd say you haven't much of a case. They'd more than likely lock you up if you took something like this to trial," Judge Wilson said.

"But it's against the law."

"Hell, I know that. But you try telling it to a town full of hard-working farmers and their womenfolk. Most of 'em's lost kids of their own. You'd be lucky if they didn't shoot you right there in the courtroom." Douglas left feeling good about that one. But the sheriff's wife was sitting in his parlor when he got home, and the way she watched him as he hung his coat and hat and poured himself a drink...

Oh well, what did it matter? He set the empty cup in the sink. It would all be over in just a few days now. The money would be here and he would make a couple of large withdrawals in the name of the railroad. Then he'd take Lillian riding where she could have her accident and he'd cry in front of everyone and they'd feel sorry for him. Then he'd be gone.

He arched his back and stared back toward the house with the white picket fence. The only thing bothering him at the moment was how much Lillian could remember and how much she might be telling Alice Blankenship and her flock of hens. Her mind had gone totally blank after he killed Bobby, but he could tell it was coming back. Little by little.

But hell, that was an accident. He was drunk and the stupid kid wouldn't stop crying. He only meant to put the pillow over his face to shut him up. Then he dozed off in the chair and when he woke, Bobby was blue and cold as ice. He really did try to wake him. But when that didn't work, he slipped him into bed with Lillian. It was a mean trick, even in his book. But it did take everyone's attention away from wondering why such an expert horseman like Colonel James D. Farthington would fall off his horse and break his neck. *Stupid idiot turned his back on me after accusing me of spying for the North during the war. He should have known better.* Doug slipped his jacket on and straightened his tie. He still didn't know who in the hell told the colonel about that in the first place.

Chapter 36

"Your old man's pretty stuck on that girl, isn't he son?" John Larkin snapped his head around as Cotton and Matthew joined him in front of the general store. He had been watching his father carry on an extended conversation with Lillian Hancock.

"Yeah, he says she reminds him a lot of Karan."

"Guess she has that same effect on several men around here."

"Pardon?"

"Al Meeks has been kinda moony over her too, but in a different sort of way. He says she looks like Ida Montgomery used to before Lowell got hold of her." The three of them stood silently for a minute listening, as Lillian laughed at something Jim had said.

"Don't reckon she reminds me of anyone I can think of. How about you, Matt?"

"Nope." The Indian shook his head.

"See you around, John."

"Sure. You two have a good day."

"Tell your dad to hang onto his wallet. I don't trust that woman's husband no further than I can throw him," Matthew said.

"Yeah, sure thing. See ya," he said as they walked away.

Chapter 37

"Does not."

"Does too."

"No she doesn't."

"Yes she does."

Vicky laid the papers she was grading aside and poked her head through the window. The children had started to gather at the far corner of the schoolyard where Caroline and Jack Caldwell stood nose to nose yelling at each other. She could see Pastor Herbert Billings approaching the school on foot. *Dear God, why are you trying me like this?* Her skirt swished in rhythm to the sound of her shoes against the wood floor. *Give me patience, or I'm going to wring her little neck.* She descended the steps two at a time as Pastor Billings stopped to watch the angry youngsters.

"Uh-uh."

"Uh-huh."

"Na-uh." He gave her a shove on the shoulder.

"Na-huh!" Caroline's high-button shoe gave a thud as she kicked him in the shin.

"Ow!" He fell to a sitting position holding his wounded leg. The giggling students parted like the Red Sea as their teacher approached.

"Caroline Jamison, what is going on here?" She grabbed the girl's ear.

"Ow, Mama! He was saying that it was good that Ida died, 'cause she didn't love her baby."

"What?" She released the ear.

"Yeah, he said she couldn't a loved it 'cause her husband sold it. And that it's good that Black Shadow took her baby 'cause nobody was gonna love it anyway. He said that Lillian can't love it 'cause it ain't her baby. But I said that it is too her baby 'cause Ida's dead so it has to be Lillian's now. And she's got to love it 'cause it's her baby, and all mamas love their babies to the highest number just like Jesus. Ain't that right, Pastor Billings?"

"Well, yes. If I understood you correctly, I believe you are right, Caroline."

"Aw, man!" Jack screwed up his face as the children laughed.

"See?" She leaned over to wag her head at him. "You're just a stupid boy and you don't know nothing."

"Caroline." Vicky tried hard to hide her grin from Pastor Billings. "Go to the classroom, right this instant."

"Yes ma'am." Her pigtails bounced as she skipped up the walkway toward the building.

"The rest of you go to class...all of you, right now."

"Aw, Mrs. Blue, do we gotta?" Bobby Sorenson said.

"Yes, now go." She waited until the grumbling students were well on their way before turning to Pastor Billings. "I'm sorry about that. I don't know what's gotten into her lately."

"I'd say a good sense of what's right and wrong," Billings said with a chuckle. It took a second or two before she could make her jaw work.

"Ah yes, well. What brings you here today? Is there something you needed to see me about?"

"Yes there was, but I feel that I already have my answer. I didn't know what to say at Ida Ollar's funeral this afternoon. It's hard to do the right thing when you don't know the person. And I didn't know the woman at all, outside of what you've told me. But I think your daughter's given me my message. 'Out of the mouths of babes.'" He glanced toward the schoolhouse. "But thank you anyway, Mrs. Blue." He squeezed her hand. "And make sure you thank Caroline for me too." She could hear him talking to himself as he walked away. "Love to the highest number."

Chapter 38

"Get in there and change your clothes. Right now!" Vicky's eyes bore down on Caroline as she pointed toward Alice's guest bedroom.

"But why, Mama? Ida's dead. She won't care none."

"That's precisely why I want you to change. We are going to show some respect for the dead around here. Besides, her funeral is to take place inside the church, and you're not going to church dressed like that." Caroline gripped the buckskin skirt between her fingers and held it wide.

"God loves Indians too."

"Yes, He does. And so do I, but you're still not going to Ida's funeral dressed like that. I don't even know why you brought it with you. You knew we were going directly from school to the funeral. Honestly, I don't know what gets into you sometimes."

"But I was wearing it when I found her, and I wore it when I went to get Doc Stevenson. I thought it would be okay to wear to her funeral too."

"Well, it isn't. So, go change." Caroline stuck out her bottom lip as she shuffled toward the door. "And wash your face and hands before you touch your clean clothes."

"Yes ma'am."

"God must be trying to teach me patience." Vicky leaned close to the hall mirror to powder her nose. "It's like having to deal with two completely different people. I was so proud of her this morning when she stood up for Ida and her baby, I thought my heart was going to burst. Now, she turns right around and does this." She glanced at Alice who was fiddling with the folds in her skirt.

"I wouldn't concern myself with it too much, Vicky. She could be doing much worse than trying to dress like a Comanche. Does this look okay? It actually needs a bustle. But those pews are so narrow that I have trouble sitting down in church when I have one on."

"It looks fine. I haven't worn a bustle in almost a year and no one's seemed to notice."

"Yes, but you're younger and shaped a little different than I am."

"Sure," she said patting her stomach. "If I wore a bustle, my rear-end would look as big as my stomach."

"Which is, I might add, not very big at all. Are you sure you're eating enough?"

"These are too hot and itchy," Caroline said, poking her head through the door.

"What is?"

"These." She shoved several cotton petticoats through the door. "Do I gotta wear them?"

"Yes, they make your skirt look fuller."

She jerked them back through the door with a grunt. "No they don't. They just make me sweat and itch and look fat."

"She's right, you know," Alice said with a giggle. "I really don't know why we think we've got to pad ourselves all over in order to look pretty."

"Don't encourage her, Alice. Caroline?" Vicky waited for a grunt of recognition from the next room. "I hope you put on clean unmentionables this morning. Caroline?" The door flew open to reveal the nine-year-old standing in her stocking feet and white linen shift.

"Why do I gotta wear them if you can't even talk about them?"

"Caroline!"

"Yes, they're clean. See?" she pulled the shift up over her stomach and danced in a circle. The skinny legs poking through the ruffled drawers caused Alice to giggle.

"Okay, that's enough. Now go get dressed. You're going to make us late."

"I'm sorry, but it was funny," Alice said.

"I know, but I have to ask. She has a habit of forgetting certain things ever since she found out that Comanche girls go natural under their buckskin skirts."

"Really?" Alice raised her eyebrows. "Mmmm, I didn't realize...but it does make sense. I just hadn't thought about it before." She dabbed the perspiration from her throat with a ruffled handkerchief. "I can't say as I'd really fault her for feeling that way. It does get awful hot under all these layers. I've often wished I could take everything off some evening and run through the trees like a jaybird myself."

"Alice!" Vicky covered her mouth as she giggled.

"It's true, and don't tell me you haven't felt all bound up yourself sometime or other. The only difference between you and me is, you might get away with it, living out on that farm of yours. I'm afraid the townspeople wouldn't understand, and my husband would have to arrest me." The bedroom door flew open to reveal a fully-clothed Caroline.

"What's so funny?"

"Nothing, dear," Vicky said, brushing a tangle out of the girl's hair. "We were just laughing at something your Aunt Alice said."

"What?"

"Nothing that would concern you. Now, go see if you can find your father and brother. We have to get to the church." She took Alice by the arm as Caroline disappeared through the door.

"You'll have to come spend the evening with me sometime when the men are off hunting or chasing bad men.

But make sure it is good and hot when you do. I've something to show you."

"Oh, and what is that?"

"You know that pond down by the oak trees?"

"Yes." Alice paused as she closed the door. "No, you wouldn't!"

"Only in the middle of the night when everyone is asleep."

"Oh my word!" The blood rushed to her cheeks as she laughed. "I would have never imagined such a thing. Not coming from you."

"Don't you dare tell a soul." They paused at the gate as Douglas and Lillian Hancock rode by in their buggy.

"I won't tell." She dabbed at the perspiration again. "But I think I will suggest that Harvey takes Matthew hunting real soon. How does next week sound?"

Chapter 39

"Anyone ever tell you how hard-headed you are?" Cotton placed his boot on the chair opposite the desk and leaned his forearms across his knee to stare at Joe Parker. The mayor shifted nervously in his chair.

"Yes, you do. Every time you come in here."

"Well, it's about time you started listening."

"About which complaint? The fact that Henry is adding more tables and chairs to the backroom at the pharmacy, or that the City Council voted not to repaint the jail this year?"

"Neither. It's about that blamed railroad you're so hot about."

"Dear God, not that again." Joe moaned and ran a hand across his face. "Look, Cotton, we've been all through this. The line to El Dorado is going through whether you like it or not. It makes good sense."

"No, it doesn't make any sense at all. If there was enough business to support two railroads around here, we'd already have two and you know it."

"Well, there will be when the rail's finished. Douglas said he'd help get the funding for another stockyard and several warehouses too."

"Now that'll be just fine, won't it?" Cotton stomped his boot on the floor as he straightened up. "What in the hell are we going to put in them after they're built?"

"Goods, dammit. People raise things around here for a living. Or haven't you noticed? Your friend Matthew's horses. Jim Larkin's cattle and Silas Wilson's hogs. You've got a field of corn if I'm not mistaken. And we're hoping to attract more people who'll grow more things so we'll have to build more warehouses and stockyards. We'll be bringing things like cotton and tobacco from down south. Why can't you understand that?"

"I can Joe, but this deal smells to high heaven. How much is it going to cost these good folks before it's over?"

"Well, for your information," he pulled a piece of paper from one of the drawers, "Douglas says he can get the Topeka Santa Fe to lay the track for around $23,000 a mile. Now, that's a deal and you know it. Some of the other lines are charging as much as $48,000 a mile."

"Sure it's a deal. But why would they want to run a line through here?"

"Because we're going to pay them."

"Oh, now really?" Cotton smirked as he pulled his pipe out of his vest pocket. "What else you got scribbled on that paper?"

"Well," he adjusted his glasses, "there's about ten miles of track which will cost $230,000. Then, we estimate that the stockyards and warehouse will run another $10,000 to $15,000. And Douglas suggested that we throw in another $5,000 for contingencies."

"I'll bet he did." Cotton paused at the door. "A quarter of a million is a lot of money, Joe. Especially for these people."

"Sure it is. But Douglas has assured us it will work. In fact," he pulled another piece of paper from the drawer. "See? He's putting up $10,000 of his own money. You're wrong on this one, Cotton. You've been a lawman so long you can't recognize an honest business deal when you see one."

"I hope you're right, Joe. I really hope you're right." He closed the door and paused on the sidewalk. "But my gut tells me you're wrong as hell."

Chapter 40

Al Meeks climbed out of the saddle and wrapped the reins around the fence railing in the shade of an oak tree.

"Oh Kansas girls, sweet Kansas girls,
With sky-blue eyes and flaxen curls,
They sing and dance and flirt and play
And when a boyfriend comes that way
They meet him at the sod house door,
Then be with him forever more."

Smokey's singing was comical enough to cause anyone to pause, but it was what the men were doing that actually caught his attention. The grizzled old man had one foot in a leather stirrup attached to the end of a long pole laying across a huge block of wood. He would put his weight into the stirrup, causing the pole to tip upward, jerking on the rope attached to the other end. Every time he released his weight, the pole would tip back down, causing whatever was on the end to hit bottom inside the hole with a loud thunk. The thunking kept rhythm with Smokey's song. After a few minutes of bouncing up and down, he stopped to wipe his face with a dirty neckerchief.

"Ready to haul 'er up?" Al had never been introduced to the huge man with the yellow beard, but the familiar accent made him pause again before opening the gate.

"Sure, bring 'er up. Ain't saying we got nothing. This dirt's harder'n a prostitute's heart." A handsome woman looked up from her potato-peeling on the front porch as Al closed and latched the gate.

"And what, may I ask, are you two doing?" He pushed the derby back on his head and stood with his hands on his hips.

"Jigging," Smokey said, as his partner began turning on the windlass. "You look as though you ain't never seen this done before."

"The only 'jigging' I've ever seen done is with music and pretty young lasses dressed in fine costumes."

"I was singing. Don't that count none?"

"Ah, was that what it was, now?"

"This is a poor man's way of drilling a well, Mr. Meeks." The other man stopped turning the crank as a section of metal pipe appeared. Both men hauled the pipe out of the ground by the rope and held it over a pile of dirt. Smokey grabbed a pole with a metal ring attached and began cleaning the packed earth out through a slit cut in the side of the pipe. "I can't afford to hire one of those companies with their steam-rigs. But my woman's going to be having a baby soon, so she can't be carrying water from the creek when I'm not around." He wiped a grimy paw on his trousers and offered it to Al.

"The name's Cary Ramczyk. I've seen you around, but I've never taken the time to introduce myself." Al felt his own hand being swallowed by the massive grip.

"That accent wouldn't be Bohemian, would it?"

"Aye, but I was a small lad when my family came to America. My wife, Anna, comes from there too."

"I thought so. My Uncle Francis married a girl from Bohemia. I was fascinated by the way she pronounced her words." He put a hand on the rope while Smokey continued digging at the packed earth inside the pipe. "Now, could you explain how this contraption works?"

"Sure." Smokey turned to spit. "This here jig's pretty simple, really. It's balanced so when you step on that end, like you seen me doing, it raises this here drilling bit," he tapped the metal pipe. "Then you let off real quick like, and it's heavy enough, so when it drops back down, it takes a bite of dirt."

"Oh, I see. Kind of like a post-hole digger."

"Now yer talking." He took a final swipe at the pipe with the metal ring. "But you gotta haul it up every once in a while to clean out the diggings with a sand pump," he held up the pole and ring.

"So that's what that's called."

"Yep." He laid the pole aside. "What brings you out here, anyway? Ain't nothing beyond this place but a bunch of jackrabbits and coyotes."

"I thought I'd take a little ride and clear my mind. Now that I've found Ida, I don't actually have any reason to stay in Leon." Al stuffed his hands into his pockets and shrugged. The corners of his mouth turned downward as he studied one of the cows grazing in the field.

"Don't you?" Smokey glanced upward before spitting on the dirt pile. "If it were me, I wouldn't step one foot outta town before I seen that varmint swinging from a rope."

"The thought did cross my mind." His eyes shot toward Anna Ramczyk, then to the well-drilling outfit. "But after that...I guess I'll be going home."

"Well, can't say as I'd blame you none. Sometimes it's better being around your own folks when you're licking some wounds. Now, ifin you'll excuse us." He swung the heavy pipe back toward the hole. "We got to get this done before that baby gets here." Al let his eyes drift toward the woman, who turned her head to blush.

"Mind if I try?"

"You?" Smokey said as he and Cary glanced at one another.

"Why, what's wrong?"

"Nothing. Just didn't think you was into getting dirty, that's all."

"Ah," he said, laying his coat and derby on the porch. "I'll have to admit that it's not what I'm normally accustomed to. But, before my father would allow me to work in his office, I had to learn the shipping industry from top to bottom." He put his foot in the stirrup and paused. "Have you ever had to unload a ship-load of cargo on a rainy day?" Both men shook their heads. "Well, I have. And this can't possibly be much harder." He shifted his weight into the stirrup and the pole shot upward, almost hitting Smokey in the chin. He let the pipe fall back with a thunk and stepped back into the stirrup again. "Besides, it'll help keep my mind off things." He let the pipe fall again.

"No, no , no," Smokey said, waving his hands. "Yer doing it all wrong."

"Why?" He let his eyes dart from the well to the pile of dirt and back again. "What's wrong?"

"You ain't go no sense of timing. You got to sing when you do it, so it falls like this." He clapped his hands up and down in rhythm.

"Oh, well, let's see." He studied the fluffy cloud drifting across the sky for a second or two. "Now what was that song Caroline was trying to teach me? Ah, yes I have it." He smile and stepped back into the stirrup.

> "Oh give me a home,
> where the buffalo roam,
> and the deer and the antelope play."

"Now ya got it," Smokey said with a nod. "Little faster now," he waved his arm up and down. "Yeah, that's right."

Chapter 41

"Where in the hell did you find this?" Douglas Hancock lifted the picture from the shelf. He was on his way to the bedroom to change for dinner when Corporal Bodard's smile stopped him in mid-stride.

"I've had it for some time. I found it when I was rummaging in my old cedar-chest this afternoon." Lillian's lilac perfume drifted to his nostrils as she joined his side. "I had forgotten all about it. I don't remember much about him, but he was pretty close to our family before the war."

"Yeah, I know."

"You don't mind that I put it here in the parlor, do you?"

"Mind? No, why should I?"

"The way you were staring at it. I thought there was something wrong."

"No, I just didn't know you had a picture of him."

"You don't mind then?" She shot a glance at him. "I know how you are about these things."

"Don't be silly. He was related to you, and he died fighting for what he believed in. The picture's fine right where it is." He returned the picture to its spot on the shelf. "Now, I've got to go get ready for dinner." He kissed her on top of the head and hurried up the stairs.

Corporal Samuel Bodard, General Jackson's personal grunt - that was a face he never thought he'd see again. Douglas had been able to talk his way into a commission in a field office under the General and win the old man's favor. It took less effort to convince the Old Man that he'd make a great spy. He was a fairly good actor and could pass himself off as a Yankee. He would cross enemy lines and discover troop movements and what ever else would be beneficial to the Confederate cause, then bring that information back to the field office. And he was able to accomplish just that, time and time again. But more importantly, he was able to sell important Confederate information to the Union soldiers on the other side. He was building quite a nice nest-egg until Lillian's cousin got suspicious and followed him one night. He had just handed a Union soldier the envelope when the stupid jackass stepped into the open to demand his surrender. Douglas paused in the middle of tying his tie. *Did he really believe it would be that simple?*

"You don't think that you can just arrest me and take me back to camp to be executed?" Douglas had asked. "You might not know it, Sam, but you're past enemy lines now. You're surrounded by Yanks." The Corporal waved his .36 caliber revolver nervously as Douglas stepped away from the Union soldier. "It's hell realizing you made a huge mistake, isn't it? You shoot that thing and they'll be all over you like flies on an outhouse."

"Come on." The soldier motioned with the gun. His eyes kept darting toward the surrounding brush.

"Sure, Sam. Just take it easy." Douglas held his hands shoulder high and took the lead. "Oh, by the way," the Corporal's gun prodded him in the back as he came to an abrupt halt, "aren't you interested in what I just gave that boy back there?"

"Hold it right here." Douglas stood still as the Corporal turned toward the Union soldier. "I'll take the envelope." Douglas grabbed Samuel Bodard around the neck with his left arm as his right took hold of Sam's wrist. The gun flew as he brought the hand down hard against the rocky surface.

"I can't believe you actually came alone." The fear in Sam's eyes gave Douglas a sense of power as he locked his fingers around his neck. "I always did think you were too stupid to make a good Corporal anyway."

After removing the Corporal's wallet, Douglas filled his pockets with rocks and dumped the body in the river. He handed the Corporal's papers to the Yankee who disappeared into the darkness. He found a picture of a girl holding a child on her lap, and a letter folded neatly inside the wallet. The writing on the back of the picture said, "With love from your cousins, Charlotte and Lillian." He stuffed the picture and letter into his own pocket and tossed the wallet into the river. He knew he couldn't go on selling information to the Yankees. There were probably others who were suspicious and he stood a good chance of getting shot as a spy. But he could go back after the war and marry the pretty daughter of a wealthy plantation owner. He might even tell her how the Corporal died a hero and how much he admired him. He laughed at the idea as he lay on his cot that evening looking at the picture in the dim lamplight. He'd have to practice on that one.

Chapter 42

"Hey!" Matthew glanced over his shoulder as he tied the reins to the hitching post in front of the general store. Charlie Stewart was leaning against a post in front of the pharmacy. The man was drunk, and having trouble with the cigarette he was trying to roll. Matthew swatted at the dust clinging to his pantlegs before continuing inside the store.

"Morning, Matt. What can I do for you?" Fred Walker smiled pleasantly from atop the stepladder.

"I need some nails and a bucket of whitewash." He picked up a leather bridle to study the tooling, then laid it back down. "Oh," he glanced up, "and you got any chicken wire? I need a roll of that too."

"Sure, be right with you." Fred created a small cloud with the feather duster before climbing down and wiping his palms on his apron. "Nails and staples are right over there. Just help yourself." He pointed to several barrels in one corner. "But I'll have to go out back to get the wire. Don't get much call for that around here. Most folks who live out of town just let their chickens run loose." He paused to clean his glasses on the same apron and grinned. "To tell the truth, most of them in town do the same thing. I woke up this morning with one of Mabel Johnson's hens staring at me through my window. Told Freda to invite it on inside and make some chicken and dumplings for supper."

"We let them run loose too, but there's some sort of cat that's been hanging around our place lately, so I thought I'd keep them penned up for awhile."

"Cat? What kind? Bobcat?"

"Could be." Matthew shrugged. "All I've seen is his tracks. Alright if I use this?" he held up an empty coffee can that had been sitting on top of the nails.

"Sure, that's what it's there for. I haven't heard of anyone around here having any cat trouble, unless it's been Edith Thompson complaining about Alice's tabby scratching around in her flowerbed."

"Guess I'm just lucky." Matthew tossed a handful on nails into the can and grinned. The man still hadn't moved. "You got that wire?"

"Wire? Oh, sure. Be right back." He disappeared through the rear door. Matthew filled the can with nails and set it on the counter, then grabbed the bucket of whitewash before Fred returned with the roll of rusty wire.

"This was the best I could do, Matt. Like I said, I don't get much demand for chicken wire."

"That'll do just fine, Fred. Just set it all to one side and I'll have Vicky stop by with the buckboard and get it on her way home. How much do I owe you?"

"Five cents for the nails. Ten cents for the whitewash. You can have the wire, seeing as I trip over it every time I need to get into that corner of the storeroom."

Matthew laid the money on the counter and touched the brim of his hat. "See you around, Fred."

"Sure thing, Matt. Don't forget to tell Vicky to stop by before she leaves town."

"I won't." He came to an abrupt halt as Charlie Stewart appeared, blocking the doorway.

"I thought I said 'hey' out there, Injun. How come you didn't answer?"

"Well, first of all, I thought you were talking to my horse, because my name is Matthew, not 'Hey'. Second, I didn't really have anything to say to you, and didn't think you'd have anything worth hearing."

"Got a pretty smart mouth for an Injun, don't you?"

"Maybe, I'm a pretty smart Injun. Now, if you'll excuse me." He tried stepping around, but Charlie refused to let him pass.

"How come you're not out looking for the Hancock baby like you're supposed to be doing, instead of hanging around town?"

"I did look for her some. But I'm not the law, and I also have a ranch to run. Besides, I haven't noticed your friend Douglas searching for her. Maybe you should go talk to him if you've got a complaint."

"Na, I'm complaining to you." He tapped Matthew's chest with his finger. Matthew's shove caught Charlie by surprise and he landed on his back with a thud. He scrambled to his feet cursing, and grabbed for his gun. Matthew's right hand landed flush on his jaw, spinning Charlie against the hitching post as the weapon rattled free across the sidewalk.

Fred Walker stood wide-eyed wringing his apron, as spectators popped out of doorways and gathered in the middle of the street. Charlie came off the hitching post swinging wildly but Matthew sidestepped and kicked him in the stomach. Charlie bent over with an "oomph" and Matthew ran him headlong into the side of the building like a battering ram.

"Having a little trouble, Matt?" Dave Price pushed his way through the crowd.

"Nope. He wasn't much trouble atall." He picked up Charlie's gun and handed it to Dave butt-first.

"That was the funniest damn thing I ever saw." Mike Steel leaned against the building laughing.

"My hell, Charlie," Larry Tyner rolled the man over with the toe of his boot, "I thought you was supposed to be tough. That's what you've been saying, anyways."

"Well, let's see." Dave glanced up thoughtfully as he stuffed the gun in his belt. "Being drunk in public, assaulting a citizen with a loaded weapon and just being a general pain in the ass. That ought to be good for a few days in the pokey. Ol' Silas will more'n likely want to lighten his wallet some, too. Here," he turned to Mike Steel, "he's your friend. You guys help carry him down to the jail."

"Good God, Charlie," Larry Tyner grunted as they hoisted the man. "You need to lose a little weight."

"Man oh man." Fred shook his head as the crowd started to evaporate. "I thought for sure you were going to kill him when he pulled that gun on you."

"Somebody eventually will kill him." Matthew glanced up from the cigarette he was rolling. "But not today. I didn't feel like it." He struck a match and held it to his smoke. "And, I hope I never do."

Chapter 43

"Matthew?"

"Mmmm?"

"Why didn't you tell me about that man in front of the store today?" Vicky leaned on one elbow to stare at him. The moonlight through the open window gave her hair a frosty look.

"Because there wasn't much to tell."

"Not much to tell? He tried to kill you."

"He was drunk, I took his gun away, and Dave has him locked in jail. End of story."

"That's not what Fred said. He said you two had a fight and you had to pound the man's head against the side of his store to get him to stop."

"Well, you know how Fred exaggerates. Besides, I didn't want to worry you and the children."

"Oooo! You make me so angry." She flopped back and held the quilt under her chin. "That's what you said about Three Horns. What's it going to take, Matthew? Someone bringing your body home and dumping it on the front porch?"

"There was nothing I could have done to stop what happened at the store today. And I don't know what good telling you about it would have done, except upset you even more than you already were."

"Upset me? What on earth do you think I am now, Matthew Blue? I don't know when I've been more angry with anyone in my entire life."

"Oh, come on now." He tried putting his arm around her but she rolled away.

"No, don't touch me! I don't want you touching, or kissing, or holding me until you learn to tell me everything that happens during the day. I don't want any more surprises. Do you understand?"

"Huh. That might make for some boring conversation. Most of my time is spent checking on the horses and cattle. Oh, I might get to see a deer or rabbit once in a while. Do you want me to tell you about them too?"

"You know exactly what I mean, Matthew Blue, so don't try being cute with me." She rolled over to glare. "Besides, that man was entirely right about one thing. You haven't been out looking for Lillian's baby like I asked you to do. Why not?"

"Have so. How do you think I got into trouble with Three Horns? Besides, all the trails we had ran cold. Cotton sent wires to everyone, telling them to keep an eye out and let us know if anyone suddenly comes up with a kid that looks something like her."

"See?" She gave him a shove. "That's exactly what I'm talking about. You could have told me this days ago instead of making me think you didn't care."

"Oh, dear God in heaven!" He rolled over to cover his head with his pillow. "I might as well go live with Three Horns and Laughing Brook."

Chapter 44

"Well that has to be the silliest thing I've ever heard of." The wrinkle between Susan Price's eyebrows grew deeper as she set the teacup and saucer on the coffee table. They were seated in Alice Blankenship's living room discussing with Vicky the situation between Matthew and Three Horns. "My husband was there and he didn't try to stop them? Boy, is he gonna get it when he gets home tonight, I'll grant you that."

"I don't know if he could have done anything, Susan. The Comanches are pretty set in their ways. Some of the others there may not have taken it very well if he had tried to interfere." Vicky passed the plate of cookies to Sally Adams. Sally was the only single woman present, and Vicky had a suspicion that the girl had a secret crush on Dave Price. Sally took a cookie and passed the plate to Lillian Hancock. Everyone present was amazed at how Alice Blankenship's persistent efforts had caused Douglas to relent and allow Lillian to join their little group.

"That may be true, but he could have at least said something. I'm still going to give him a piece of my mind."

"Please don't be too hard on him, Sue. He might have been frightened. I certainly would have been," Sally said, taking a tiny bite from a ginger snap.

"He'd better be scared of me."

"What do you plan on doing, Vicky?" Alice asked, refilling the cups with hot tea.

"I don't know. To tell the truth, I'm the one who's scared to death. I've already lost one husband, and I don't want to lose this one. It'll kill me if something happens to Matthew."

"I'll tell you what I'd do, if it were me," Lillian said in little more than a whisper. "I'd go to that man's wife and have a talk with her." They all turned to stare at her before glancing at each other, then back to her again. "I'm sorry. It must have been a silly idea."

"No, I think it's a brilliant idea, Lillian," Alice said.

"Really?"

"I thought about it myself...sort of...but I wouldn't know where or how to find her." Vicky's eyes darted around the room. "And there's no way I can ask Matthew to take me."

"Well, what about Dave, Susan? Doesn't he know where their village is?" Alice set the teapot on the table and sat on the sofa beside Lillian.

"Uh-uh," Susan said, shaking her head. She dabbed her lips with a napkin. "I mean, he told me where they are, but I don't think you could get him to take you there. He was scared to death the whole time. He says he has nightmares about having to face Black Shadow in the dark all alone and not being able to find his gun." She paused to glance at each face. "Now don't any of you tell a soul I said that," she said quickly.

"What about Smokey? I'll bet he knows how to get there," Sally said.

"I believe you're right." Alice went to the screen door and yelled at the children playing in the back yard. "Caroline? Come here a minute. I need to ask you to do a favor for me."

"Yes, Aunt Alice?" The girl pressed her nose against the screen.

"Run down to the livery and tell Smokey I want to see him right away. Hurry, now."

155

"Run down to the livery and tell Smokey I want to see him right away. Hurry, now."

Chapter 45

"Well, I'm surprised to see you here. I was just heading out to Cary and Anna Ramczyk's place. I thought you'd be out there digging the well." Smokey looked up from the wagon wheel he was greasing as Al Meeks leaned his long frame in the doorway.

"Got that done already. Busted through the hardpan right after you left yesterday and hit tons of fresh water." Smokey dipped his hand into the bucket filled with tallow and pine tar and applied a healthy dose to the axle.

"Really? That's wonderful. How much deeper did you have to go?"

"Not too far. I calculate the whole well's only sixty-odd feet. Out on the plains we used to have to go more'n a hundred most of the time." He wiped his grimy paws on a dirty rag. "Here, give me a hand with this wheel instead of just standing there jawing."

"Sure." Al grabbed one side by the spokes and both men slid it into place. "You say you lived out on the plains for awhile?"

"Yep. Had me a soddie with a little patch of ground. Had a woman and boy too." He tightened the nut and drove in the cotter pin to lock it into place.

"I didn't know you were ever married."

"Can't say as I was...not Christian-like in a church, anyways. Wia'ne was full-blood Shoshone. We just sort of took together first time I laid eyes on her. Pretty little thing. Gave her father four mules, poke of tobacco and ten beaver skins for her."

"You bought your wife?"

"It was more like a dowry. The higher up in the tribe, and the prettier the girl, the higher the bride-price goes up. Knew of one chief who got thirty horses for his oldest daughter." He dug a chew out of a pouch and shoved it in his cheek. "Anyways, as I was saying, that's what her dowry was, and she was worth a sight more."

"Where are they now?"

"They're buried out on the homestead. Both caught the fever and died about ten years ago."

"I'm sorry."

"Weren't no need in my staying around there anymore. So I just sort of drifted this way and been here ever since. Besides, I never liked fighting the dust storms. Ever been stuck in a real Kansas dust storm, boy?"

"Well, yes. Just the other day..."

"Naw, that weren't no dust storm. That was just a little breeze. Why, I seen it blowing dust so thick out on the prairie, that I come up on a prairie dog once digging a burrow ten feet in the air. No kidding," he said as Al started laughing. "Another time I seen a flock of crows flying backwards just to keep the dust out of their eyes. Yes, sir. I'll tell you what, if you're ever caught in one, you'll never want to be in another. That's why I packed up and left." They were interrupted by Caroline flying through the open door.

"Aunt Alice says she wants to see you, Smokey. Hi, Mr. Meeks," she added with a big smile.

"Don't say." He spit and wiped his mouth on his sleeve. "And I don't reckon she told you about what?"

"No, but she acted like it was kinda important. Said for you to hurry."

"Huh. Heard she was having one of her hen parties today, so it can't be too important." He wiped his hands again on the same dirty rag and hitched up his coveralls. "Better do yer visiting with this young lady, Al, while I go see what Alice wants."

"Smokey was just telling me about his homestead," Al said as they walked aimlessly down the street. "He said he was married and had a son."

"Uh-huh. That's what my Uncle Harvey says too."

"He said that his wife was a Shoshone, or something like that."

"Yep. Same as my dad." He stopped to push the derby back on his head.

"I thought your father was a Comanche."

"He is. The Comanche and the Shoshone are the same thing. You didn't know that?" He shook his head. "They are. It's just that the Shoshone live way up north, in the mountains around Wyoming and Montana. And the Comanche live around here, all the way to Texas. Or, they did until they started making them live on the reservation. But they're all the same. They speak the same language and they still remember being one great big bunch of people once upon a time."

"Oh, really? And what happened that caused them to split up?" They started walking again.

"Well, according to Daddy, there are three different stories. One says it's because one boy accidently killed another when they were playing. Another says they split up because some people were fighting over a bear someone killed. And another says it was because of some terrible disease like smallpox." She shrugged her shoulders. "Who knows? They all could be true for all I know."

"So, your father's people moved south and became the Comanche. Hmmm, interesting."

"Yep, and I'm glad, 'cause my mama wouldn't of got to meet him if he was way up north. Besides, who wants to be called a snake?"

"A snake? Who in the world is calling you a snake?"

"No one. That's what the Shoshone are." She wrinkled her nose and giggled as he stopped in front of the general store and put his hands on his hips. "That's what they're called. The Snake People."

"And what, pray tell, does the name Comanche mean?"

"Well, nothing that I know of. 'Cause that's not their real name. It's just something the Spanish started calling them years ago. Their real name is Nerm, which means human beings. And I think that sounds a whole lot better, don't you?"

"Yes, I think I'd rather be called a human than a snake any day. Come on, I'll buy you some candy."

Chapter 46

"Aw, sit yourself down and have a drink." Chris Hari snickered and gave the empty chair a shove with his toe from under the table. "Geez, Charlie," he said as the sullen man plopped down. "You're kinda expensive. That old pig-farming judge charged us twenty dollars to bail your hide out of jail. You shoulda just shot that indian. It couldn't have cost much more."

"That's exactly what I'm gonna do." He glared as Mike Steel and Larry Tyner started laughing. "What's so damn funny?"

"You'd have to bore him in the back from fifty yards away from what I saw," Mike said.

"That so?" He jumped to his feet and put his hand on his gun. "How about me taking your head off right now?"

"Sit down, Charlie. You're making more of an ass out of yourself than you already are." Chris removed the matchstick he'd been chewing and glared at him.

"Not until I settle this with Mike."

"Settle what? Is boring me gonna take care of that injun?" Mike folded his arms and leaned against the wall. "Besides, I ain't so sure you can out-pull me."

"I said, sit down!" Chris slammed his palm against the table and yelled.

"I owe you." Charlie pointed a finger at Mike as his right hand quivered just above his gun.

"Damn." Chris shook his head as he pulled his own gun and pointed it at Charlie. "Now, either you sit down, or I'll take your head off right here in front of God and everyone." Charlie's eyes darted between Chris' gun and a grinning Mike Steel. "Now!" Chris pulled the hammer back.

"Later," Charlie said, still pointing at Mike as he took the seat.

"No, there ain't gonna be no later," Chris said. "You're gonna do exactly what I say, or you're not gonna be doing anything at all. Understand?" He paused to glare at him before filling one of the glasses. "Here." He shoved the glass across the table. "Drink that and keep your mouth shut." He waited until Charlie had finished his drink.

"What you're going to do is exactly what I say you're going to do. 'Cause if you don't I'll kill you before that indian ever gets the chance. Is that understood? Is it?" Charlie nodded. "Good. Because we've got too much to lose just so you can try to prove you're tougher than some Comanche...or Mike. Besides," Chris refilled Charlie's glass, "from what I hear, Mike might be right. He isn't just another indian. Anyone of us would probably have to shoot him in the back."

"The hell you say," Charlie snickered, as he downed his drink.

"Yes, the hell I say. And I'm not going to let you screw this up." Chris pointed his finger across the table. "If you want to prove how tough you are, you can do it after we've got the money and are on our way out of town. Understood? Do you understand me?" He waited for Charlie's nod. "I hope so. You can have it out with him and Mike both, if you want. But not until this thing is over. Now, go get yourself something to eat. And take a bath. You stink."

They waited until Charlie had left the room. "You know," Mike said as he took a seat and started shuffling the deck of cards, "I'll bet one of us has to kill him before this is over. He's like a boil that's ready to pop."

"Na." Chris shook his head. "That Comanche's going to do it for us. I can feel it just as sure as Sherman's walk to the sea."

Chapter 47

"Ain't no blamed way. I ain't gonna take Mrs. Blue or none of you females out anywheres near them Comanches." Smokey stood defiantly in front of the circle of women.

"And what about Matthew. How are you going to feel if Three Horns kills him? What will you say to Vicky or her children then?" Alice said.

"Na, Three Horns ain't gonna kill Matt. He'd have to shoot him in the back to do that, and Three Horns ain't that kinda coward."

"What about Three Horns' wife and children, Smokey? I'm worried about them too. How would they feel if he died?"

"Hell, (begging yer pardon ma'am), but they's just injuns. They ain't got no feelings."

"Ahhhh," Susan threw her hand up to her mouth as the women stared at the man.

"I beg your pardon. My husband is Indian, and he does so have feelings. He feels things deeply," Vicky said. "And besides, weren't you married to an Indian yourself at one time?"

"I didn't mean it like that. I've knowed a lot of good injun women, and Wia'ne was just as kind and gentle as any of you. It's their men I'm talking about. Besides, I always figured that Matthew got his feelings from having a white woman fer a mother."

"I don't believe this," Susan said, shaking her head.

"Well, it's the Gospel truth. And you'd think the same if you'd a seen them fighting and hurting folks the way I have. 'Cause no one that's really human could do such things."

"Perhaps it's because they feel things so passionately that they are such fierce fighters." Lillian Hancock's quiet voice caused everyone to fix their eyes on her. "I know that was the way it was with my father."

"Well, maybe so, but I still ain't gonna take none of you out there. And besides, Mrs. Blue, that husband of yours would skin me alive if he knew I was even thinking such things."

"That's alright, Smokey, you don't have to take me. I'll go by myself."

"Begging your pardon, ma'am, but how do you propose to do that? Yer just a woman."

"Ooooo, that does it." Susan Price jumped to her feet. "What makes you think a woman can't find something as large as an Indian village? I find things much smaller around the house that my husband couldn't possibly find if his life depended on it. Of all the nerve."

"Now, don't get so het up. I..." He had suddenly become invisible as the women chattered and laughed amongst themselves.

"That's just like a man. They all claim to be such great trackers and yet Harvey has to ask me where his socks are nearly every morning. And I show him that they're still in the same drawer that they've always been," Alice said with a giggle.

"You ought to see how Matthew acts when he can't find the sugar. He'll take every can and jar out of the cupboard when the sugar bowl is sitting right in the middle of the table. Then he'll start complaining that no one ever puts things away where they should be. But guess who has to put the things back inside the cupboard?"

"Oh, my gosh," Susan said, laughing so hard she spilled her tea. "Dave's just as bad." She stooped to wipe up the spill with her napkin. "He'll forget where he puts things and start blaming Joshua for taking things that are impossible for him to reach."

"I guess it doesn't change when a person gets married then, does it?" Sally Adams said. "I just thought it was something that went with age. You know, my dad's always doing the things you're saying that your husbands do, and I just thought it was something that old folks do."

"Oh, my word child," Alice said, holding her sides. "It doesn't have anything to do with age, it has to do with the male gender. I'll just bet you Harvey couldn't find his socks when he was a little boy. How about you, Lillian? Does Douglas forget where he puts things too?"

"Well, I'm not too sure about things, since we have a housekeeper. Come to think of it, though, he is constantly asking Joan to fetch whatever it is he's needing at the moment. But what he does do mostly, is forget what he said, or what happened just yesterday. Now, I'm aware that I can't remember things that happened six months or a year ago in Virginia, but Douglas can't seem to remember what happened ten minutes ago. I'm constantly having to remind him, and he gets so angry when I do. But he'll get even angrier if I don't."

"Yeah, I see a little bit of that in my father," Sally said with a nod.

"Oh, I'm sorry we're being so rude, Smokey. We were just having a little fun. You can go back to what you were doing when I sent Carol looking for you. Here." Alice handed him the plate. "Take a couple of cookies with you."

"You ain't gonna go trying to find them Injuns on yer own, now are you, Mrs. Blue?" He said, choosing the cookies carefully.

"Well, I didn't say that I wouldn't, did I?" Vicky said with a giggle. "I'm still thinking about it."

"We just might all go," Susan said matter-of-factly.

"Yes, let's do it. You too, Lillian. I'll bet we could find their village and be back here before nightfall if we left early in the morning," Sally said, bouncing in her seat.

"Cornsarned womenfolk are just plain crazy." Smokey closed the door behind him. "That's exactly why I'm happy I'm not hitched up to one of them crazy varmints. I'da taken a switch to Wia'ne if she ever acted that way." He took a bite of the sugar cookie. "They shore can cook, though."

Chapter 48

Just a little closer. Matthew edged his horse toward the bobbing head. The air hung thick with dust as a thousand hooves raced across the prairie. He was close enough to hear the labored breathing of the beast as he raised his lance. His heart leaped when the buffalo suddenly changed direction and plunged directly at his horse. The animal beneath him screamed as the sharp horns ripped into its flesh. He met the ground face-first as thundering hooves swept around all sides.

He was on his feet in an instant, running with the herd, trying to find his way to the edge and freedom, but an ocean of wooly beasts had engulfed him. He dodged one to his left, then another on his right. His lungs were filling with dust, choking the life out of him. His legs were starting to buckle when a strong hand latched onto his arm and he was swept forward, half running, half suspended in air. The hand released its grip as they approached a crop of rocks on a small rise of ground and Matthew dropped to his knees gasping for air. He raised his head to catch a glimpse of his savior. Three Horns grinned and raised his lance high with a piercing yell before darting off to rejoin the hunt. "Aiiiiee-yiiiee-yiiiee!" Matthew waved his fist in the air and yelled, cheering him on. He had lost his favorite horse and lance. But he had other horses and could make another lance. He was a man who had been resurrected from the dead.

Matthew woke feeling warm and peaceful. The scene in his dream returned, then drifted away like a dried leaf in the wind as so many others had. It would return again. They all had. He was again reminded that he was two completely different persons. The young Comanche warrior who fought battles, went on hunts and played games with his friends, and Manhunter. The two crossed paths every once in a while, confusing others and complicating things. The Comanche was a simple man who took things as they came and asked little in return. Manhunter's life was much more complicated. He had tried desperately to make Vicky and those close to him understand, but he didn't know if that was possible.

He studied the shadows cast by the moon as they danced on the curtain dividing their sleeping quarters from the rest of the house. Vicky's golden hair lay in unruly waves across both their pillows. Her soft breathing filled his own chest with compassion to the point where he thought it would burst. She was right. There had to be another way to end this thing with Three Horns. After all, he owed the man his life.

Chapter 49

"Well, why didn't you say something about it sooner?" Matthew scowled from where he was kneeling beside the creek. Smokey had just informed him of his conversation with the women in the Blankenship house the previous day.

"Because I didn't think it was important. Besides, we're supposed to be trailing a cat that's been nosing around your horses."

"I don't care about a cougar that's too old and lame to hunt anymore. My wife's safety is more important."

"You'll care a whole bunch when he gets hold of one of them colts or one of them young-uns and tears them all to hell, now won't you? Besides, it don't make no sense for them to go off hunting a bunch of Injuns. I think they was just funnin' me."

"You don't know my wife very well, do you?" Matthew put his foot in the stirrup and leaped into the saddle.

"Where you going?"

"To find my wife."

"That's not too damned hard. She's down there teaching school."

"Like I said, you don't know my wife." He dug his heels into the horse's flanks and raced toward town.

"But it don't make no sense." Smokey spit in the dust at his feet and ran a gnarled hand across his face. "But then, nothing makes any sense anymore. Women folk back-talking their men and running all over creation looking fer Injuns. Mountain lions bigger'n bears down here in the grasslands nosing 'round ranches instead of being where they belong." He grabbed the reins to his horse and started following the tracks away from the creek. "Maybe we should just go off somewhere where their ain't no crazy folks around. Whadda ya say, ol' girl?" He patted the horse's neck.

~   ~   ~

Matthew brought his horse to a halt in the middle of the street to stare at the spectacle. Vicky sat atop the buckboard loaded with women. Alice Blankenship was standing upright and arguing with her husband who was refusing to let loose his hold on the lead horse. "You ain't going and that's that. So ya'll can just get outta that contraption right now. Ya hear? Go on," he waved his left arm, "get outta there and go back home to your families where you belong."

"Harvey Blankenship, I know how to use this whip." She held the coil high in the air for everyone to see. "If you don't let go of that horse this instant, I'm going to welt you real good."

"I'll be damned and go to hell if you are! And I'll be good and double-damned if I'm gonna let my wife talk to me like that, especially in front of the whole town." Matthew edged the horse closer as the red-faced sheriff jerked his beloved hat from his head and threw it in the dirt. The men on the sidewalk laughed all the harder as the women gasped their horror at the lawman's profanity.

"Sally, what in God's name do you think you're doing? Get down out of that wagon." Henry Adams came out of the pharmacy and yelled at his daughter. "You're supposed to be next door helping your mother at the lunch counter."

"I'm sorry, Daddy, but this is something I believe in. It has to be done. Don't you understand?"

"This is your doing, isn't it?" He shook an angry finger toward Matthew.

"Just found out about it a little while ago myself." He turned toward Vicky who, up to this point, had been sitting quietly holding the reins. "What's going on? Why aren't you teaching school?"

"You know why."

"I know what Smokey told me. Now I want to hear it from you."

"I'm going to see if I can't talk some sense into Three Horns. And if I can't talk to him, maybe his wife will listen."

"Why don't you try talking to me instead?"

"I did, and you said that if Three Horns came looking for you, you'd have to fight him and one of you would more than likely die."

"That's right."

"Well, I don't want that to happen. And if you won't listen, and he won't listen, perhaps his wife will. I can't believe she wants to lose her husband anymore than I do. So, just get out of our way. I've already made up my mind."

"Yes, I can see that, but why take these other women with you and make their families worry?"

"We chose to go, Matthew. Vicky never asked us, but we women have to stick together." Susan nodded her red head. Matthew could see a disbelieving Douglas Hancock from the corner of his eye staring open-mouthed at his wife in the back of the wagon.

"So would you please ask Cotton to let go of Charlie? I wanted to be back sometime today, if possible." Vicky's blue eyes resembled dark pools from beneath her bonnet. "There's nothing you can say that will stop us."

"Sure," he said turning his horse so his right side was facing the wagon. "Let them go, Cotton."

"What?"

"I said, step away from the wagon." Matthew drew his forty-four and pointed it at the horse. Several women screamed as people began to scatter.

"Matthew, don't!" Vicky jumped to her feet as he pulled the hammer back.

"Hey, come on, Matt. You can't do something like that." Cotton tried to grab hold of his arm but he pulled away.

"Why not? They're my horses. I raised them both from the time they were colts. Now, get out of the way."

"Matthew Blue, don't you dare." Vicky leaped from the wagon. "If you just so much as scratch either one of my horses, I...I'll never speak to you again so long as I live."

"And if I let you wander off by yourselves, none of you may live long enough to speak to any of us again. You're not going, Vicky, and that is that. I'll stop you one way or the other, even if I have to kill both of these animals. You can believe that above anything else."

"Yes, I can see that. But you can believe this one thing, Matthew Blue. Neither I nor the children will be home this evening. And I'll not be coming home until you figure out a way to settle this thing between you and Three Horns without you killing each other. Come on, girls," she said, turning away with a swish of her skirts.

"And that goes for me too, Harvey Blankenship. You can sleep in the jail tonight," Alice said, as she climbed down.

"And double for me." Susan jumped out to follow with Sally and Lillian close behind. The women headed straight toward the Blankenship house, with Lillian being the only one to peel away to her own home.

"What the hell did I do? I didn't say a word." Dave stood in the middle of the street with palms open toward the sky.

"Damned Comanche. You ain't caused me nothing but trouble since the day I met you." Cotton scooped his hat from the dust and stomped toward the jail.

Chapter 50

"Dammit!" Douglas flung his hat across the room. "The very idea of Lillian sitting in the back of that wagon in the middle of town with that...that rabble. What was she thinking? She wasn't, I'll tell you that!" He turned to point a finger at Chris. "That woman isn't capable of thinking, drawing attention and making a spectacle of herself like a fool."

"Calm down, Dougie. Here, have a drink," Chris said, filling two glasses.

"Calm down nothing. How do you think something like this makes me look in the eyes of the townspeople? Tell me that, if you can. Just when we're about ready to pull off the deal of a lifetime."

"Okay, I'll tell you how it looks." Chris held his glass high in a salute before downing its contents. "It makes you look just like a normal human being. A man just like the sheriff and that Indian friend of his. You're married to a beautiful woman with a mind of her own. That's what they're thinking. Now, that's not too bad, is it? Have your drink. It'll calm your nerves." Douglas emptied his glass and listened, as Chris refilled both glasses.

"You do realize that this could be the best thing that could happen to us, don't you?"

"How so?"

"Well, it's bound to draw their attention away from what we're really doing, especially that sheriff and his deputy. If they're busy trying to make peace with their womenfolk, they're not going to be nosing around our project."

"Yeah, I didn't think to look at it from that angle." Douglas took a sip of his drink. "And besides, they're supposed to be out looking for Lottie."

"That's right." Chris downed his drink and set the glass on the table. "If I was you, I'd raise a little hell about them being in town so much instead of out trying to find whoever it was that took her." He paused at the door to put his hat on. "That'll keep them even busier, whether you want the kid back or not. Remember, Doug, family can be a real pain sometimes, but they're real nice to have around at other times."

Douglas turned toward the painting hanging over the fireplace as Chris closed the door. Old Silas Hancock had insisted they all pose for a family portrait even if they didn't act like one. "Here's to each and every one of you." He held his glass high. "Mom...Dad...and to you too, darling Tim. May you all rot in hell." He downed the whisky and slammed the glass on the table.

"Everyone of you was against me from the start. You never even tried to understand how I felt. And you know what? I don't give a damn. And you know why? Because you're all dead, and I'm alive." He poured himself another drink and sat in a chair where he could study the painting.

It was by pure accident that Douglas had found the will in the top drawer of the desk that day and opened it up. He had actually been looking for a blank sheet of paper. He shook with fury when he read the part where his father had willed the entire plantation to his older brother Timothy.

"Timothy has always been more stable than you," Silas Hancock had said when he confronted him in the kitchen. "It's no secret that you drink and gamble away every cent you can lay your hands on. And I don't approve of the company you keep either. That woman you brought out here last Sunday, what was her name... Violet? Where did you meet her Douglas? In The Scarlet Palace? No," he shook his head slowly, "your brother gets this place when I pass on. You'll get a fair cash settlement that you can throw away any way you choose."

"Didn't turn out exactly like you thought. Did it, old man?" He saluted the painting a second time before downing his drink.

Chapter 51

"I'm sorry, I just don't like him, and it sticks in my craw to go around looking for his kid, while he sits on his duff doing nothing." Matthew sat in the sheriff's office with his feet propped up on the desk staring at Cotton over his cup of coffee.

"I agree with Matt. I wanted to slap him up beside the head this morning when he was out there accusing us in front of everybody of not trying to find that baby. There's a skunk in the woodpile somewhere, and it's starting to stink up the place," Dave said.

"Didn't say I liked him none myself, did I? Fact is I wouldn't trust him anymore than a Confederate three-dollar bill. But he's got the mayor and half the town eating out of his trough, thinking they're gonna get another railroad and some fancy warehouses." Cotton held out his cup for Dave to refill.

"Well, ain't they?"

"When pigs learn to fly," Matthew said.

"You too?" Cotton's face brightened as he leaned over the desk. "That's one of the things that's been eating at my insides. Now, I ain't saying that we won't get a line to El Dorado someday, but why in the hell would they want to leave off pushing toward every large city in these United

States of America and build another line to Leon? It just doesn't make good business sense."

"But he's putting up a large hunk of money himself, isn't he?" Dave refilled their cups and set the pot on the desk.

"Sure, but look at what he's getting in return." Matthew set his cup down and began rolling a cigarette. "He puts up ten thousand dollars, but we give him control of a quarter of a million." He licked the paper and dug a match out of his vest pocket. "Doesn't sound like too bad a deal to me. Besides, we'll get a line to El Dorado when the line figures there's enough business to pay for it, and it won't cost us a penny."

"Matt's right. Now, let me ask you boys something. What do we really know about Douglas Hancock?" Cotton drummed his fingers and waited for an answer.

Matthew leaned back and blew a cloud of smoke in the air. "That much." Dave was silent.

"That's right. He comes into town with his smooth talk and pretty wife who can't remember nothing from a month-of-Sundays, and starts throwing a lot of money around. Next thing we know, he's talking about bringing in a line to El Dorado with a big terminal and stockyards and tie-ins with the south. Says he's got plans for turning this berg into a large city, and everyone just eats it up. Trouble is, we ain't got much of nothing most folks in the big cities want, except for maybe Matt or Jim Larkin. And it ain't ever been much of a problem for Jim to hire a couple of drovers to herd his cattle and horses over to El Dorado or down to Coffeyville. Or, he can ship them by rail over to Dodge City where they got themselves a proper market." He paused to take a sip of his coffee.

"But Joe Parker says this new line will get our cattle to market a lot faster," Dave said.

"Maybe, but let me ask you something, Matt. When's it ever been too hard to take your horses to market?"

"Never."

"See?" He made a sweeping motion with his right hand and leaned back. "And you tell me why folks down south would want to ship their goods all the way to Leon, Kansas, when they ain't even heard of us? It just don't make good business sense."

"So, what you're saying is, that you think we're not going to get the tie-in to El Dorado, but Douglas Hancock's going to get our money," Dave said, striking a match on the sole of his boot.

"I ain't saying that...just yet, anyway. But like you said, there's a polecat in the woodpile, and he's starting to stink the place up." Cotton set the cup on his desk and leaned back in his chair.

"It's mostly Jim Larkin's money. Mayor Parker and a bunch of people talked him into putting up his place for collateral, cattle and all. And I heard this afternoon that Fred Walker put his store into the pot too," Matthew said.

"So, what are we going to do about it?" Dave got up to pull a bottle and glasses from the cupboard.

"I'll tell you what we're gonna do." Cotton tapped his index finger on the desk. "Tomorrow, you're going to tell everyone you're going out to look for the Hancock baby. Tell them you got some sort of lead. Lie to 'em just a little. But you're actually going over to El Dorado and wire every agency in Virginia. I want to know everything we can possibly know about Douglas Hancock. I want to know what he eats for breakfast and what he likes in his coffee. I even want the names of the all the whores he's ever slept with."

"Okay, sure. But why El Dorado? We've got a telegraph right here in town," Dave said, filling the glasses.

"Because the telegraph office happens to be located next to the mayor's office, and Paul Thornton tells the mayor about every wire he sends and receives. You know Joe Parker's gonna tell Douglas what we're up to the minute you start. Take that damned Englishman with you," he added as an afterthought. "He's under my feet every time I turn around, wanting to know when we're gonna try Lowell Ollar.

We're gonna take him to trial when I'm sure we've gotten enough evidence out of him to put a noose around his buddy Doug's neck too." He slammed his palm down on the desk.

"And what about me? Want me to go with him?"

"No, you just do what you're doing."

"And what's that?" Matthew said.

"Keeping those women stirred up. When they're good and mad they feel like they got some sort of mission to be on, and my wife's got two bees in her bonnet right now." He got up from his desk and arched his back. "She's been able to get Lillian Hancock outta the house and make friends with her. Seem's like ol' Doug is scared of her being around my wife for some reason. I wouldn't know why." He grinned. "But I want them to stay stirred up for a while. It'll make a good diversion from our investigation. And I want to see what Alice can worm out of Lillian at some of their hen parties." He paused to glance around the room. "Only thing is, did you have to get 'em so damned mad this time? Where in the hell's everyone going to sleep? Damn women anyway. Trying to go off and get themselves killed." He paused to light his pipe.

"I knew we was making a mistake last year by telling them they could vote in local elections. And my wife's just as bad as the rest of them, getting all the womenfolk together to carry signs and make banners. Next thing you know, they'll be wanting to vote for president. I still can't believe that folks over at Argonia elected Susanna Salter mayor. A woman mayor! Can you believe it? Should've let them go get scalped by the Comanches."

"Oh, I don't think White Cloud would let anyone in his camp hurt them," Matthew said.

"It's not really White Cloud I was worried about. But you know as well as I do that we'd play hell getting them back from some of those braves. And besides that, there's no telling what could happen to them out wandering around like that. Women should be home taking care of their families, and that's that."

"Yeah, I've got a mind to turn Susan over my knee and paddle her backside real good," Dave said with a scowl.

"And Shadow's gonna move into town and run for mayor." Matthew laughed as he set the empty glass on the desk and stretched his legs. "That girl's more'n likely the one who'll be tanning your hide if you try bossing her around. I agree with Cotton, though. Most women are damned hard to get along with. But I wouldn't want it any other way, would you?" He hung his gunbelt and hat on a peg on the wall. "I'll take that corner over there. You two can fight over the cot in the empty cell next to Lowell Ollar."

"I'll take the other corner and Dave can have the cot."

"Why? With your bad back, you should get the cot. I'll take the floor."

"No you won't. That man in there ain't had a bath in a month of Sundays," Cotton pointed toward the cell, "and he smells like an old outhouse. I'm taking the floor; you get the cot."

Chapter 52

"We were all taking bets on whether they was gonna lock you up or not, Doug. Sure had us scared there for a minute." Chris picked up the stack of chips and let them fall through his fingers. "What'd you want to go and do something stupid like buying a kid for anyway? I know you don't like the little buggers."

"Already told you." He took a sip of brandy and set the glass on the table. "Like you were saying the other day, it looks better in this type of game if you're a family man and," he held his glass high, "a respectable member of the community. Bet you didn't know I've even got my own spot reserved on a church pew, did you."

Chris choked on his drink as he laughed. "Hell, I might even show up Sunday just to get a look at that," Mike Steel said.

"Well, what are you planning to do with the kid when this game's over? I know you're not planning on taking her with you. I can see that written all over your face." Chris refilled the glasses.

"I don't know. Leave 'em here, I guess. Who cares?" He shrugged.

"Them? You're not thinking about leaving Lillian too, are you?" He nodded. "Damn, Doug, you're one hard son of a bitch."

"Yeah. Here's to you." He toasted his glass again and laughed. *You have to be hard if you're going to survive.* He had learned long ago that to get ahead in this world you have to get rid of any attachments. And those who didn't, like his brother, got swallowed up.

He was still working in General Jackson's detachment when he received word that Timothy had been wounded at Fredricksburg. The report said his brother was lying near death in a neighboring field hospital. He begged permission to go see him, and sure enough, just like they said, there he was lying there in a hospital tent all shot to hell.

"Well, look at you," Timothy croaked as Douglas hovered at his bedside. "Doesn't look like you've seen any action. Old Jackson must treat you real good."

"Oh, I've seen my share of action, dear brother. Why, just the other day I had to strangle one of the enemy with my bare hands." He held up his delicate hands and smiled.

"Fat chance. Those hands haven't seen any work in years." He grimaced with pain.

"No, really. He had the drop on me and I couldn't take the chance of firing a shot because we were behind Yankee lines. So I jumped him. You should have seen the look in his eyes as I choked the life out of him." He leaned close and smiled broadly.

"The only difference between you and me Tim, is that I'm smarter than you. I take the time to choose my battles and who it is I'm going to fight. You, on the other hand, have always run head-long into any kind of fight you might happen onto. Now look at you." He stuck out his bottom lip and frowned. "You've got Yankee holes all through you and you're going to die." He shook his head slowly from side to side and added, "Guess I'll just have to run the plantation all by myself when the old man passes on."

"You bastard. I'll live long enough to see that you won't get hold of one inch of land." "He tried to sit upright, but fell back coughing.

"No, dear brother of mine. You won't even make it out of that bed you're lying in." He left the tent laughing.

He waited until the early morning hours before slipping back inside. There were thirty or forty patients in the room and one exhausted male nurse who was asleep in a chair. He grabbed a pillow from a pile of bedding as he wove his way to his brother's cot. Timothy's breathing was shallow and raspy. Douglas took a quick look around before shoving the pillow downward. He held it firmly, listening to the muffled sounds as one weak hand struggled to push him away. Then the hand fell limply over the side of the cot and everything was quiet. Douglas wove his way back through the cots and replaced the pillow on the table before returning to his own tent. The next morning he hung his head in sorrow as the quartermaster informed him of Sargent Hancock's death. He even stood at attention and saluted the body as it was carried from the hospital tent. *Goodby Timmy. Too bad you couldn't have seen who it was who put you out of your misery.* Douglas smiled. The deed had actually put them both out of misery in one sense. He wouldn't have to see Timothy's smug face or hear his grating voice as he berated him again.

Chapter 53

Matthew stood by the gate scowling as Dave said his goodbyes. Vicky had smiled and waved through Alice's open door, but refused to come outside and talk, let alone give him a hug or kiss. Caroline looked forlorn as she clung to his arm.

"I'm sorry, Daddy. I missed you terrible last night. I told Mama we ought to go home. I want to ride Sugar, and play with Mark in my own house."

"I know, baby, but your mother has her reasons and she believes she's right. So, you go on to school and behave yourself. We'll get this settled as soon as we can."

"Good morning, Matthew. Did you sleep well?" Vicky asked, closing the gate behind her.

"Tolerable. How about yourself?"

"Oh, just wonderful. Did you know that Alice has a down mattress on her guest bed? I do believe it was the softest bed I've ever slept in." Her smile was too perfect. "Well, we must be going. I can't keep the students waiting too long, you know."

"Why the hell not? You kept them waiting all day yesterday."

"Matthew," she said covering Caroline's ears, "I know you're upset, but I wish you'd watch your mouth around the children."

"That wasn't half near as bad as what I was thinking."

"Really? Then you can have the rest of the day to learn how to control both your temper and your language." She took Caroline by the hand and turned away. She stopped to glance at him over her shoulder when they neared the far corner of the yard. "If you learn to do those two things, I just might decide to come visit you at the ranch tonight."

"It'll be one god-awful walk if you do. I sent the team and buckboard back home with Smokey early this morning."

"You didn't."

"Did so. How else can I expect to keep you from going off and doing something stupid?" Several passers-by stopped to stare as they glared at each other. "I'm not going to shoot all of our horses just to keep you in line."

"Well, you can just go ahead and shoot up the whole world if you want. That's all you men are good for anyway, isn't it? But if you think sending our buckboard and team home is going to stop me from trying to talk some sense into Three Horns, you've got another think coming, Matthew Blue. I'll find a way to get out there and talk to him and his wife if I have to walk the whole way, because God knows I can't talk any sense into my own husband."

"In that case, I guess I'd better consider hog-tying you to a post, or maybe shooting your leg off."

"Ahhhh," her mouth fell open as she grabbed her daughter's arm.

"Daddy didn't mean it, Mama. He's just mad," Caroline said as Vicky dragged her along at a brisk stride.

"Well, what are you looking at?" The man and woman standing in the middle of the street hurried away. "This is going to be a long week. Might as well go see Three Horns myself and get it over with."

Chapter 54

"I've never seen such bloody-tall corn in all my life." Al Meeks stood gazing at the stalks towering three feet over his head. The cornfield was about fifty yards behind the Blankenship house at the edge of town. "How'd you get it to grow so tall?"

"It just does, that's all." Cotton reached up to pluck an ear and peel back the shucks. "I plow the ground and plant the seeds, then the Lord and some good Kansas weather does the rest." He turned to show Smokey the ear. "Be ready in about a week, I'd say."

"How many acres have you got planted." Al craned his neck trying to see the end of the field.

"About twenty." Cotton held the ear for him to see. "Ever been to a husking party?"

"No, sir. What's that?"

"He's one of them furners that ain't never done anything what's fun a'tall," Smokey said, digging a plug of tobacco out of his shirt pocket. "It's where everyone gets together to harvest the corn. And if you ain't never been to one, I'll tell you what, it's one more good time." He shook his head and took a healthy bite out of the plug. "We'll have us a hoe-down, after the corn's in the crib, with hot cider, dancing, and some of the best fiddle playing you ever heard."

"That right?"

"Yeah." Cotton nodded as he studied the ear in his hand. "Say," his eyes shot upward. "I thought you were supposed to be going to El Dorado with Dave."

"I'm all ready. I'm just waiting for him to finish saying goodbye to his wife."

"That boy's going to drive me to drink yet," he said, checking his pocket watch. "It'll be dark before you get there...if you ever do."

"We will. When's this husking party you're talking about going to take place?"

"We've got to get the corn in first," Cotton said.

"But that's the fun part." Smokey's eyes grew large and he drew close to Al. "Ya say you've never been to one of these husking parties?" Al shook his head. "Everyone shows up, 'cause it takes everyone to harvest Kansas corn. Now Cotton grows some mighty tall corn, I'll grant you that. But I've seen it so tall folks had to use stepladders and cut the ears off with a crosscut saw. And ol' Harley Jones down near Independence used ta tie a four-horse team to each ear just so he could drag it to the crib. Yes, sir. Now that was some corn, I'll tell you that."

Chapter 55

"Why don't you sit down, you damned Comanche? You're making me nervous," Cotton said from behind the stack of paper on his desk. Matthew continued pacing back and forth, staring at the darkened street. "Don't know how you Injuns won as many battles as you did, if they're all as restless as you." Matthew stopped to glare at him.

"Kinda sticks in your craw, don't it, boy?" The Indian kept his gaze fixed on him. "Well, if it makes you feel any better, it does mine too. And I already made up my mind that I ain't gonna put up with sleeping on this hard floor too many nights. Those women can just get mad and scratch their mad spots for all I care." He went back to shuffling his papers and Matthew continued his pacing.

"Well, now, would you look at this." Cotton held up a communications bulletin. "Marshall over at El Dorado has a couple of punchers locked up in the pokey. Seems they got drunk and pried open a cage at some circus and turned a lion loose. Says they thought it'd be kinda fun to see if they couldn't put a rope on it like ol' Buffalo Jones claims to do with cougars. But the damned thing got a way from them and now no one can seem to find it. So they're telling everyone to keep an eye on their cattle and what not."

"He's out at my place," Matthew said without taking his eye off the street.

"What?"

"I said, he's out at my place."

"That's what I thought you said. Who's out at your place?"

"That damned cat you've been telling me about." He shot a glance over to Cotton and went back to watching the street.

"It's a she, not a he. And how in the hell would you know if a full-grown African lion was out at your place when you ain't been there in two days?"

"Because we all heard it the night Ida Ollar died. And Smokey came back from there this afternoon saying he found a half-eaten colt down by the creek."

"Aw, that's too bad, Matt." He shook his head. "Well, it's nearly ten miles from your spread to El Dorado. What in God's name is it doing all the way out there?"

"Hell, I don't know. Why don't you go ask it?" There was a long pause as Matthew watched the street.

"You want me to go with you in the morning and see if we can find it?"

"No, you've got too much work here. Smokey and I can handle it." He glanced back over his shoulder. "But you'd better send them a wire and tell them if they want it back alive, they'd better high-tail it over here from El Dorado right now, because if I find it first, I'm going to kill it." He turned back to the window. "It's bad enough losing a horse or two, but I've got two small kids and a wife to think about."

"I'll do it first thing in the morning. And I can't say as I blame you at all. I'd grab my Winchester and go after it in a second, if you'd just say the word." He went back to his papers as Matthew continued to wear out the floorboards.

"Dammit, boy. If you can't sit down, why don't you burn up some of that energy walking the streets? You can play deputy for me and take Dave's place tonight."

"Don't I need a badge to do that?"

"Hell no. Just get out of here and give me some peace." Cotton poured himself a cup of coffee as Matthew disappeared into the night. "Dad-gum Injun. Don't guess you can cause me anymore trouble this time of night."

~   ~   ~

Matthew was leaning against the tree rolling himself a smoke when he saw them. The two shadows glided down the street and vanished into the tall bushes next to the Hancock house. The larger one of the two emerged a few seconds later to slip through the gate and disappear behind the house. Matthew tossed his unlit cigarette on the ground and grabbed his Sharps rifle that had been leaning against the tree.

Chapter 56

"Now, you stay right here, and don't say nothing unless you sees somebody coming. Then, you yell real loud to let me know. Got that?" Benjamin Polk whispered. Jessie's large eyes shone in the moonlight as she nodded her head. "Good. Now, give her here." She deposited the tightly-wrapped bundle in his arms.

"Shhhhh, shhhhh, not a word out of you either," he said as the baby let out a whimper. "In just a minute you is gonna be back in that same bed I took you out of just a few days ago."

Stepping out of the bushes, he slipped the latch on the gate and crept inside. The soft-soled moccasins glided silently across the lawn and darted around the corner toward the bedroom window. Benjamin steadied the baby in one arm while trying to raise the window with his free hand. It refused to budge. Sliding the blade of his hunting knife between the lower and upper panes, he rocked it back and forth until it caught on the lock. He paused to take a breath before rocking it once more with a little more force. The latch flipped back with a click. He slid the window open and peered inside.

"Here you goes," he said, depositing Lottie in the crib.

Stepping back outside, he slid the window shut and darted to the corner of the house where he paused. Glancing around at the blackness, he dashed through the gate and latched it behind him.

"Jessie?" His eyes roamed the empty spot where he'd left his sister. Now, where'd that child go? "Jessie, where is you?"

"Looking for someone?" The deep voice caused his heart to jump to his throat. Whipping the knife out of his belt, Benjamin spun on his heel. "Uh-uh," the large buckskin-clad man shook his head. "Don't even think about it." He was holding Jessie with one arm and pointing the biggest gun he'd ever seen right at his chest.

"Let my sister go." He waved the knife back and forth.

"Not a chance. Now, you want to put that thing back in your belt? You don't know how to use it in the first place." Benjamin's eyes fell to the blade and back to the man with the gun. His dark hair hung to his shirt collar and his copper skin glistened in the moonlight. "I don't want to hurt you, son, but I will if you don't put that thing away."

"No." He stepped back and readied himself. "You ain't gonna hang me, and she had nothing to do with it."

"Who said anything about hanging?" The man looked puzzled. "I just want to ask you some questions. Quit wiggling." Benjamin lunged forward as the man glanced away, and whipped the knife waist-high. The man released his hold on Jessie and side-stepped the charge with amazing speed as he brought the rifle around. The loud popping sound inside of Ben's head was followed quickly by a blinding pain that sent him to his knees. The last thing he remembered was the smell of damp earth as another blow between his shoulder-blades knocked him flat to the ground.

~   ~   ~

Benjamin woke with a throbbing headache and the sound of his sister's shrill voice ringing in his ears.

"Please ma'am, don't let them hurt my brother. We was only tryin' to give that baby back."

"What I want to know is why you took Lottie in the first place?" Benjamin blinked hard and shielded his eyes from the lamp the woman was holding above his head. Her violet eyes roamed across his face like dark, transparent pools, as she dabbed at the side of his head with a damp cloth. She tossed her head, causing a strand of golden hair to flip over her right shoulder. "You didn't have to try to kill him, did you?" She shot an angry gaze toward the tall man leaning against the wall. He growled and held out a cup for another woman to fill with coffee.

"Guess she's still mad at you, Matt," the white-haired man at the table said with a laugh.

"I'm angry with the both of you." She stood and Benjamin let his eyes fall down her slim form. She was a fine woman, someone most men only meet in their dreams. She moved away and he was sorry.

"Why are you angry with me? I didn't do anything."

"She's got every right to be upset with you, Harvey Blankenship. I am too." The other woman filled another empty cup before slamming the pot down on the stove. "Here, Caroline," she said, handing the cup to a skinny girl seated at the table. "See if our guest is awake enough to drink this." The girl squatted on her heels in front of him before handing him the cup.

"You okay?" He nodded and took the cup from her hands.

"Thanks." He studied her over the rim of the cup.

"Careful, it's hot."

"That your ma?" He motioned with his head.

"Uh-huh."

"Thought so. You look like her. Just smaller." He sat up and leaned back against the wall. Jessie came over to curl up against his side. "This here is my sister, Jessie."

"I know. We already met while you was knocked out. I'm Carol and that's my brother, Mark," she said, pointing to the boy sleeping on the sofa. "And that's my pa." She pointed toward the big man who was trying to explain something in a soft voice to the angry woman. "Well, he's actually my step-dad, 'cause my real father's dead. But I call him Daddy, 'cause he married my mother and I can't remember my real one too well. He's the one who bonked you on the noggin, but he's really nice when you get to know him."

"He's Indian?"

"Comanche," she said with a nod.

"Is he the law around here?" He grimaced and held his hand to his head.

"No, we raise horses," she said with a laugh. "Well, he does chase bad guys every once in a while. He used to make his living that way before he and Mama got married, but now, he just raises horses." She paused and smiled warmly. "Uncle Harvey" she pointed to Cotton, "is the sheriff."

"Aren't you scared that man will bite you?" the one she called 'Uncle Harvey' said as he scooted his chair back to cross his legs.

"Na, he ain't mean, Uncle Harvey. I can tell." She had a warm smile.

"Oh? How's that?"

"I don't know. Same way as I can tell when a horse is good or bad. I just know. You know, don't you?"

"I don't know, do I?" he raised his eyebrows and turned his head toward the Indian who shrugged.

"She just does, don't you know that, Uncle Harvey?"

"Well, I guess you're a pretty nice fellow, then," he said, knitting his eyebrows together as he studied him intently. "But you've given me a real problem. Your sister has already told us why you took that baby and why you was trying to return it. But kidnapping is a hanging offense, son, and if I haul you into court, ol' Silas Wilson's going to order me to string you up. Now, I really don't want to do that, but I represent the law around here, and I just can't turn you loose.

Then, on the other hand, we've got a couple hundred angry white folks out there who would more'n likely try busting you out of jail so they could hang you themselves, if they knew we had you. Now, we were just discussing all this with these womenfolk," he motioned with his head. "They're are all for turning you loose, but me and Matt are in agreement. The law's the law. What do you say?"

"If...if we could just find Mrs. Ollar, she'd tell you that child's rightfully hers. That'd set things right, wouldn't it? I was only trying to give her back her baby."

"Well, it might make a difference at that, if it could be done. But you see, Ida Ollar's dead." Benjamin felt a chill sweep through him as the sheriff kept talking. "That little girl sitting right in front of you found her lying on the road outside of town, and these fine folks tried their best to help her. But even Doc Stevenson, as good a man as he is, couldn't save her. She's gone, son. And their isn't another person in the whole world to witness for you and your good intentions, except maybe that rotten husband of hers. We've got him locked up in the jail right now, and we're more'n likely gonna hang him for beating his wife to death. You really don't want to leave your life in his hands, do you?" He paused while Benjamin studied the boards in the floor.

"Didn't think so. Nope, you've given me a real problem, son. I shore don't want to hang you, but I don't see any other way out of this mess.

Chapter 57

"Now you go on to bed and get some rest," Vicky said, kissing Caroline on the forehead. The sleepy girl fumbled her way into the loft as she tucked Mark into his cot and kissed his cheek. "We'll be having to get up in just a few more hours as it is, to make it back to town in time for school."

"Aw, Ma, do we gotta go?" Caroline hung her head out of the loft and whined.

"Yes, we do. I'm the teacher, and you're one of the students. Now, go to sleep." She blew out the lamp and began undressing. The bed was going to be lonely tonight with Matthew gone. She missed him terribly. She slipped her nightgown over her head and sat on the edge of the bed to stare out the window into the night. He was out there somewhere with Jim Larkin taking the Polk children back home. Cotton had thought it wise to get them out of town before anyone even knew they had been there. She watched them go before borrowing Alice Blankenship's buggy and heading to the ranch.

"But Matt wanted you to stay here while he was gone. That's why he sent your wagon and team home without you," Cotton said.

"That's not why he sent the team and wagon back, and you know it. He did that because he was angry."

"Well, I don't know if I should let you go out there by yourselves anyway. Got word that there's some sort of critter nosing around your place. That's one of the reasons Matthew's been in such a tizzy."

"Harvey Blankenship, there's always some sort of critter nosing around our place. Now, I've spent many a night alone in my own house with my children while my husband was off somewhere with you, rescuing the world. I am very capable of taking care of myself." She laughed as the sheriff thoughtfully stroked his chin. "Look, I'm the school teacher and there is no possible way I'm going to wear this same old dress, or make my children wear the same clothes, all week long. Besides, I'm not sure that husband of mine has milked the cow or fed the chickens the past two days." He let her go, but not without a stern warning.

"You be careful, now. Go straight to your house, and I want to see you back here first thing in the morning, 'cause if I don't, I'm coming after you. Understand?"

"Yes, I understand." She shook her head and started the buggy moving. "Geesh, you'd think he was my father." Vicky ran her hand across the quilt where her husband normally lay before crawling under the covers.

She was still angry with him for acting the way he had in town. God knew how she was fuming inside. None of the ladies really believed they were actually going to White Cloud's camp, except maybe Sally Adams, and that silly girl would believe anything. They wouldn't have known how to find his camp in the first place, but they did want to make a statement. They wanted their husbands to know there had to be a better way to settle arguments than killing one another. That was all they had wanted, that is until the men started acting so stupid --- Cotton standing in the middle of the street yelling at his wife, and Matthew, that very morning, threatening to shoot her in the leg, in front of God and everyone. Of all the nerve. She didn't know if she could ever forgive him. She wiped a tear from the corner of her eye and rolled toward the empty spot in her bed. *Lord Jesus, I miss him something awful. Make him come home safely.* She fell into a troubled asleep.

~   ~   ~

The sun was just beginning to turn the eastern sky pink when she bolted upright in bed. Caroline made a muffled noise from the loft as Vicky rubbed her eyes with her knuckles and scanned the room, not sure what it was that woke her.

"Hush Tippy." The dog was standing in the middle of the floor growling at the door. There it was again. It was a deep rumble. Something that she had never heard before. "Quiet," she said, as the dog let out a series of loud barks. Throwing back the covers, she ran across the floor in her bare feet to open the door and peer out toward the corral.

"No, get back." She gave the dog a shove with the side of her foot as he tried to nose past her. He backed away reluctantly with his fangs bared and hair standing on end. She fixed her eyes once more on the corral. Caroline had forgotten to leave the gate open after feeding Sugar and the mare was going crazy. It took a second before Vicky's eyes caught the movement. There it was, creeping low across the yard, keeping to the shadows. It moved slowly at first, even stopping once, then it dashed quickly toward the pen where the mare was desperately kicking the rails. The big cat lowered its chest to the ground and prepared to pounce.

"Oh, my God." Vicky reached for the shotgun hanging above the door.

"What is it, Mama?" She could hardly hear her daughter over the noise the snarling dog was making.

"Stay in bed, baby." She lifted the gun from its rack and stepped onto the front porch. The horse was whistling and snorting now.

"What's the matter with Sugar?" She heard the thud of bare feet hitting the floor.

"Stay inside and take care of your brother," she said. Mark was sitting up in bed now and crying.

Vicky took several cautious steps out into the yard and raised the gun to her shoulder. *No, you forgot to cock the hammer.* She lowered the shotgun and put her right thumb on the hammers. The cat let out an ear-splitting roar and bolted over the top rail. It latched onto the mare's neck and twisted the horse to the ground.

"No, leave her alone!" Vicky ran to the middle of the yard where she tried to aim the gun at the twisting mass of muscle. The dog darted past her to leap through the railing. "Tippy, get back here." She lowered the gun, afraid she might kill the dog or horse instead of her intended target. The dog was only in the melee seconds before it came flying out to land beside the gate with a cry of pain.

"Please God, help me," she said, running toward the pen. Tippy made a second valiant effort to attack but received another vicious blow from a huge paw that sent him rolling. She jammed the gun against her shoulder and pulled the triggers. Nothing. She had failed to cock the hammers when the cat pounced.

She pulled both hammers back and rested the gun against her shoulder. Her finger was starting to squeeze the trigger when her eye caught the glimpse of something white flash by.

"No, no, no! Leave my horse alone!" The frantic girl was now tugging at the gate.

"Caroline, get back! Get away from there!" The lion let go of the horse's neck and backed away, eyeing the two humans who were invading her kill.

"Go away! Leave her alone!" She tugged at the rope that held the gate shut.

"Get away from the gate."

"Get up, Sugar. Please get up."

"Get away from there. Do you hear me?"

Vicky poked the gun through the railing. *Steady now. Remember what Matthew taught you.* She took a deep breath and rested the butt against her right shoulder. The cat was making a low rumbling noise as its tail twitched nervously back and forth. *Squeeze the trigger slowly.* She readied herself. The gate suddenly flew open and her daughter dashed inside. The huge cat leaped into the air. "No!" Vicky jerked the triggers on the ten-gauge. Both barrels exploded and she hit the ground hard as her daughter screamed. She rolled her head to one side. The big cat had landed on top of Caroline.

Chapter 58

Vicky clawed at the shotgun lying in the dust as she scrambled to her feet. Her ears rang and her shoulder felt like it had been kicked by a mule. "Dear Jesus, God, please help me!" She dragged the gun by the barrel as she half ran and staggered toward the gate. She hadn't heard the horses enter the yard and the sight of the bronzed body flashing past her caught her by surprise. The Indian jerked the lion's head back to cut its throat before pulling the huge cat off Caroline. Vicky stood numbly blocking the gate as several more bodies bumped passed her, the last one knocking her into the gatepost.

"Stupid white woman. You used too big a gun. Now the hide's no good," said the first man, pointing toward the gaping hole in the lion's stomach.

"Thank you, Jesus." She let the gun fall and bolted to Caroline's side. The girl was covered with blood. "Caroline. Caroline, baby. Are you alright?"

"Oh, Mommy, Mommy." She let go of the knife she had been holding and threw her arms around Vicky's neck. "I was so scared."

"Are you okay, baby? Where are you hurt?"

"I'm fine, Mommy. It was squashing me. I couldn't move." She released her hold as the Indian who was kneeling beside Sugar said something. "No, no, you can't be dead." She threw herself across the horse's body.

"The girl speaks Comanche?" the first man said.

"Yes, she does." He wore a beaded breast plate and a buffalo headdress with three horns.

"You speak Comanche?" He gestured toward Vicky with his knife.

"No, just a little." She snapped her head around at the sound of her son's crying. A huge black man, who had been sitting on a horse watching, got down to carry the toddler under one arm and drop him at Vicky's knees.

"Well hello, sister," he said kneeling beside the dead cat. "Where did you come from? You died valiantly like a true African, didn't you?" He stroked the lion's side.

"You're Shadow, aren't you?"

"Yes." His eyes darted back toward Vicky. "You know of me?" She nodded.

"And you're Three Horns?"

"War Chief of the Kwahadi." He stood erect and tall.

"Why are you here?" She tried to sound calm as she retrieved the shotgun from the dust with a shaking hand.

"To see Manhunter. Is he now hiding in the house, while his woman fights the large cat?" The comment brought laughter from the others.

"No, my husband isn't here. What do you want with him?" She held the gun with both hands.

"I've come to kill Manhunter and take his scalp for my belt." He put his hands on his hips and thrust out his chest.

"I won't let you do that." She cocked the hammers on the gun and pointed it at him.

"You cannot kill me, white woman. The gun has no bullets." He jerked it from her hands and flung it across the corral before grabbing her by the hair. He pulled her head back and held a knife to her throat as he spoke to the others in his native tongue.

"No, leave her alone." Caroline scrambled on all fours to retrieve her knife from the dirt. "Don't hurt my mother."

"You wish to fight with Three Horns girl, instead of watching your mother die?"

"Yes."

"Caroline, don't..." He gave Vicky's hair a yank, cutting her off.

"White women talk too much." He gave her a shove. "Comanche women know when to be quiet."

He stood before Caroline with his hands on his hips before kicking her feet from under her. The girl rolled and bounced upright like a cat whipping the knife at him. The point came dangerously close to catching his loin cloth as he reached for her. He jumped back while the others laughed and grabbed their crotches. They circled each other, Caroline bent-over and holding the knife chest high. The man suddenly caught her by the arm and flung her to the ground in a cloud of dust. She rolled, trying to regain her footing, but Three Horns pounced on top of her and wound his fingers in her hair. He jerked her head back and held the knife to her throat.

"No, please don't." Vicky dove at them, but Shadow grabbed her around the waist and held her fast. Caroline set her lips into a thin line and glared straight ahead.

"You're not afraid to die?"

"No." He released his hold on her and stood to tower over the girl.

"You're not afraid of Three Horns either, are you?" She shook her head. "That's good." He turned to the others. "She was willing to fight to save the horse, and," he pointed the knife toward Vicky, "she fought to save her mother. But she's not afraid for herself." He held out a hand to help her up. "Manhunter has taught you well, little princess. You have the heart of a Comanche." He turned to Vicky. "Mother should be proud."

"I am." It sounded more like a sob. "If...you all would like...please come up to the house. I'll fix you something to eat." She motioned for her daughter to join her.

"But, Mama, what about Tippy?"

"Later, Caroline. Come..." She dragged the shotgun into the house by the barrel and let it fall on the floor before throwing herself across the bed and letting the flood come.

Chapter 59

"Why are you so set on fighting my husband?" Vicky set the second pan of biscuits on the table, which vanished as quickly as the first. Caroline was stirring another pot of cornmeal mush while bacon popped and sizzled in the frying pan.

"He questioned my honor." Crumbs fell from Three Horn's lips as he spoke.

"He said you challenged him with your lance. Is that true?" The man's eyes shot around the table toward the others. "Wouldn't you do the same, if he had given the challenge to you?"

"He questioned my honor!" He slammed his palm against the table.

"I'm sorry." She turned away toward the bacon. "I didn't mean to make you angry. But it seems silly that two grown men would want to fight and maybe kill one another instead of sitting down to talk." She watched him from the corner of her eye as she turned the bacon. "I've already had a husband who died in such a fight, and I was hoping to keep this one." The man took an angry bite from the biscuit and chewed viciously.

"I hate to keep bothering you and upsetting your breakfast." She knelt beside his chair. His eyes once again shot toward the others before falling back on her. "But I can't help wondering how Laughing Brook would feel if you were hurt or killed. I know how it would affect me, and it just breaks my heart to think of her like that."

"You know my woman?"

"We've never met, but I feel I know her. Matthew has told me a lot about her...and you. He says you were friends." She returned to her bacon. "He says that you used to hunt together. That you played games as children and even fought as warriors." She put the plate of bacon on the table and watched it vanish. "Is that true?"

"Yes," he said, stuffing a piece of bacon in his mouth. "Manhunter was a brave warrior. He should have stayed with the Comanche and had a Comanche woman, like Prairie Flower." He pointed at her with another piece of bacon.

"Oh?" She raised her eyebrows and turned away. "I guess I could dye my hair black and paint my skin. Would that help?" Shadow's laughter made her jump.

"If you do, paint yourself my color. That would shock everyone, wouldn't it?"

"A Comanche woman would not humble herself before another man like you." He pointed to where she had been kneeling. "She only sits at the feet of her husband or father."

"Oh, did I break one of your rules? I'm sorry. I was honoring you as a Chief. My people have always bowed before kings," she paused to let the statement take root, "but I would humble myself and do more to save my husband. I would fight you the same as my daughter, the same way I fought others before you. And, if needed, I would die for him." She held the pot as Caroline spooned more mush into their bowls. "I'm sure Laughing Brook would do the same." She let the men finish their meal in silence and waited until they retreated outside before readying herself and the children for school.

"The dog will be lame for awhile, but he will live." Shadow was sitting on the porch rubbing Tippy's neck when she opened the door. "I put some herbs in his wounds, but he licks them out as soon as they're there. You'll have to wrap him."

"Thank you. You're a kind man."

"Me?" He rose from the porch laughing. "You don't know me, lady." He was still laughing as he walked to his horse. Three Horns trotted his pony to where Caroline stood staring at the empty corral.

"My braves have taken your horse away for you, little princess. It will be a great loss, but your life will be filled with losses, and you must learn to accept them." He caused the pony to sidestep toward Vicky. "You are a wise woman, but this thing between Manhunter and myself is between men, and we must meet and settle it as men."

"I understand. But it will not keep the women from weeping." He turned and galloped away.

"Look." Mark pointed as they headed toward the barn to get the buggy. The lion's skin was tacked to the plank wall.

Chapter 60

Douglas stuck his whole head into the basin of cold water then straightened upright, letting the drops trickle down to wet his shirt and vest. It had gotten totally out of control, like a runaway boxcar heading downhill with no way to stop but crash. He held up his hand and slowly made a fist. He had it right there. Just a few more days was all he had needed. A quarter of a million dollars for the taking. It would have been easy to leave Lillian behind. No one would believe she knew anything about the deal in the first place, let alone had anything to do with it. He had planned on growing a beard, buying new clothes and using a different name. Hell, he could have gone anywhere with that kind of money and done whatever he wanted. No one would ever have been able to find him.

"You don't look so good, Doug. You'd better calm down." Chris Hari's voice made his skin crawl. *Hell no, I don't look so good, and you're one of the reasons, you stupid son of a bitch. Why'd you have to show up and spoil everything?*

"That's a nice looking kid your wife's rocking. You say you just got up this morning and there she was, holding her in her arms? And you've got no idea where it came from?"

"That's right." Douglas threw a towel over his head and began rubbing vigorously.

"And she doesn't know either?" Douglas shook his head. "I'd say you got yourself one hell of a problem. Someone knows where that kid's been. And I'll bet it had some help getting back inside the house last night too. You know, the word is that they're going to hang Lowell for killing the real mother."

"What are you driving at, Chris?"

"Just this." He struck a match against the paneling and lit his cigar. "When Lowell finally realizes they're gonna stretch his neck, who do you think he's gonna try to pin that murder on?"

"Hell, I didn't kill her. Besides, I'm an upstanding citizen of the community and personal friend to the Mayor. He's nothing but an old broken-down drunk. Who do you think they are going to believe?"

"Well, I don't know. But you've already given him a hundred and fifty dollars. God and everybody else at the drugstore knows about that. And you've got the kid in the next room. They might start thinking you paid that drunken husband of hers to kill her." He paused to puff on the cigar. "Folks are bound to find out about that kid reappearing sooner or later and start asking questions."

"So? The kidnapper must have gotten a guilty conscience and brought her back. We've already been through all this before. I'm just a compassionate sort of fellow and everyone around here knows it. I just happened to see what type of condition that child was going to be raised in, and I cut a few corners as far as adoptions are concerned. Who's going to condemn me for that? I'm a goddamn hero in this town, Chris. Get used to it." He leaned close to the mirror as he ran a comb through his hair.

"Yeah, maybe. But Steel says the word is that old sheriff's been sending wires to Virginia and asking all sorts of questions about you and Lillian. It won't be long before he starts getting some answers. You got to be pretty popular after you left, you know."

"What do you mean?" He paused in the middle of tying his tie to glare at Chris.

"Well, hell, Doug, the way you took off owing everyone money, folks just naturally started talking. It wasn't long before they started putting two and two together. You know, like who it was that shot Drake Larsen and ran off with the money. Then some corporal who happened to serve under General Jackson in the same outfit as you...now what was his name? Baker? Yeah, that was it, Gary Baker. Anyway, he showed up saying that you were under suspicion of being a Yankee spy. Is that true, Doug? Were you a stinking Yankee spy? A yellow-livered traitor?" Chris' eyes narrowed as he rolled the cigar back and forth between his fingers.

"You're awful quiet for a man who's just gotten called the lowest name a true Southerner can think of. Well, no matter. But he was telling everyone that another corporal by the name of Sam Bodard was trying to get the goods on you when he came up missing. It was his belief that you had something to do with the missing corporal."

"Go on."

"Then, he starts telling everyone that he wrote Colonel Farthington and told him all about you. Said he believed the old man deserved to know that his son in law was a Yankee dog. Then the old man goes out for a ride with you one afternoon and turns up dead. Now, I'd hate to go on thinking what everyone back home's been saying, but they're saying that my buddy Doug did for the old colonel. Is that true? Did you?"

"You're just fishing. You don't have anything on me." Douglas went back to his tie. "Besides, you're no saint yourself. You were in on the game as deep as I was."

"True, I was in on the card games. I'll admit I dealt from the bottom of the deck some. I even lifted a few wallets from some of those carpetbaggers. But I never was no

Yankee spy, and I never killed no one who didn't deserve to get what was coming to him. But you on the other hand…" He snickered and shook his head. "Hell, one of them darkies you had working in your house was claiming it was you that killed that baby. He says you were angry because the kid wouldn't stop crying. Then he said you stuffed his body in bed next to Lillian and told her she musta rolled over on him in the middle of the night and smothered him. Hell, the kid was only crying because he was sick, Doug. Then the same darkie went on to say that he saw you shoot that nanny of Lillian's in the head the day you were leaving, for no good reason. Damn, Doug," he shook his head in disbelief, "how'd you get so mean?"

"Well, what if I did shoot her? She was always sticking her nose into my business and trying to tell me how to treat my own wife. Who gives a damn about a fat old nigger woman in the first place. And that kid was so sick he was probably gonna die anyway." Both men spun on their heels as they heard someone gasp behind them. Lillian was standing in the open doorway holding the baby in her arms. "Dammit! What did you hear?"

"You killed Ma'amaw and Bobby?"

"No, he was just telling me what some imbeciles are saying back around the plantation. Go on back into the other room and shut the door."

"But I heard you, and that's not what you were saying. You said…"

"I know what I said. Now, dammit Lillian, get back to the other room. This doesn't concern you." He took a couple of strides toward her, but she stood her ground with chin held high.

"Anything concerning my son and my nanny concerns me. I believe I also heard something about my father. Is Chris telling the truth Douglas?" She took a deep breath. "Well, is he?"

Douglas glanced over his shoulder at Chris and sighed before giving Lillian a resounding slap across the left cheek that knocked her to the floor. He started for her hair, but froze at the clicking of a gun beside his ear. He turned slowly to stare down the barrel of Chris Hari's forty-four.

"Don't ever do that again. Now, get over against that wall." He motioned with the gun and waited until Doug was completely across the room before helping Lillian to her feet.

"Here," he said, handing Lottie to her. "I might be a black-heart in a lot of ways, Lillian, but I've never struck a woman, and I'll not stand for it now."

"Thank you, Chris. I haven't always liked what you did, but you have been a true friend to me."

"I always will be." He leaned over to kiss her bruised cheek. "Now, go to your room until we're gone."

"Why, what are you going to do?"

"I'm not going to hurt him, if that's what's concerning you." She stood firm, while her dark eyes searched his face. "Believe me, Lillian. I won't for your sake." She left the room, talking softly to the crying baby.

"What now?" Douglas said, folding his arms.

"We're going to go have a drink. Then, we're going to the bank and make that withdrawal."

"What? The money won't be here for another week or two. I checked."

"It won't be there at all Dougie, don't you get it yet? It's over. That old gray-headed sheriff has you in his sights, and he's ready to pull the trigger. He'll have you tried and hung before that money ever gets here. Now, come on." He motioned with the gun.

"Hell, you don't know what you're talking about."

"I don't, huh? This isn't the South where things move at a snail's pace. This is the West where they try and hang you the same day."

"I don't think so." Douglas crossed his legs as he leaned against the wall. "We'll wait until the money gets here before going to the bank."

"No," Chris said, pulling the hammer back to the last notch. "There's something I forgot to tell you. That corporal and a passel of others are headed this way on a train right this minute to watch you hang. They're gonna stand up in court and tell about your spying, killing and robbing."

"What? Where'd you hear that?" Douglas stood up straight.

"Charlie and Mike were having breakfast when they overheard that young deputy's wife telling that gal that works behind the counter about it. What's her name...Sally? Anyway, it seems that old sheriff has had her husband and that tall drink of water from England over at El Dorado the past few days. They've been burning up the telegraph wires finding out everything about you. He wants to hang you real bad, Doug, and you know what? Half this town's good old Southern boys, just like you and me. And you being a Yankee spy? Hell, they'll throw a party and dance around your feet while you're swaying in the breeze. Now, wait, don't go soft on me," he said, as Douglas slumped into a chair. "We still have to get to the bank and make our withdrawal. I realize that they won't have all the money we were expecting, but they'll have some. And seeing as you won't be around much longer to help us out, the boys and I decided that we should get something for our trouble."

"Here," he said, tossing Doug his coat and hat. "Let's go have that drink. The bank opens in another hour."

Chapter 61

"Good morning, Sally. Here, let me help you with that." Dave Price jumped to his feet as the young girl pushed the door open with her hip. "Breakfast for our guest?"

"Yep," she said, sitting the tray on the desk. "All except this." She slid a pastry-filled plate from the tray.

"Oooo, bear-sign."

"Your wife made me promise you'd know it was from her." She adjusted the collar on her green dress and crinkled her nose at him. "You're pretty lucky to have her."

"I know," he said over a mouthful. "But if I didn't, I'd be after you. Nobody makes bear-sign better'n you."

"Oh yeah? Think I'll tell her you said that."

"Don't you dare. That little redhead would skin me alive." He wiped his mouth on his sleeve and grabbed the keys from the desk drawer. "Ready?" He unlocked the outer wooden door and pulled it open. "After you, ma'am," he said, stepping backward with a bow.

"Thank you, sir," she said with a laugh, and scooped the tray off the desk. Suddenly the tray crashed to the floor as she screamed.

"What the hell?" Dave pushed her aside with his left arm and drew his gun before entering the cellblock. Lowell Ollar's body hung limply by bed sheets tied to the bars in the upper window. "Dammit," he said, dropping the gun back into the holster. "Sally?"

The girl stood frozen, holding a hand over her mouth and whimpering softly.

"Sally!" He grabbed her by the shoulders and shook her two or three times good and hard. "Snap out of it. I need you to go find Cotton as fast as you can. Understand?" She nodded. "Good. He should be home with Alice. Get going, now, and hurry."

He made sure she was headed in the right direction before removing the keys from the outer door and slipping them into the cell-door. "Stupid bastard. Well, at least you saved us the trouble of hanging you ourselves." He gave the key a twist and the lock snapped open with a loud click. The hinges cried as he gave the door a shove and let it bang against the bars on the other side of the tiny cell. Dave paused to glance around before entering.

"Musta stood on your piss-bucket to do yourself in," he said, glancing toward the metal bucket lying on its side in the center of a yellow puddle. "Hell, why'd you have to do it on my watch? Why couldn't you have done it last night when Cotton was here? Well, I don't guess I've got to ask you to hold still so I can cut you free, do I?" He pulled out his knife and bent over to straighten the bucket to stand on. He raised up and Lowell's heavy boot caught him under the chin, propelling him back against the iron bars. The last thing he remembered was the feel of the cold stone floor as it rushed up to meet the side of his face. Then, everything went black.

Chapter 62

Lowell laughed as he reached for the end of the sheet tucked inside the back of his shirt and gave it a pull. The slipknot gave way and the sheet running under his armpits and hidden by his dirty shirt let him drop to the floor. It was an old trick he had learned from an escape-artist years earlier. The separate strip of sheeting tied around both his neck and the one holding him off the ground would have given anyone the impression that he had really committed suicide.

"Thank you, deputy, sir." He gave Dave a mock salute before slipping his jacket and hat on. "And since you're such a kind and generous man, I don't believe you'll mind one little bit if I borrow these," he said, stuffing Dave's knife in his pocket and pulling the gun from its holster. "Sorry I can't stay around to see the hanging, but I must really be going. Hope you have a great day, sir." He laughed as he turned the key, locking Dave inside the cell.

He took only a split-second to glance around the office before locking the wooden door and tossing the keys into the stove. He paused once again at the front door to study the street before pulling his hat down over his eyes and closing it behind him.

The day was just getting started. Henry Adams was sweeping the sidewalk in front of the pharmacy as a lonely buggy rattled its way down the street to stop at the general store. *No time for a drink this morning, Lowell*, he told himself, as he quickened his pace past the temptation. "Dammit!" Up ahead, coming to meet him was that sheriff, being led by the young girl in a green dress and white apron.

No, no, he hasn't seen you yet, Lowell. Just calm yourself. He's heading for the jail because he thinks you're dead. But you can't let him see you, so you just do a little shopping until they're gone. He slipped inside the general store and started looking at a bridle and tack display in the front window where he could watch. "Look, it's him, Mama!" The shrill voice caused his heart to jump. *Ignore it, Lowell. They're almost past.* "It's the man who killed Ida. He's supposed to be in jail."

"Goddammit!" He spun on his heel to point the gun in her direction. "Shut your mouth before I kill you." The storekeeper disappeared through the rear door as the blond-headed woman tried to herd her two children into a corner for safety.

"Please, we'll keep quiet," she said as she tried to stop the little boy from crying.

"You'd better hope so." He kept the gun pointed their way as he craned his neck to see out the window. They were past the general store and well on their way to the jail. The storekeeper suddenly rounded the corner of the building yelling. He was waving his arms like a wounded chicken as he ran to meet the sheriff. Cotton stopped to stare, then drew his gun and turning to face the store. He motioned with his left arm, and the girl and storekeeper vanished inside one of the neighboring buildings. Lowell glanced toward the drugstore across the street as Henry Adams stopped his sweeping and hurried inside. He licked his lips wishing he had a drink.

"Lowell? Lowell Ollar, come out with your hands up."

"See what your big mouth's done. I would have been out of town in a few more minutes, but now someone's sure gonna get hurt," he said as the skinny girl crouched closer to her mother.

"He won't hurt you if you do what he says. I know him," the woman said in a hoarse whisper.

"Won't hurt me? Hell, woman! He's gonna hang me. How much more hurt can you get?"

"Lowell, don't make me come in there."

"Just go out the back door and I won't tell him where you went."

"Shut your mouth!" He waved the gun wildly making them crouch lower. "I've got to think." He leaned against the counter and ran a shaking hand across his stubbled face. "Think, dammit, think." His eyes roamed the shelves until they landed on a row of bottles labeled cough medicine. He struggled with the paper wrapping on the neck of one of the bottles before pulling the cork with his teeth.

"Do you think that is going to clear your mind for you? It's nothing but corn whiskey."

"Dammit woman. One more word out of you and I'll shut your mouth for good." Some of the liquid trickled out of the corners of his mouth as he tilted the bottle a second time. He could hear the excited voice of the storekeeper trying to explain something to the sheriff.

"What?"

"I said, I believe Vicky and her children are still inside the store with him."

"Dammit, why didn't you tell me this sooner?"

"I thought they were right behind me, but I can't find them anywhere."

A grin crept across Lowell's face as he turned toward the captives huddled against the wall. "Come here, girl." He motioned with the gun.

Chapter 63

"What the hell's going on out there, Hank?" Charlie Stewart asked as the pharmacist peered through the dusty window.

"That feller who was locked up in jail," Henry Adams glanced over his shoulder, "you know, the one who used to sit and drink with you boys once in a while? Well, it looks like he's busted out and he's got some folks holed up over at the general store."

"No kidding?" Chris Hari rose from his chair to join him at the window. "Hey, you guys, come on and look at this. He's got that little girl by the hair, and he's holding a gun to her head." There was an immediate shuffling and scraping as the men crowded around.

"Jesus Christ, is he crazy?" Mike Steel said.

"Must be. That's Manhunter's family he's messing with. I wouldn't want to be him when that Comanche gets back," Hank said, pouring himself a drink.

"Where'd he go?" Chris slid his empty glass down the counter for a refill.

"Manhunter? Don't rightly know. Word is that him and Jim Larkin headed out north to look at some stock sometime last night. They expect them back later today, if what Sally said is right."

"Whadda ya think he'll do to him?"

"Hard to guess with that Injun. But what I hear is," he leaned close and lowered his voice, "that he was married once before. And while he was off scouting for the Army, this drifter shows up and kills his wife and baby."

"Aw Gawd, that's too bad," Charlie said shaking his head.

"Anyway, the sheriff we had around here at the time couldn't seem to find the killer. Don't actually think he cared much, seeing as she was Injun same as Manhunter. But that Comanche wouldn't give it up. It took him most of a month, but him and Cotton finally found the man who killed them." He turned away to wipe a glass with a grimy towel.

"Well, what the hell happened when they caught him?"

"The rumor has it that Manhunter slit his throat." Hank drug his index finger across his throat.

"Hell, this town's finally getting exciting," Larry Tyner exclaimed. "Wanna stick around for another day or two?"

"Na, this might be an excellent time to finish our business and get outta here. Everyone's going to be busy thinking about Doug's friend. What time you got?"

"Let's see," Larry said pulling his pocket watch. "About 9:15."

"Another forty-five minutes." Chris paused before downing his drink. "Yep, it's going to be a real good day. Why don't you give it another half-hour, then take the boys and go get the horses, then meet us in front of the bank. In the meantime, Doug and me will mosey on over so we can be first in line when the teller opens the door."

"You trust him?"

"Hell, what's not to trust? He's got to leave town one way or the other. If he stays here long enough, he'll be sharing a cell with our buddy Lowell."

"Shut up, Chris!" Douglas glared across the table.

"Oh, I'm scared," he said with a grin. "Yes, it's going to be a great day. I can feel it in my bones."

Chapter 64

"You ain't so brave now, are you girl?" Lowell took a long pull on the bottle, then leaned forward to blow his alcoholic breath in Caroline's face. "Now that I ain't locked behind those bars, and you got to deal with me face to face, you're scared to death, ain't you?" She sat stone-like in the middle of the floor without blinking. "Well, answer me. Ain't you?" He prodded her with the gun.

"Leave her alone. You'd be frightened too," Vicky said.

"No I wouldn't. 'Cause I woulda' been minding my own business and not got involved in other folk's affairs in the first place. But this brat went to telling that sheriff she seen me kick Ida out of the wagon and leave her beside the road. Now, didn't she?"

"That's because she did see you do it."

"Maybe so, but it weren't none of her business."

"Anytime one human mistreats another, it becomes everybody's business. Especially the way you treated your wife. Come here, Carol."

"No." He gave Caroline a shove with his boot as he started to get up. "She stays right here where I can keep an eye on her. And if you don't shut your mouth like I done told you, I'm gonna shut it for you."

"Shhhhh, it's alright," Vicky said, caressing Mark's head. She gave Caroline a reassuring glance as the girl re-assumed her statue-like pose. "Your daddy will be here soon, and everything will be okay."

"I said, shut up!" Lowell tilted the bottle and drained its contents before shuffling to the door. "Hey, you still out there?"

"Yes, we're here. What do you want?" Cotton's voice sounded close.

"I already told you. I want some money, grub and a horse. I also want free passage outta town."

"But that's not possible, because you haven't met our demands yet. You have to let Mrs. Blue and her children go first."

"What? Hell, are you stupid or something?" He laughed and grabbed Caroline by the hair.

"Ow, ow, that hurts," she cried as he dragged her toward the door.

"Maybe you don't understand, sheriff." He stood Carol in the doorway and jammed the muzzle in her ear. "It's getting late. And if you don't start doing something real soon, I'm gonna start tossing them out one by one, dead."

"Alright, take it easy. I'll send someone to get your horse right now. But you'll have to wait until the bank opens before we can get your money."

"No, dammit!" He gave Caroline's hair a tug and flung her to the floor. "You're the law, and that bank will open anytime you say. So go get the money or I start killing me some folks."

Please, God, please don't let him hurt my children. I'm not asking for myself, Lord. But they're just babies. Vicky blinked back a tear. She could see Douglas Hancock and Chris Hari as they left the drugstore and walked gingerly toward the bank on the opposite corner.

"Ha, it's working, just like I knew it would." He leaned his head out the door and yelled. "I want five hundred dollars and not one cent less." Douglas held up a hand and nodded. "Hot-damn, I'm gonna be rich." He staggered toward the shelf to grab another bottle.

Where's my husband? Oh, God, please send him here before it's too late.

Chapter 65

"Poverty's a real eye-opener, isn't it?" Matthew said, tossing his right leg over the pommel and dropping to the ground. There were holes in the side of the shanty letting one see the sunlight peeking through the cracks in the boards in the opposite wall. The tall lanky boy working in the small garden let the hoe fall from his hands and ran to the house.

"Damn, I didn't know people actually lived like this." Jim Larkin's mouth hung open as he let the reins of his horse trail the ground. He took a few steps toward the house and turned back toward Matthew.

"I mean, I've seen poor people before. I was poor once myself, but..."

"This is nothing. You ought to see how some of my people survive. Here she comes." A black woman emerged, followed by the boy and a small bare-foot girl. The three of them ran to engulf Benjamin Polk and Jessie in bear-hugs. "Shall we go meet them?"

"Well, yeah, sure."

"Hello, ma'am. My name is Jim Larkin, and this here is Matthew Blue," he said, removing his hat.

"How much trouble is my boy in, mister?" She eyed Jim carefully while holding a protective arm around Benjamin.

"I can't rightly answer that ma'am. You'd better ask Matt that question. I'm just along for the ride," Jim said, turning his hat in his hands.

"Oh?" she raised her eyebrows and eyed Matthew up and down. "And how is it that you's in charge. Did he go and cause some trouble with you folks?"

"No," Matthew chuckled. "I just happen to be friends with the sheriff in Leon, and he asked me to bring your son and daughter home. He was afraid that some of the people in town wouldn't understand what happened and might try to hurt them."

"I'm afeared I don't rightly understand what happened myself. My name's Martha Polk, and these two younguns that you brung with you is my children. And these other two are their brother and sister, Joshua and Joy. Would y'all like to come in out of the sun?" She motioned toward the house.

"Sure," Matthew said, glancing toward Jim.

"I would be pleased to ma'am." He reached for his horse but the lanky boy beat him to the reins.

"I'll take care of him, sir, and yours too, mister." He nodded at Matthew.

The inside of the shanty was clean, but smaller than imagined, with beds and pallets lining three walls and a small table in the center. Pots and pans hung by rusty nails close to the small wood-burning stove and a wash pan sat next to a metal bucket on a board balanced across wooden boxes. The cool breeze seeping through the cracks made Jim wonder what kept them from freezing to death in the winter.

"Would y'all like something to eat? I can whip up some bacon and I got a few biscuits left over from this morning," she said shoving, a few sticks inside the stove.

"Sure, that'd be fine," Matthew said, nodding toward Jim.

"Ben, you need to draw a bucket of water so these folks can wash up," she said, handing him the pail. "In fact, you and Jessie need to scrub some of that grime off'n yourselves too."

"Yes'm," he said, ducking as he went through the door.

"Jessie, you run yourself over to Mira's and see if she ain't got some eggs I can borrow. Hurry now, child."

"No need to go to all that trouble, ma'am," Jim said.

"It's no trouble at all. Go on girl, get yourself moving." She shooed her out the door. "Besides, we don't get many visitors out this way, especially white folks like yourself. Only white folks we used to see much of was Ida and that no-account husband of hers." She put the pan on the stove to heat. "Guess he up and took her completely away, 'cause we ain't seen hide nor hair of that woman for a while now. Y'all wouldn't know anything about her now, would you?"

"Mrs. Ollar's dead, ma'am," Matthew said, glancing at the floor and back to the woman.

"Here's your water, Mama," Benjamin said, setting the pail on the makeshift counter.

"Thank you son." She pulled up a box and sat opposite them at the table. "Dead? How? What happened?"

Jessie returned with two small eggs and began frying the bacon while Matthew related the story of Caroline finding Ida beside the road, up to her death and burial in the cemetery beside the church.

"That poor soul. I always did feel sorry for her," she said, wiping her eyes on her apron. "What's gonna happen to that devil she was married to?" she said as she took the cooking duties from her daughter."

"Well, Sheriff Blankenship has him locked up in jail right now," Jim said, accepting the cup of coffee offered by Jessie. "And Matthew's daughter is going to testify that she saw him push her out of the wagon. Then, Ida herself told everyone including our deputy that it was her husband that gave her the beating before she died. So when it goes to trial, we're thinking that he'll get convicted of murder. They'll more than likely hang him."

"I hate to say it, but good. We're God-fearing folk, Mr. Larkin, but that man's a devil and needs to be hanged. You should have seen the way he treated that woman."

"I can imagine."

"No, you can't." She cracked the eggs into the skillet. "My husband and me was raised on a plantation in Georgia. We was owned, you understand that, Mr. Larkin?" She turned to glare at him, misty-eyed. "Our master was a hard man, but he never treated us niggers the way that man treated his woman. May God forgive me for the hate I feels in my heart, but I hope Lowell Ollar burns in hell."

"I'm sure God understands the way you feel, ma'am. I'm sure we all do."

"Now, maybe you folks can tell me," she said, setting the plates in front of the men, "what's gonna happen to this boy of mine? He done something terrible-wrong, and I tried to make him undo it. But I guess he went and got himself caught, or else you wouldn't be a-coming here." Jim stuffed a biscuit in his mouth and glanced at Matthew.

"Well, he did break the law, on two counts, you understand. First, he broke into a house, and then he kidnapped a baby."

"I knows that. That's why I was afeared that he'd get caught and you'd hang him. But you brung him back. Why? What's gonna happen to him?"

"Nothing, I guess." Matthew laid the fork in his plate and shrugged his shoulders. "We couldn't really figure out what to do with him. If he stood trial, he would either go to prison or be hung. More'n likely hung, knowing the way things go. But, we knew he really didn't mean any harm by what he did. So?" He shrugged again and picked up his fork.

"He's not telling you the whole story from what I hear," Jim said, choking down the last of the biscuit.

"Oh? And what might that be?"

"It was their wives that told them to let your son go. They would have had to contend with a couple of angry women at home if they locked him up."

"I see. So you're gonna let him go, just like that? You're not gonna be coming back and taking him from me later on, are you?"

"No, ma'am," Matthew said over a mouthful of biscuit and bacon. "But I wouldn't advise him to ever try anything like that again, no matter how good his intentions are. He's lucky it was me who caught him breaking into that house last night. If it was the owner or someone else, they might have shot him."

"Thank you kindly for not hurting him," she said, her bottom lip trembling. Then suddenly she jumped up from the table and slapped her son on the side of the head.

"Ow, Mama! What was that for?"

"You listening to that man, boy? You could have got yourself killed, and what for? The good Lord done already got the whole thing handled and there was no need in you messing in His business. That woman's already gone to heaven where she ain't gotta feel no more pain. And that man of hers is gonna hang. So, what's you gotta say for yourself? Huh?"

"No need to hit me, Mama. That hurt," he said, rubbing his head.

"I'm afraid I had to bonk him on the noggin, ma'am. You hit him on the same spot."

"You had to hit him on the head? Why, what for?"

"He pulled his knife on Mr. Blue, Mama," Jessie said.

"He did what? Lord have mercy," she said, holding her hand over her breast.

"I thought he was gonna hurt me and Jessie, Mama."

"Benjamin Polk," she said, grabbing a cast iron pan from one of the nails, "I'm gonna beat some sense into you if it's the last thing I do."

"But it wasn't like that. No, Mama," he said, holding up an arm and backing toward the door.

"You ain't never going anywhere again, you hear?" The pan glanced off his arm to clang against the doorpost. "You're gonna stay right here on this patch of ground and do nothing but plow and dig the rest of your born days." They heard the pan clang again followed by a cry of pain as the two combatants exited the make-shift porch.

"I'd say that was punishment enough, wouldn't you?" Jim said, handing Matthew a cigar. "I'd sure as hell hate to have that woman mad at me."

~   ~   ~

"How much land do you own?" Jim paused after he'd already put his foot in the stirrup.

"About twenty acres, give or take a few," Martha Polk said, pointing toward another row of shacks toward the north. "Over to Mira Johnson's place, she and her husband's got some forty-odd acres but no mule. Their mule up and died two winters ago, about the same time my man did. So we kind of share our old mule, but he's starting to feel kinda poorly lately hisself."

"And you folks feed your families on this land with what I see? No cow or chickens?"

"Oh, we got a dozen chickens or so, it's just that they don't lay many eggs. And we had a cow, but she up and died in that blizzard we had two years ago. We just ain't had the means to get another. But, the good Lord, he takes care of us."

"Yes, I almost lost a third of my own herd during that freeze. I don't know what kept you folks from dying alongside your cow," he said, letting his eyes drift over the shanty. The blizzard of 1886 had been a particularly vicious one. Someone at Dodge City was claiming that the state had lost twenty-percent of its livestock by the time the snow melted. "But I'm sure the Lord does take care of you. Nice meeting you ma'am," he said, touching the brim of his hat. They had only gone about a quarter of a mile when he brought his horse to a halt and turned to catch another view of the little homestead.

"How far would you say it is from here to my place?" he said, as Matthew trotted up beside him.

"Oh, maybe ten, twelve miles, give or take a few. Why? What's rolling around in that head of yours?"

"I'm wondering if they wouldn't mind taking care of a few head of cattle for me. I don't know. What do you think?"

"Be careful. They're proud people and they might think you're trying to give them charity."

"What's wrong with that?"

"Nothing, if it's done right. Look," he said shifting in the saddle, "if you want to give them work, fine, give them work, but let them keep their pride. They're free people Jim, and you're not a master on some plantation."

"Huh," he said as he started his horse forward. "Give an Indian a little education and he thinks he knows everything. I'll just bet you didn't know that I'm short-handed and really could use a couple more drovers, did you? Now, I got a hunch that Benjamin and his younger brother might make pretty good hands. Could probably even set that mother and those girls up raising chickens and what. I happen to like eggs myself. What's wrong with that?"

"Not a damn thing, Jim. Not a damn thing."

Chapter 66

"He must have taken the keys with him, because we can't find them anywhere," Fred Walker said, trying to catch his breath. "Susan's in a real tizzy."

"Can't say as I blame her. I ain't in a real good mood myself," Cotton said, shading his eyes against the sun. "Any idea how Dave is?"

"Well, he's come to, but he's got a bunged-up chin and a nasty bump on the noggin. The side of his face is black and blue too, probably when he hit the floor is my guess. Outside of that, I reckon he'll be alright."

"Mmmm, knowing Dave, he's likely mad enough to chew through those bars without a key. It's probably good that he is locked up, or else he'd be trying to bust right in there and get Vicky and them kids killed."

"Well, what do you plan to do?"

"Do? Well, I plan on doing exactly what he says, just so long as it keeps those kids alive."

"You mean you're actually going to give him some money and a horse and let him get away?"

"The money and horse, yes. Get away, no." He gestured toward the horse Silas Wilson was leading down the street. "That's his mount."

"Isn't that his own horse?"

"Yes, the same one he came pulling the wagon with. It's old, sick and half-starved. I think I could outrun it on foot myself. Any other questions?"

"What about the money?"

"I believe Douglas Hancock and his friend are in the bank taking care of that right now. The main thing is to stall him as long as we can, and hopefully get Vicky and the children out of there. Then when we get him out in the open, it's a different story."

"Whadda you think will happen if Matthew gets back and they're still in there?"

Cotton glanced up from the cigarette he was rolling. "Well, I'm hoping to have this cleared up before that happens." He shoved the smoke between his lips and struck a match. "If not, there probably won't be any trial or hanging to worry about."

Chapter 67

"Isn't that just terrible what's happening over at the general store?" Neal Thompson said. The little man with hawk-like features and thick wire-rim glasses held the door open to let Douglas Hancock and Chris Hari inside. "I don't normally open the bank doors until straight-up ten o'clock, but I've been listening to that crazy man's demands. And when I saw you wave toward the sheriff, well, I took it for granted that you were going to get the money he's asking for ransom." He closed and locked the door behind them.

"Yes, that's right. That's what we're here for." Douglas glanced toward the clock on the wall. 9:45.

"Well, come right on over here and we'll see what we can do." He ran behind the counter and opened the shutters covering the service window. "Now, how much was it that man was asking for? Five hundred?" he said, unlocking the cash drawer.

"Yeah, but I kind of thought that as long as we're already in here, we might as well take care of our own business before the crowds get here." Chris leaned his elbows against the counter.

"I'm afraid there are never really any crowds to speak of. But I guess we can accommodate you. Now, let's see, if you'll just fill this out for the records, Mr. Hancock," he said, shoving a pen and a withdrawal slip across the counter, "I've already counted out the five hundred, so all we'll..." he stopped as Chris leaned through the window and shoved the muzzle of the forty-four in his face.

"I'm afraid we will be making a much larger withdrawal than Mr. Ollar's five hundred dollars. But it is a start." He took the money and stuffed it into his coat pocket.

"Mr. Hancock?" The banker's eyes darted from the gun to Douglas and his arms shot straight up.

"I'm afraid I'd do exactly what he says, Neal. He's dead serious."

"Bu...but..."

"Just step back away from the counter and keep your hands where I can see them. Doug?" Chris motioned with the gun and Douglas rushed around the counter to empty the cash drawer into a bag. "How much is in the vault?" Chris held the gun level as he joined them behind the counter.

"I don't know."

"Don't give me that. You count every cent each night. How much?"

"Four...no, five thousand."

"How much?" He cocked the hammer.

"Okay, two hundred thousand. The money for Mr. Hancock's railroad arrived yesterday."

"What did I tell you, Doug?" Chris glanced at Douglas with a grin. "Open it. And don't give me any horse-shit about it being on a time-lock either. This town's not big enough to warrant one." Neal's hands trembled badly as he turned the knob and he had to try three times before the heavy door opened.

"There, now that wasn't too bad, was it? Sit down over there and keep your mouth shut." He motioned with the gun and Neal slumped against the wall as he mopped his face with his handkerchief.

"Now, one more thing." Chris shoved a writing pad in front of Neal's nose after they had finished emptying the vault. "Put the combination on here, and it had better be right, because your life depends on it. I don't want you hollering and yelling until we're way out of sight, so I'm locking you inside the safe."

"Oh, God, no!"

"Yeah, now get busy." They waited until he finished and Douglas had tried the combination. "See, now that wasn't so bad, was it? Look, I even added the part about locking you inside myself."

"You're not really going to lock me inside, are you?"

"Go on." He motioned with his gun.

"Please mister, oh God, please don't lock me in there."

"Get in there." He gave him a shove and closed the door.

"You're not going to leave that note where everyone can see it, are you?" Douglas said as Chris stopped to tack the note on the front of the counter.

"Sure, why not?"

"Why bother? He doesn't mean anything to anybody." Douglas wadded the note into a ball and tossed it in the corner.

"Damn, Doug. You're a hard man."

The street was deserted except for the sheriff who was leaning against a post watching the store front. Charlie Stewart and Larry Tyner were headed their way, leading three horses. Mike Steel was mounted and waiting at the far end of the street.

"I'll hold the bag and wait here while you walk this over to the store." Chris handed him the wad of bills. "And make sure the sheriff sees you telling your friend to let that woman and her kids go."

"Are you kidding? I'm not giving that drunk five hundred dollars."

"It'll throw them off guard for awhile. They'll be thinking you're some damned hero instead of a thief. Besides," he said patting his gun. "If you don't, I'll kill you right here in front of God and everybody."

"Sure, alright, just so it comes out of your share." He took the money and held it up high as he crossed the street. "Here it is, Lowell," he said loudly. "I got your money. Took it out of my own account just so you can let Mrs. Blue and her children go. Can you hear me Lowell?"

Chapter 68

Al Meeks stood hunched over with his hands on his knees gasping for breath. "I just heard what happened. Is there anything I can do?"

"Yeah, get my wife and as many people as you can find over to the church and start praying," Cotton said.

"Is that all? Isn't there something else you need?"

"No, not right now."

"You sure that's enough?"

"Well, if it ain't, then we're in one hell of a mess."

Chapter 69

"Here's your money, Lowell. Chris said to let the woman and kids go," Douglas said, handing him the wad of bills.

"Did he now? And what if I don't?"

"No skin off my nose. I'm just passing the word on. See you around."

"And where the hell do you think you're going?" he said as Douglas turned his back and started walking away.

"Oh, I don't know. We thought we'd take a little trip. You know, leave this town for a while." He shoved his hands in his pockets and shrugged his shoulders. "Well, I guess they're waiting on me. See you, Lowell. Good luck."

"Wait." Lowell was stepping through the door, but turned back.

"What for? You're out of jail. You've got your horse and the money you asked for. What more can you want?"

"I might want to go with you. We're supposed to be friends, remember?"

"Not likely, Lowell," he shook his head with a snicker. "Besides, you're still holed up inside this store with Mrs. Blue and her brats, and you've got to figure out how you're going to get out of town without getting shot."

"Oh, so that's the way it is, huh?'

"Looks that way. Sorry." He started to turn away, but Lowell pointed the gun at his head and pulled the hammer back.

"Like hell, you say. Get over here."

"Aw, Lowell, you don't want to do that. You're only wasting time."

"Now!"

"Okay, okay," he raised his hands. "Now what? How's this going to help you?"

"You're going to be my ticket out of town." He shoved the muzzle close to Douglas' face.

"Careful with that thing." He tried to push the barrel away but Lowell kept waving it around.

"No one would dare try to shoot me if they thought I was taking such a fine up-standing citizen like you along as hostage." He laughed and began shoving bottles from the shelf into his coat pocket. "But first, I wanted you to see what I do to people who cross me. This woman and her nosey daughter tried to have me hung. They told that lawman it was me who killed Ida. Can you believe it, that I would kill my own wife?"

"You? Na, you're such a nice guy, Lowell."

"That's right. I'm Mister Nice Guy," he laughed. "Now, I want you to see this." He whirled to point the gun at Vicky. "Say goodbye, bitch."

Caroline sprang from the floor to grab his arm as she struck at his stomach with her right hand. "Ahhhh, dammit!" Lowell folded over and grabbing himself as the bullet bit harmlessly into the floor, sending a shower of dust and splinters into the air.

"Run, Mama, run," the girl said, diving behind the pickle barrel. Her mother wrapped the boy in her arms and rolled behind the counter.

"Damn bitch stabbed me." Lowell pulled a bloody hand away from his stomach to stare at him. The scraping of heavy boots caused them to turn.

"Don't move!" Cotton stood in the doorway with a gun pointed at Lowell. "Stand back, Doug."

"No, you got it all wrong. It's you who are gonna stand back." Lowell raised his gun to the side of Doug's head. "'Cause if you just so much as sneeze, I'm going to blow his head clean off."

"He's crazy enough to do it sheriff," Douglas said. "By damn, I think he really is."

"You bet I am. Now move out." He gave Douglas a little shove with the muzzle.

"Vicky? Caroline?" Cotton said, stepping back onto the sidewalk.

"They're fine. It's Lowell who's in bad shape." Douglas paused and Lowell jammed the barrel against his ear.

"Move! Wait, hold it," he said, shifting so that Douglas was between him and the sheriff. "Grab my horse and lead it over to where Chris is waiting. And don't get no funny ideas, 'cause I ain't got nothing to lose."

"You don't look so good, Lowell. Maybe you should go see the doctor."

"Don't you worry about me. All I need is to get out of town, then I'll be fine."

"Sure, okay, Lowell. Whatever you say."

"What the hell are you bringing him along for? That sheriff's gonna follow us all the way to hell with him tagging along," Larry Tyner said, as they reached the men waiting on the other side of the street.

"I didn't plan on it. He sort of invited himself."

"Just shut up, and get moving," Lowell said, pulling himself up in the saddle with a groan.

"Aw, jeez, Lowell. What the hell happened to you?" Chris said, staring at the bloody shirt.

"He let that skinny girl with the pigtails poke him in the breadbasket with a toad-sticker," Douglas said with a laugh.

"Leave him. Hell, he'll just slow us down," Charlie Stewart said.

"I'm fine. I'll keep up with the likes of you any day."

"Yeah, sure." He spurred his horse into a dead run toward the south end of town.

Douglas surveyed the street one last time before digging his heels into his horse's flanks. The sheriff had already disappeared inside the store and people were scurrying out of doorways like ants on a hot summer day. He touched the brim of his hat as they shot by his own house. *Goodbye, Lillian. Can't say I'll be sorry for never seeing you again.*

Chapter 70

Matthew pushed his way through the crowd in front of the general store to find Cotton seated on the pickle barrel. He was talking to an ashen-faced Vicky who sat huddled on the floor with the children. They were scrunched against the counter like a group of frightened kittens. "Daddy!" Caroline bolting to bury her face in his stomach.

"Matthew, thank God you're here." Vicky latched her arms tightly around his neck and kissed his face repeatedly as Mark held onto his leg. "It's been a horrible day. That monster killed Caroline's horse and attacked her before I could shoot it. I thought she was dead, Matthew. Then, Three Horns and Shadow came with several Indians. They were looking for you, and when Three Horns found out you weren't there, he held a knife to our throats and threatened to kill us. Then he said we should be proud of Caroline and they ate everything in the house. And when I got here this morning to give Mr. Walker a list before school, that dirty man from the jail tried to kill us."

"What?" He glanced toward Cotton as he tried to pull away from his wife's grasp.

"You just missed it," Cotton said.

"Missed what? I don't understand." He held Vicky's face between his palms and wiped back the tears with his thumbs.

"Our friend, Lowell Ollar, decided to bust outta jail. He had Vicky and the kids holed up here inside the store as hostages for more'n an hour before riding out of town with Doug Hancock. They took Chris Hari and the rest of that gang with them. Their dust hadn't even settled when you and Jim came riding in the other way. But I'm having a little trouble understanding the rest of it myself. You'll have to get it from her when things calm down."

"Oh, God," he said, engulfing Vicky and the children in his arms.

"We're okay, Matthew. Just frightened, that's all," Vicky said in a hoarse whisper.

"He broke out of jail? Anybody hurt? What about Dave?" he said, glancing back over his shoulder without easing his hold on Vicky.

"He's kinda buggered up some, but he's gonna be alright. Biggest problem seems to be in locating the keys. He let our guest lock him inside one of the cells. I guess Lowell must have taken them with him, because no one can find the key ring. Fred Walker and Susan are down there right now trying to figure a way of getting him out."

"Excuse me, Matthew, but I'd like to take a look at your family for a moment," Doc Stevenson said, plopping his bag on the counter. Matthew started to rise, but Caroline clung to his arm like a burr.

"I hurt him, Daddy."

"Hurt who?"

"Mr. Ollar. He was trying to shoot Mama, so I hurt him and hid behind the barrel." She held up a trembling hand that had a smear of blood on its palm and began to cry.

"You used the knife?"

"Yes," she nodded.

"That's okay, baby. He was trying to kill your mama. He probably would have killed you and Mark too, if he could have gotten away with it. I'm going to see about your Uncle Dave. I'll be right back. Okay?" She nodded and Matthew leaned over to give Vicky a lingering kiss before following Cotton outside.

"Hey, don't y'all got businesses to run? Go on now, give the Doc and them folks some privacy," Cotton said, shooing the crowd back from the door.

"Cotton, you seen Neal around anywhere?" Smokey said pushing his way through the grumbling spectators. "I heered about him havin' to give up some of that money to them fellers, so I moseyed over to see if he didn't have a heart attack havin' ta watch it walk out the door. But he ain't there and the door's unlocked."

"That's strange." Cotton glanced toward Matthew. "He never goes anywhere without locking up."

"You telling me? He's tighter'n Miss Mollie's corset." Smokey kept talking as they crossed the street. "He once made me put my hoss up for collateral when I wanted to borrow twenty dollars to tide me over for a month or so. I told him she was worth a sight more than that, but it didn't make him no never-mind. See, I told you," he said, scraping his boots against the deserted floor.

"Strange," Cotton said shaking his head. "Did you check out back?"

"Checked everywhere, including the outhouse, and he ain't nowhere to be found."

"Well, run down to the jail. Maybe he's down there trying to help free Dave."

"No need to," Jim Larkin said stamping the dust from his boots on the sidewalk. "I just came from there, and he wasn't at the jail."

"Seems like he also left without sweeping the floor," Matthew said uncrumpling the wad of paper he'd retrieved from the corner. "Damn!" He shoved the paper into Cotton's hand and bolted over the counter to start tugging on the safe handle. "What's the combination? Hurry!"

"Eight left, twenty-three right, sixteen left," Cotton said in an even-voice as they rounded the counter. Matthew spun the cylinder and gave the handle a jerk. Nothing.

"I must have done something wrong. Read it to me again, slower." Cotton repeated the instructions and Matthew turned the knob slower this time. Still nothing. "Dammit! What am I doing wrong. Are you sure that's what it says?" he said wiping his palms on his pantlegs.

"Yeah, right here." He held the paper out for him to see.

"Next time, turn the knob one time to the left, twice to the right, and back three times to the left and see if that doesn't work," Jim said over Matthew's shoulder. "They sometimes set them up that way." Matthew glanced at him before spinning the cylinder. Eight left, one time. Twenty-three right, two times, and back sixteen left three times. He grabbed the handle and paused before giving it a yank. The lock snapped open with a loud click and all four men exhaled with a sigh of relief. He pulled the door open and Neal Thompson rolled to the floor in a heap.

"Quick, get him on his back," Cotton said, as frantic hands seemed to pull at the man from every direction. "Give him some air." The sheriff grabbed the front of Fred's belt and pulled his mid-section off the floor. "Breathe, dammit. Breathe!" He lowered the body and raised it again higher. Neal began flaying his arms in the air with a gasp.

"Let me out! Oh God, oh God! Let me out of here," he said, bolting upright. Then, seeing the men around him, he buried his face in his hands and broke into sobs.

"It's alright, Neal. I'd have done the same thing. You're gonna be okay," Cotton said, patting him on the back. He shoved his hat back on his head and took his time studying the intent faces staring at the banker. "Why don't y'all go down and see if you can't figure some way of busting Dave out of that cell. I want to ask Neal some questions after he calms down."

Matthew ignored the questions of several citizens as he led the way to the jail with a brisk walk. He pushed his way past a group of children gathered at the door and stepped inside. Susan Price was busy filling the coffee pot with clean water. "My Lord, it's good to see you. How's Vicky and the children?"

"They'll be fine. How's that saddle tramp of yours doing?"

"He's got a lump on his head the size of an egg and a bad bruise on his cheek, but I think it's his pride that's suffered the greatest wound."

"I should hope so," he said, poking his head through the door to stare at the deputy.

"Not one word out of you, do you hear? Not one word," Dave said, pointing a finger at him.

"Shouldn't have to say anything. You've probably said anything I could think of to yourself as it is," he said with a grin. "How long they got you locked up for, anyway?"

"Damn you."

Matthew laughed and ducked the metal cup that Dave flung through the bars.

"We're waiting for Gordon Miller to bring a hammer and chisel from the blacksmith's shop. Maybe he can break the lock or something. Can one of you help me build a fire? They left the door open and it went out," Susan said, as she stooped over to study the inside of the pot-bellied stove.

"Sure thing. Here, let me do it for you," Jim Larkin said grabbing an armload of sticks from the kindling box.

"Wait," she held up her hand as he started to shove the first stick through the door. "Here, let me see that." She took the stick and began poking around the ashes. "I thought I saw something," she said, holding the key ring high from the end of the stick.

"Well, thank God for women. I'd have never thought of looking in there. Your husband would've had to stay locked up for several more days until I got around to cleaning the ashes if it was left up to me," Jim said, dropping the sticks in a pile.

Susan sloshed the keys in the water bucket and took her time drying them before heading toward the cell, where she paused.

"Well, come on. Let me out of here," Dave said, as his eyes bounced between her face and the key ring.

"Is that all you have to say, David Price? I'm the one who found the keys inside the stove. Everyone else spent their time looking through the desk and trash can time and time again."

"Well, yeah. You found the keys. So great. Now let me out of here."

Susan put her hands on her hips and stared at Matthew who shrugged and raised his eyebrows. "You married him. I don't know what to do with him. You do know that his horse is actually smarter, don't you?"

"I'm beginning to think so."

"Hey, what's the matter with you two? Come on, open the door so I can go catch that guy."

"I believe they're telling you that you ought to be more grateful," Jim said, pulling a cigar out of his vest pocket and inhaling its fragrance.

"I am. I'm awful glad she found the keys. Now come on, open the damn door."

"I'm beginning to think maybe Caroline's dog's a might smarter too," Matthew said, turning away. "I'll go catch him and bring him back for you, Dave."

"Hey!"

"You might have tried telling your wife how much you love and appreciate her before ordering her to 'open the damn door'," Jim said, striking a match against the wall.

"She already knows that."

"Would you like me to throw the keys back into the stove for you, Mrs. Price?"

"If you would please, Mr. Larkin."

Matthew could hear the angry deputy yelling as he left the sheriff's office and headed down the street to check on his family.

Chapter 71

"You wait up a minute, Matthew. You ain't going out hunting those men by yourself," Cotton said, returning from the jail with several rifles. He handed one to Al Meeks and another to Silas Wilson. Dave Price was leading several horses down the street, saddled and ready to ride. Jim Larkin had returned to his ranch and would meet them several miles out of town with extra mounts ready for the long run. Vicky stood on the steps of the general store with an arm around each child. All three had their eyes locked on the man seated on the large pinto that kept stamping its hooves nervously and shaking its head.

"Better hurry up then. They've got an hour's head start."

"Look, Daddy's horse knows there's going to be a chase, doesn't he?" Caroline said.

"Yes, he's done this before."

"Why's Daddy look so mean? He's never that way around us."

"It's because that man tried to hurt you and your brother."

"What about you? He was trying to kill you."

"Yes, he tried to hurt me too, but that's what has him upset. You need to ask God to help him not hurt those men out of anger."

"Why not? They locked Mr. Thompson inside the vault, and no one's any meaner than Lowell Ollar. Remember what he did to Ida?"

"Yes, I remember very well. But it's still not how God would want us to act, now is it?" They grew silent as Matthew guided the prancing horse over to where they were standing.

"You and the kids stay put while we're gone. I'll be back as soon as I can."

"You be careful, Matthew Blue. I don't want to have to raise these children without you."

"I'll be coming back. I almost lost the three of you today without knowing it. I don't want that to happen again. Understand?" She nodded as he turned the horse out to the middle of the street. "Don't you worry, I'll be back."

"Well come on, you lazy yahoos. Let's go get 'em," Cotton said, digging his spurs into his horses flanks.

Vicky stared at the empty street long after the dust had settled. With a deep sigh she took both kids by the hand and started toward the small white house with the picket fence at the end of town.

"We're going to Aunt Alice's house?" Caroline said.

"Yes, we're going to see your Aunt Alice while we wait for your father. Your Aunt Susan and cousin Joshua will be there too. We'll all wait...and pray."

"What about Lillian? Is she coming?"

"I don't know. Perhaps we should make a special effort to invite her. She probably needs prayer more than anybody."

Chapter 72

"Hey, wait up a minute." Chris Hari turned his horse back to where Lowell Ollar had fallen from the saddle. The man lay in the middle of the road, moaning and cursing.

"Hell, leave the sonofabitch. We didn't want him along anyway," Larry Tyner said as he drew up beside them. They were only six miles out of town heading south toward Arkansas, and knew the posse couldn't be far behind.

"I am, but you don't understand," Chris said, digging a hand into Lowell's coat pocket.

"No you don't. That's my money," Lowell gasped and tried to pull his gun.

"Oh, thank you, that might come in handy, too." Chris snatched the gun out of the dying man's grasp. "And the knife too." He shoved the weapons in his belt before continuing his search for the money. "Come on Lowell, where is it? You're not going to need it where you're going. Ahhh," he said, pulling the wad of bills from the inner pocket.

"Damn you. You just gonna leave me here like this for the posse?"

"Well, I wouldn't know what else to do with you. Besides, it doesn't look like you're going to be around much longer. Kinda fitting, isn't it Lowell?" Chris climbed back in the saddle. "You've always hated women and beat the hell out of them every chance you got. Now, a little girl's done for you. I think it's funny as hell." He laughed. "Say howdy to the devil for me."

Lowell clawed his way several feet, before collapsing, and lay cursing as he watched the men disappear from sight.

Chapter 73

Matthew's pinto fell into a ground-eating lope that left the posse far behind. There was no need in wasting time looking for tracks. These men were not trying to hide their trail. They were simply trying to get as far away from Leon as quickly as possible. The time for hiding tracks would come later when darkness fell, or when they crossed the Little Walnut, but for now, they would punish their mounts in an effort to distance themselves from the posse.

Matthew shot a glance over his shoulder. Jim Larkin had been true to his word and had joined them at the bend with his son and six fresh horses. They waved as he passed. Now, they were nothing but dots cresting the rise behind him with Cotton and the posse. He drew back slightly on the reins. The magnificent beast he was riding could keep this pace all day, but it would kill the horses of the other riders. He smiled. The mounts of the fugitives would give up long before his horse would begin showing signs of tiring. He pulled back on the reins, bringing the horse to a complete halt. Lowell Ollar's blood-soaked body was lying in the middle of the road.

Matthew edged his horse to the side of the roadway and drew his gun. He let his eyes roam the scenery, taking in every rock, tree and clump of brush as he waited. It wasn't likely that they would waste time laying a trap, but many a man had been killed stopping for a wounded or dead man. He could hear the hoof-beats of the posse when he finally slid from the saddle and led his horse to where Lowell was lying, He nudged him with his boot, then squatted and rolled him to his back. There was a gaping knife wound in his stomach. Matthew looked up as the posse slowly circled him and Cotton dismounted.

"Well, that's one we won't have to worry about hanging." Cotton hitched his gunbelt.

"Guess not." Matthew rubbed a handful of sand between his palms to remove the smear of blood.

"What killed him? Gun or knife?"

"Knife." Mathew had a sick feeling in the pit of his stomach.

"Caroline?"

"I reckon." He wiped the dust from his hands on his pants. "Dammit Cotton, I don't wanna tell her she killed a man. She's only nine years old."

"We could hang him from that tree over yonder," Jim Larkin said, pointing toward an oak a few yards off the road to their left.

"Without a trial? I ain't never done that sort of thing before. What do you think folks at the U.S. Marshall's office would say?"

"My hell, Cotton, he's already dead! What difference is it gonna make? It's Matt's girl we're worrying about, not how you're gonna explain hanging a dead man." Jim bit the end off a cigar and spit it on the ground.

"Don't worry about it, I'll think of something," Matthew shrugged. "I was the one who taught her how to use the knife in the first place."

"No." Al Meeks drew his gun. He took aim and fired a shot into the dead man's head. "There, all of you are my witnesses. I shot and killed Lowell Ollar. That child should never know she did any more that scratch him with her knife." He holstered his gun and folded his arms.

"Well, don't know about these young'uns, but my eyes are shore 'nuff good, Albert," Smokey said as he stuffed a chew in his jaw. "The way I see it, you didn't have no choice in the matter, 'cause that skunk was going for his iron when you bored him."

"I saw it that way too. How about you, Jim?" Dave said.

"Couldn't have been any other way."

"Alright, that's settled. Let's rustle before we have to chase 'em all the way through Arkansas," Cotton said.

"What about Lowell? We just going to leave him here?" Fred Walker said.

"Unless you want to carry him on your horse." Cotton leaped into the saddle. "We'll pick him up on the way back. Come on, we're wasting time."

"There's coyotes and buzzards and..."

"Then we won't have to worry none 'bout burying him, will we?" Smokey said.

Matthew waited until most of the men were mounted before turning to Al Meeks. "Much obliged," he said, touching the brim of his hat with a nod.

"Think nothing of it. I would have killed him for Ida's sake if I'd the chance." He turned his horse to follow the posse, but paused to glare at the dead man. "I hope some beast does drag you off. You're not worthy to be buried in the same cemetery with her."

Chapter 74

It was about a half hour later when Matthew spotted them. They had left the road five miles back and were walking their tired horses through a sandy wash. "Well, one thing's for sure," he said patting his horse's neck, "they don't know the land. They've gone in a circle, heading right into White Cloud's summer hunting ground." He shaded his eyes and searched the trail behind him.

"Well, no sign of Cotton or the posse. Guess it's up to us," he said, pulling the Sharps rifle from its sheath. He climbed out of the saddle and slid a round into the chamber. "Kind of reminds you of old times, doesn't it" He dropped to one knee and took careful aim. The buffalo gun leaped in his arms with a loud boom. The horse closest to the top of the steep bank rose on its hind legs and toppled backwards, knocking the nearest horse off his feet. Matthew reloaded as the men scrambled for cover. His next shot dropped another horse that had made it to the top and was being chased by a tall, lanky man. The man fell and rolled as he scampered back down the bank to take cover beside his partners.

Matthew sat quietly waiting, as the men fired volley after volley from their handguns, kicking up tufts of grass and dust fifty yards shy of their intended target. He glanced over his shoulder to see the posse pushing their horses through the tall grass. It would all be over in a matter of minutes. The men pinned inside the wash would be no match for the well armed posse. All he had to do now was wait.

Chapter 75

"What the hell's he using? A cannon?" Douglas Hancock ducked his head as another round sent a plume of dirt high into the air. He popped his head over the bank and cranked off three quick shots from his thirty-six caliber handgun, then ducked back down.

"Relax, you're wasting ammunition," Mike Steel said with a scowl.

"Well, what do you expect me to do, let him kill us all?"

"There ain't a damn thing you can do with that little pop-gun of yours. He's got us pinned down pretty good with that Sharps," Charlie Stewart said, loading his Winchester. "I ain't even sure if I can reach him with my forty-four-forty from here."

"Better think of something right quick. The posse's coming," Larry Tyner said, peering through a clump of brush. A round from Matthew's gun cut one of the branches and sent him tumbling down the bank. "Goddamn son of a bitch!" He said brushing the sand from his eyes. Douglas poked his head above the bank and fired two more shots. Another round from Matthew's gun kicked up dirt dangerously close and sent him sliding back down.

"Ever fought a Comanche before?" Mike asked as Douglas beat the dust from his hat.

"No, why?"

"Well, I have. And it ain't no picnic, I can tell you that. Those Comanches have a saying, that 'A brave man dies young.' They don't expect to live very long. That's why they're such fierce fighters."

"What's that got to do with us?" He scampered back up the hill to take a peek.

"Oh, just about everything. That Injun up there's just playing with us. He could kill any one of us, if he wanted. He's just keeping us pinned down, waiting for the posse, and he ain't gonna give up. So, you're either gonna have to kill him or he's gonna get you." Douglas turned to glare at him. "Trouble is, he's got that Sharps that'll pick you off a mile away." He turned to the whole group as another round sent sticks flying from one of the shrubs. "I remember riding alongside a bunch of soldiers once back in Texas. They was chasing a Comanche raiding party. This one old warrior dismounted and took off his moccasins. That was a sure sign he didn't intend to leave that spot alive. That old devil was one hell of a fighter. He wounded three soldiers and their commanding officer before he died. Took more than twenty bullets to croak him. In the meantime, his friends were able to get away."

"It's a nice story, but it doesn't seem to be helping matters at the present." Douglas half-slid and half-walked back down the bank.

"Well, it seems to me that some of you are going to have to stay here and fend for yourselves." Chris Hari rose from his perch.

"What the hell you talking about?" Charlie said, cocking the rifle lever.

"I simply mean I've still got my horse, and I plan on leading him down this wash until I can find a place to get out and ride away. Now, if the rest of you can figure out how to ride out of here on two horses, you're welcome to come join me. Otherwise, good luck."

"I've still got mine, so I'm coming with you," Douglas said, reloading his gun.

"So that's how it is, huh Chris?" Mike was lying on his back rolling a cigarette.

"Yes, that's how it is Mike. How'd you think it would be if it ever came to something like this?"

"Oh, I don't know. I just thought that we'd kind of watch each other's backs, that's all."

"Hell, you're old enough to know better than that. It's each man for hisself when you shuck right down to the cob," Larry said, sliding down the bank to join them. "We still got that nag of Lowell's. I say the three of us draw straws for it. Short straw rides," he said, plucking some sticks from a dead bush.

"Fine by me. Just hurry, they're here." Charlie fired another shot from his Winchester.

"Here, you first," he said, holding out his hand to Mike, who pulled one of the sticks. He then scampered over to where Charlie was and let him choose, then all three men compared their choices.

"Well, looks like I ride," Charlie said with a grin. "Here, you might need this." He handed Larry the Winchester. "Good luck."

"Na," Larry said, as they watched the men disappear down the wash. "He's the one that's gonna need the luck. That nag ain't gonna make it another three miles before it becomes buzzard-bait." He took a position behind the same clump of brush that Charlie had hidden behind and aimed the rifle. "Damn, they're working their way toward us," he said, pulling the trigger. He was instantly lifted from his feet by a fifty-caliber ball from Matthew's gun and sent sailing to the bottom of the wash.

"Always knew you was kinda dumb, Larry. That's why I'm sitting here enjoying my smoke and you're dead. Now the way I see it, I didn't go into no bank to rob it. And I ain't got none of the money on me, so they can't pin none of that on me. And I wasn't stupid enough to climb up there and try to shoot it out with that Comanche. Hell, that damn gun could kill an elephant. So," he took a drag off his smoke, "when they get here, they'll find my gun hasn't been fired. They only thing they can get me on is taking a ride with my friends." He crushed the smoke in the sand as the sound of walking horses drew closer to the wash.

"I might spend a few years behind bars. But I'm still alive and you're lying there with a hole in your chest big enough to drive a plow-team through."

"Hey, down in the wash. Come out with your hands up."

"I'm alone, Sheriff, and I don't aim to fight. Come on down and sit a spell. I think there's a bottle over there in the bag hanging on that dead bay."

"He's telling the truth, Cotton." Smokey stepped out from behind some bushes. Mike hadn't even heard him coming down the bank. "Just hold still, son. I don't want to hurt you none," he said, resting the muzzle of the rifle against his chest as he bent over to remove the pistol from Mike's holster and sniff the barrel. He was instantly engulfed in a cloud of dust as the posse clamored down the bank to join them.

"Here, it ain't been fired in a week of Sundays," Smokey said, handing the gun to Cotton.

"That right? Then who was doing all the shooting?" The sheriff pushed his hat back on his head.

"Him," he justured toward Larry, "and Charlie Stewart, some. But it was mostly Douglas Hancock. He's too stupid to figure out you can't fight an Injun with a buffalo gun when all you've got is a pea-shooter."

"So, you was going to sit tight and let us arrest you. Is that right?"

"Suppose so. Besides, I ain't guilty of nothing but riding my horse that I know of."

"You were with those men who robbed the bank and held Mrs. Blue and her children hostage. That makes you guilty in my book. Now, turn around so we can tie your hands."

"There ain't no need to do that, Sheriff. I can't go anywheres unless you say I can. Easy," he said as Dave gave the rope a tug. "I got skin for hide, not leather."

"Looks like three of them headed down the wash this way leading their horses," Matthew said adjusting his saddle cinch.

"Coulda told you that. They plan on crawling out somewhere round the bend and making a break for the border. Only problem is, that hoss Charlie's got is the same old bag of bones that belonged to Lowell, and it's about ready to croak as it is."

"There's another problem no one's counted on up to this point." Matthew pulled himself up into the saddle. "They're heading toward White Cloud's summer hunting grounds."

"Ya don't say. And I suppose Three Horns is leading this year's hunting party." Smokey rubbed his beard.

"Last time I checked he was. You can stand around trying to figure out what to do with him if you want, but I'm going to try to catch them before Three Horns does." Matthew dug his heels into his horse's flanks and the pinto sent a spray of dust and sand from his hooves as he darted down the wash.

"Hell, why worry? Them Comanches will save us the trouble of hangin' 'em," Smokey said.

"Well, I'm worried. I don't want another Indian war on my hands. Throw him on the back of one of the extra horses and let's ride," Cotton said, stomping off toward his own horse.

"Hey, someone got a bandage on 'em?" Jim Larkin was trying to roll up his son's bloody shirt sleeve.

"Sure, what happened to him?" Smokey said.

"The last shot from that saddle-gun bounced off a rock and winged John." Smokey ripped the boy's sleeve up past the elbow and wiped the blood away with his grimy neckerchief.

"Yep, more of a burn than anything else." He pulled a wad of chew from his cheek and slapped it over the wound and bound it with the neckerchief. "Be better'n new in a few days. Let's rustle."

"I can't ride with my hands like this," Mike said as Dave helped him on the horse. "I'll fall off and keep slowing you down."

"How about it?" Dave said turning toward Cotton.

"Cut him loose. But shoot him if he tries anything."

"You don't got to worry none about me, Sheriff. I'm just out to see the fun from now on."

Chapter 76

Matthew slowed his horse to a walk. It was easy to see where the men had made their way out of the wash. The fools had ridden up the sandy bank with no regard for the safety or welfare of the horses. He dismounted and led his horse out of the wash, then paused to study the tracks. One of the horses was limping badly. He climbed back into the saddle and pulled the Sharps from its sheath. He could hear the rumble of hooves coming down the wash as he injected a load into the chamber. "Come on, boy," he said, touching the horse's sides with his heels. "Let's go hunting."

Chapter 77

"Hey, wait up!" Charlie stood up in the stirrups to yell. The horse could hardly walk, let alone run. "Sons-of-bitches." The men didn't look back as they urged their mounts on through the thick grass. "Leave me out here alone. I'll cut you heart out for this, Chris. Damn you, just you wait and see." He drove the animal on for another quarter of a mile where it fell with a shudder and lay heaving a bloody froth from its nostrils.

Charlie unhitched the canteen and slung it over his shoulder before trotting through the knee-high grass. Chris Hari and Douglas Hancock were small shadows drifting from sight over the distant rise to the west. He paused to look behind, as the sound of a galloping horse drifted toward him on the breeze. The Indian on the brown and white paint was not more than a hundred yards away and coming fast. "Well, this might be my lucky day after all," he said, dropping the canteen. He waited with his hands on his hips until Matthew brought the horse to a halt a few feet away. Matthew shoved the Sharps back into the sheath and slid from the saddle.

"About ready to quit running?" he asked, stepping away from the animal.

"From you anyway. Ain't got much of a chance of outrunning that hoss on foot."

"Where's your friends. They run off and leave you?"

"Appears that way don't it?"

"Not very good friends if you ask me."

"No one's asking you, but it does kinda stick in my gut some. I'd like to borrow that hoss of yourn' so I can go tell them how much I appreciate them doing me thisaway," Charlie said, moving so that the sunlight shone in Matthew's eyes.

"Well, I don't think I could let you do that. But if you'll just be patient, I'm sure Cotton will lend you on one of the extras he's got with the posse. And if you're nice and polite, he might even put you in the same cell with your friends, so you can give them your compliments back in Leon." Matthew adjusted the brim of his hat with his left hand while moving to a better vantage point himself.

"That don't sound like too good a deal to me. Na, I'll take my chances with you," Charlie said, interlocking his fingers and stretching them. "Besides, the way I see it, I owe you one."

"Well, if it'll make you feel any better, I'll just tell everyone I was a bad little boy for whipping you and letting Dave throw you in the pokey." The grin left Charlie's face.

"It ain't gonna be so easy today, 'cause I ain't drunk."

"Neither am I."

"I've been hearing how tough you are, Manhunter. Are those stories really true? How tough are you anyway?"

"I'm tolerable. But there's a lot of people in the world, Charlie. You can always find someone a little better, if you look long enough."

"I ain't been able to find anyone better'n me, Manhunter, and I've been looking for a while now." Charlie's hand dropped to his forty-four but Matthew's first bullet caught him on the left vest pocket and spun him sideways. The second smashed into his ribs on the right side, knocking him off his feet.

"I...I...I...I," he said gasping for air as Matthew rolled him over on his back. His chest felt like it was on fire.

"Damn fool. What did you have to prove?" Matthew ripped his shirt open to study the wound. "That you're fast with a gun? I tried to tell you. But if it wasn't me, it would have been someone else. Now look at you. I'm still alive, and you're dead." Charlie's eyes went blank as his head rolled to one side.

Chapter 77

"Hear that?" Chris said, galloping his horse close to Douglas. "Sounds like a forty-four or forty-five."

"So, what's that mean?"

"It means they caught up with Charlie. He more'n likely tried to make a stand of some sort, but seeing as there was only two shots, they probably got him."

"Don't expect me to shed any tears. I'm glad to be rid of him."

"Damn, Doug, he was one of our partners."

"One of yours, not mine. I couldn't stand the man."

"That's nothing new. You couldn't even stand your own mother."

"That's true. I couldn't."

They urged the tired animals into a lope for another fifteen minutes, then slowed to a walk. "Well, here he comes," Chris said with a nod of his head. Douglas turned in his saddle to see the familiar figure on the brown and white pinto drawing closer.

"Damn! Doesn't he ever get tired?"

"Not hardly. Mike was right about him. That redskin will chase us into hell and out the back door, if he gets the chance." Both men whipped their horses into a labored run that only lasted for a matter of minutes before Douglas' animal gave way beneath him.

"Here, grab the money and come on," Chris said, holding out a hand to help him up. Douglas untied the bags and threw them over his shoulder. He grabbed Chris' hand, before drawing his gun and firing point-blank into the man's side. Chris fell from the horse with a groan.

"Should have kept going, Chris. That's what I would have done." Douglas leaped into the saddle and dug his heels into the tired horse's sides. "Stupid bastard."

Chapter 78

Three Horns had the sights of his forty-four-forty locked on the antelope and was starting to squeeze the trigger when the animal bolted. Someone on the opposite side of the hill had fired a shot that spooked his prey.

"Ahhh," he said leaping atop his horse. He only knew of a few Indians who carried pistols and none of them use the small weapons for hunting. With close to ninety hungry mouths to feed, the horse and lion taken from Manhunter's home would soon be gone. Now, the antelope that would have added much needed meat to the camp was also gone.

Chapter 79

Douglas leaned close to the horse's neck as a bullet whined overhead to kick up grass in front of him. "Come on," he said whipping the animal up a hill. Another bullet whizzed by followed by a boom, this one dangerously close. "Move, dammit!" He lashed even harder. He crested the hill and almost ran into an Indian mounted on a white horse. Both animals whinnied and shied from each other. Without thinking, Douglas turned and fired his gun directly into the man's chest. He was instantly surrounded by more Indians who seemed to come from everywhere. One particularly fierce-looking brave rode over to stare at the fallen man. *Funny*, Douglas thought. *I've never seen a black Indian before.* The man lying on the ground wore a buffalo skin headdress with three horns sticking out of it. The black Indian let out an angry yell before knocking Douglas from his horse with the butt of his rifle.

Chapter 80

"Is he dead?" Cotton said as he dismounted. He let the reins trail the ground and swatted at the dust clinging to his clothes as the rest of the posse arrived, one by one.

"We got ourselves a problem," Matthew said as Cotton squatted beside him.

"I'll say we have. The federal marshall's gonna be asking why a member of my posse left a string of bodies clear across Kansas."

"He didn't shoot me," Chris said through clenched teeth. "Doug did after his horse gave out." His breathing was labored and a bloody froth appeared around his mouth and nostrils when he coughed.

"Nice fellow to have as a friend, isn't he?" Al, said squatting at the man's feet. He pulled a silver flask from his coat pocket and offered it to Chris who shook his head.

"I'll say he is. Looks like your pard's done for you son. Want to make things right before you go to meet your Maker?" Cotton pulled his pipe from his pocket and wiped the dust from its bowl.

"Douglas was a Yankee spy in the war. Colonel Farthington, Lillian's father, found out about it and Doug killed him. He also killed a man in Virginia named Drake Larsen, a business partner of ours. We ran a gambling scam of sorts." He grimaced with pain. "It was mostly fleecing the carpetbaggers out of some of the money they stole from us in the first place. Anyway, Drake had almost twenty thousand on him that belonged to the six of us. We knew Doug took it, and that's why we came looking for him. You know he actually killed his own son and made Lillian believe she did it? Oh, damn it hurts," he said, catching his breath.

"Who's idea was it to lock Neal inside the safe?" Cotton took time packing tobacco in his pipe.

"Mine, just to give us a chance to get away. I left a note tacked to the counter, telling where he was, and the combination. Doug tore it down and threw it away. Did you get him out in time?"

"Barely."

"Good."

"Hey, Cotton, we got company," Dave said, pointing toward the top of the hill where eight Comanche braves sat on horses.

"Where the hell did they come from?"

"That's what I was trying to tell you," Matthew said.

"You talk to them yet?" Matthew nodded. "Well, what do they want?"

"Douglass ran right smack into them while I was chasing him, and for some reason, he shot Three Horns."

"He what?" Cotton dropped his pipe. Dave and several others started muttering and milling nervously. "Is he dead? Did he kill him?"

"Just take it easy, and don't make any quick moves," Matthew said evenly. "He's hurt plenty bad, but he wasn't dead when I last talked to them. Anyway, they've got Douglas and they're waiting to see what you're going to do."

"The Indians got Doug? Well, I'll be damned," Chris said with a hoarse laugh. He then coughed and fell limp.

"Yes, I guess you probably are." Cotton closed the dead man's eyes, then beat the unlit tobacco out against a rock and rose to his feet. "Well, lead on. Let's go see what they want."

"You men fall in behind in single file, and for God's sake, keep your hands in plain sight. Don't even scratch an itch, unless one of them can see exactly what you're doing, and then be doubly careful," Matthew said walking his horse up the hill. The braves parted to let them pass, then fell into a silent escort behind the posse. Matthew trotted his horse down the grassy slope for a mile and a half before turning in behind a grove of cottonwood trees lining the creek bank. The sight of teepees and children playing with barking dogs would have been a pleasant sight for him if he were not on such a solemn mission. One of the braves let out a yell and charged his pony past them on a dead run. Matthew held up his hand and brought the posse to a halt.

"What now?" Cotton said pulling up beside him.

"We wait."

"Wait for what?"

"Them." He nodded as the brave emerged from the camp with White Cloud and Shadow.

"Damn, he still looks good, doesn't he?" Cotton said, as the chief galloped his black horse out to meet them.

"Why does Manhunter and the white chief come to White Cloud's camp?" Shadow pranced his horse back and forth in front of them. "We have no use for white eyes here. Be gone."

"The white chief comes to offer his regrets for the grievous wrong that has been committed by another white man to one of our people today." Matthew spoke in his native language. "This man is a bad man and we were trying to catch and punish him when he happened upon your hunters."

"Good. You have said your piece, now leave. We will punish the man for you."

"That is good, Shadow. I know Comanche justice is a good thing. But the white chief wishes to see you carry out the punishment so he may return and tell his own people. You see, this man has hurt and killed many white people also." The brave stopped the pony's pacing to study Matthew's face.

"No, you lie. You would not let me have Comanche justice on a white man."

"I do not speak lies, Shadow. Why would I ask to be present if I lied? Three Horns is a Comanche brother and did nothing to deserve being shot."

"Three Horns swore he would kill you before the whole village."

"Yes, but that was between Three Horns and myself. That had nothing to do with this white man."

"Enough, let the white men pass." White Cloud raised his hand. Shadow gritted his teeth and gave Matthew a shake of his lance before turning his pony toward camp.

"Now, tell me what the hell's going on? I know White Cloud and half this group speaks English. Why'd you talk in that Comanche jabber of yours?" Cotton asked.

"I did it so you couldn't understand and butt in."

"So I wouldn't butt in? Who do you think is in charge around here, anyway?"

"White Cloud. Look around us. There's close to thirty armed warriors in this camp. I aim to get back to my wife and children in one piece. Now, I know what the law says," he said, halting his horse in front of a large teepee. "but I think the safety of you and your men would mean more to the wives and the citizens of Leon, than getting the chance to see Douglas Hancock get hung."

"So, what'd you do, tell them they could have Doug all to themselves?"

"Something like that." He turned to give Cotton a warning glance. "You can get mad and explode back in town all you want. Just be careful what you say and what you do right now, because these people are plenty angry. Three Horns was a war chief, and they're not taking this too well." Matthew slid to the ground and faced White Cloud.

"I thank White Cloud for allowing us to witness justice, but I wish to see Three Horns before I see the white dog who hurt him." The chief nodded and led the way toward a tent where a crowd of people stood out front. Matthew motioned for Cotton to follow. White Cloud held the flap open for them to enter. Gray Eagle, the camp medicine man, stood over the prostrate warrior chanting, while Laughing Brook sat to one side holding their two small children in her arms. Their oldest, a young boy, stood behind her with wet cheeks. Matthew knelt beside the man to look him in the eye.

"Ah, does Manhunter come to gloat over my death?" Three Horns said in a whisper.

"No, Manhunter comes to weep with your wife and children. He will cry for the loss of a great chief with the rest of the warriors."

"But Manhunter and I were to meet in battle. How can this be?"

"The battle of two warriors often ends in respect and friendship. I think that's how ours would have been. We would not have killed each other. We are brothers." He grabbed the man's hand and held it tight.

"Perhaps you are right, Manhunter." A tear trickled down toward his ear as he closed his eyes. "It is time for me to cross over."

"Goodbye, my friend. I will see that Laughing Brook is taken care of." The hand went limp. Matthew rose as Gray Eagle changed his chant from one of healing to a death prayer. Cotton let the flap fall closed behind them as Laughing Brook let out a spine-tingling wail.

Matthew tilted his head back and spread his arms outward as his cry lifted skyward. "My brother Three Horns has gone to our Grandfather. My heart is broken and I shall miss him greatly." He dropped to his knees and cast dust in the air. The words to the song of the eagle returned as though he had sung it only yesterday. He rocked from side to side with his palms turned upward toward the sun, to aid the spirits in carrying his friend to the other side. He then sang a song about Three Horns. It told of the times they rode

together and the games they played. He sang of Three Horns'
bravery on the battlefield and the many hunts they had been
on. The sun crept across the sky, but the words kept welling
up inside, until finally, he finished by telling of his friend's
death. He died bravely like a true Comanche, trying to find
food for his hungry people.

The crowd had gathered in a tight circle surrounding
the front of the teepee, mostly out of respect for Three Horns.
But there were also those who Matthew suspected were
waiting to see what he intended to do next. He slapped the
dust from his knees before snatching Three Horn's lance
from where it leaned against the teepee, and turned toward
Shadow.

"Now it is time to visit the white man who did this."

"Welcome, my brother. At last, Manhunter has come
home," Shadow said with a grin. He lifted his own lance
high. A dozen or more warriors joined in the celebration as
the group moved beyond the row of teepees to where they
found a badly beaten Douglas Hancock tied to a post.

Chapter 81

"Well, now that you've started this whole thing, what's gonna happen next?" Cotton's lips were set in a thin line and the crease between his brows had become noticeably deeper. They were seated inside the largest teepee where several braves and a couple of minor war chiefs were giving their argument for the death penalty.

"It will be up to White Cloud. He will try to get everyone to agree, but he has the final say."

"And what about me? Don't I get a chance to say anything? I am supposed to be the law 'round here."

"Shhhh, don't talk so loud. You're disturbing the proceedings."

"Well, excuse me," Cotton said, folding his arms. A handsome young brave who was busy acting out his account of what happened, fell suddenly to the ground with a cry of pain. "What the hell?" The young man bounced back up and took his place among the witnesses seated in the circle and another took his place.

"Everyone we've heard so far claims they were present and actually saw Douglas shoot Three Horns. They were hunting antelope when they heard gunshots far off. Shadow says he recognized my Sharps, but it was far away, so they never thought much about it. Then they heard someone fire a pistol just over the next hill and Three Horns went to investigate. That's when Douglas Hancock appeared and shot him. Grey Wolf claims Douglas was holding the pistol in his hand when he ran into Three Horns."

"I suppose they're all for stringing him up."

"Something like that." Matthew placed a hand on Cotton's arm as White Cloud began to address them. "He says it's your turn. He wants everyone to know what the white chief has to say. I don't have to tell you to be careful."

"I've done this type of thing before, boy," he said, rising to his feet. "Here, you tell these folks what I got to say." Cotton waited until Matthew had completed the introductions, then cleared his throat.

"I've known White Cloud nigh onto twenty years now. I sat in his tent and ate bread with him back when I wore the blue army uniform. I was present when his son, Little Wolf was born. I was also present, and ordered my men to stand at attention, while Manhunter sang the death chant as Little Wolf went to meet his Grandfather. White Cloud knows I am an honorable man." The chief nodded his assent.

"I am honored that White Cloud would ask for my counsel when one of his own people has been killed. That just goes to prove that White Cloud himself is an honorable man. Now, the fact is, that fellow you got tied up out there is a no good coyote that's done nothing but hurt folks all his life long. We were chasing him when he ran right smack into your hunting party. I was hoping to take him back to Leon to stand trial for murder. Then I was gonna take him out and hang him. Now, I'll do just that, if you let me. And I'll add to the charges against him that he murdered Three Horns, and all these witnesses here are welcome to come and testify in court. And everyone of you are invited to watch me hang him. That's my counsel, and that's what I'm asking you to let me do." He waited while the men discussed the proposal amongst themselves. There were a few nods here and there, mingled with those who were adamantly opposed to the idea.

It was Shadow who finally stood to his feet and addressed Cotton in English.

"Very fine speech, Sheriff, very fine. But you failed to tell these people one little detail. If we allow you to take this man back for trial, there is no guarantee that he will be found guilty and be hanged, is there?"

"No, but..."

"Especially for killing an Indian. Now, he might be hung if he did indeed kill a white man, but be honest with me, Sheriff. These people would be wasting their time telling a white man's court about the killing of a Comanche war chief. They would probably give him a medal. Isn't that true?"

"Yes, I suppose it would be that way in some places, but folks in Leon think differently. Take Manhunter here. Folks there like him."

"Yes, let's take Manhunter." Cotton felt his blood pressure rise as the man laughed. "A half-white Comanche with his mother's eyes, who's married to a white woman? He lives in a house with a wooden floor and eats a white man's food while his wife teaches school. I'm sure they like him. What about me, Sheriff? A runaway slave who has chosen to live among those you call savages? Would they feel the same about me?"

"You might be surprised."

"Yes, I'm sure I would," he laughed again, more loudly, "when someone puts a bullet in my back. But we're getting off the subject." He turned to Matthew. "Go ahead, Manhunter. Tell them what the white chief said about a fair trial." The man laughed again when Matthew finished. "You should go into politics, Manhunter. You skirted the issues very well. But all that aside, that's not why I'm really opposed to you taking our prisoner back to town with you."

"What is it then?"

"Let me tell you." He stepped back into the center of the circle and raised his arms and spoke to all present while Matthew interpreted into English. "The white man brought my people from a far country and made them slaves. So I ran from the white man's harsh hand that beat my back with whips and put a rope around my neck. I came here," he pointed to the ground, "to live with my Comanche brothers. They are my people now. But the white people came here also, and they killed the buffalo. They also killed our wives and our sons and took our land. They said we have to live like animals on a small piece of land that no one wants, far away from our hunting grounds. They say if we will do this, that they will give us blankets and food. The white man thinks he can take care of the Comanche like he takes care of his dogs." The comment brought a loud murmur from the crowd. "Now the white chief says he will take this man back to be tried in a white man's court. He will tell them how he killed Three Horns. Will the white chief also take care of us like the rest? Will he take justice out of our hands also? That is all I have to say. That is my counsel." Angry voices bounced around the tent as Shadow seated himself with a smile.

"Let me remind White Cloud that if I don't take Douglas Hancock back to stand trial, and if the Comanche kills him, the government of The United States will send men here asking questions." He held up his hand as several braves jumped to their feet, but it was White Cloud's angry voice that calmed them enough for Cotton to continue.

"This is not what I want; you know that. For years I've overlooked the fact that you've refused to join the others on the reservation. I've even talked General McKerney into looking the other way. But the U. S. Marshall is going to ask me what happened out here today, and I don't want to have to tell him you folks killed that man. It's my job to hang him, not yours. I don't like it any more than you do, but that's just the way it is."

After a few more minutes of arguing among themselves, White Cloud asked for Manhunter's opinion and Cotton sat quietly as Matthew addressed them in their native tongue. The crowd grew silent and more than a few smiled and nodded their heads. Matthew sat down and everyone waited as White Cloud weighed the matter in his head. He finally asked for his pipe.

"I have decided to follow Manhunter's counsel. It is the wise choice to follow." Everyone nodded their agreement. "We will smoke on it." He took an ember from the fire and lit the pipe.

"Alright, what's this wisdom of yours that everyone finds so all-fired pleasing?" Cotton said as the pipe was passed around. "Did you tell them they can have his scalp?"

"No, not one of them is going to touch a hair on his head. He'll stand trial."

"Good, when can we take him out of here?"

"You can't. We're not going to try him; God is."

Chapter 82

Douglas Hancock kicked and fought against the rawhide thongs as the warrior gave them a jerk to make sure they were tight. He had been tied to a post all night with little food or water. Now, he was lying on his back, stretched across a decaying log a mile outside the Comanche camp. "You can't leave me here like this," he said, as Cotton propped his foot on the log to stare at him.

"Don't think I've got much say in the matter, son. I did my best to argue your case, but that brave you shot died, and he was a Comanche war chief. You're lucky they're willing to let The Great Spirit handle the matter, 'cause I've seen them skin a man alive for doing less."

"What are they going to do to me?" His breathing was labored as he tugged against the ropes.

"Nothing, is my understanding. You're on your own now. If you can break free before you croak in the sun, or before some varmint gets to you, they'll accept it as God's will and let you go. Of course, Manhunter will be around just in case you do, and he'll cart your sorry carcass back to Leon to stand trial. Then I'll get the pleasure of hanging you myself. So, your goose is cooked no matter how you look at it."

"You can't do this. You have to get me out of here."

"Now, how am I supposed to do that? Fight the whole blamed tribe? I'd only get a bunch of good folks, including myself, killed, and frankly, I don't think you're worth that much trouble."

"Please, I'm begging you."

"That's kinda hypocritical don't you think? You killed at least four people I know of, and probably more. Now you're begging me for mercy? Na." Cotton shook his head and frowned. "It kinda goes against my grain leaving you here like this, me being sheriff and all. But I mulled it over these past few hours, and I don't reckon I'll start another Indian war just to save your hide. I'd only have to hang you anyway. So, I'm gonna take the posse back to their camp and wait. Manhunter'll let me know how you fair."

"Jesus, no," he said, as Cotton turned away.

"Guess these Comanches are more civilized than I thought," Smokey said, biting into a plug of tobacco. "I run across a situation sorta like this down Texas way a while back, where a rancher kilt a young Apache for no good reason. And they taken him out and buried him up to his neck near an ant hill and propped his mouth open with a stick." He spat and wiped his mouth with the back of his hand. "Didn't take them ants long to find out where dinner was, I can tell you that."

"Go to hell. When I get out of here, I'm going to kill you real slow," Douglas said, tugging on the tongs.

"But I ain't seen no ants hanging round here to speak of." Smokey paused to look skyward as a shadow swept across them. "You know, it's a funny thing about turkey buzzards. Most folks think they like eating dead things, but that ain't really so. Now, you take that feller up there." He pointed skyward. "He likes fresh meat just same as you and me. Only thing is, the Lord made him kinda big and slow, so's he can't hunt and kill things like a hawk or an owl. So he has to settle for what he can get, which is mostly dead critters. But when he finds something that's crippled and can't get around too good or fight back, why he'll settle for a fresh steak any day. Well whadda ya know. Look," he said, pointing toward several other large shadows starting to circle overhead. "He's done called his entire family to supper. See you 'round, Doug." He spat once more and turned away.

"You can't do this to me," Douglas yelled, but it was as though the man couldn't hear him. "I'm begging you, cut me loose." Smokey paused to spit once more, then kept walking toward the group of Indians sitting near a campfire a couple hundred yards off to his right. "I know you can hear me, you bastard. Get back here and cut me loose." The man kept walking.

Douglas stared up at the sky. There were five of them floating in a wide circle. *Never heard of such a thing. He's only trying to make you frightened, Douglas. Don't give them the pleasure.* He pulled and twisted his wrists back and forth until they burned, but the thongs only seemed to get tighter. He fell back against the log in exhaustion and gazed upward. He blinked several times against the sun before deciding there were actually six buzzards circling in their odd formation. Was it his imagination, or were they closer? He glanced toward the men seated at the campfire.

"Come back here and cut these ropes, damn you. Do you hear me? Cut the ropes." His screams seemed to float away on the breeze to die.

Chapter 83

"What sort of game is that they're playing?" Al Meeks said, watching the group of Indians gathered around the deerskin. He and Smokey were the only ones who chose to stay with Matthew. The brave he was watching grabbed a handful of sticks painted with colorful stripes with strange markings carved in their sides. He held them high for everyone to see, before tossing them across the playing surface. The men immediately began arguing and gesturing toward the deerskin.

"It's like shooting dice. A crap game," Matthew said. "The points are tallied by the way the sticks fall. Certain colors touching each other mean more points than if the sticks are separate. And if the markings are facing upward instead of toward the skin, the player gets extra points."

The player finally gave in with a sigh of disgust, as another player gathered up the sticks and gave them a toss. Then whole scene repeated itself. "The arguing, of course, is a major part of the game. It wouldn't be the same without it."

"Do they ever get angry enough to fight?" Al said, as one brave began pounding on the skin with his fist.

"Seldom. Right now they're just having fun. No one's really mad at all."

A brave at the next group stood and pointed toward the prisoner. One of the vultures had landed and was hopping toward Douglas. Everyone jumped to their feet at once and began arguing amongst themselves and gesturing toward the man. "Now they're betting on whether or not that bird is going to get him, or whether the gods are going to save him," Matthew said. The bird took flight as Douglas shook his head violently and screamed. Several Indians laughed as they received payment of beaded belts, wristbands and other trinkets from the losers. They seated themselves and the games continued.

A half an hour or so later another Indian jumped to his feet and pointed. Two buzzards were already on the ground and a third was landing. The betting grew heavy as the birds hopped toward Douglas. "Do you think..." Al started to say, but Matthew held out a hand to silence him as he craned his neck for a better view.

One of the birds took to flight as the prisoner shouted and jerked like he was having convulsions. The second bird seemed braver and flapped his huge wings to land on the fallen log just above Douglas' head. "Oh, Jesus," Al said as the black creature began pecking at the man's face. The third creature leaped to plant his claws in Douglas' chest and started tearing at his shirt collar with his hooked beak. The air suddenly turned black as the remaining birds dropped from the sky to join in the meal. The small band of Comanches grew quiet and solemn as the vultures covered the log like a black shroud. They began collecting their blankets and game pieces and wandered silently toward their village.

"Is congratulations out of order, Manhunter?" Shadow said.

Matthew was silent.

"Yes, I suppose it might be. But I didn't believe you would actually allow the gods to judge the man, regardless of what he had done. I thought you'd disappear and slip up from behind the log to cut the bindings and let him go." Matthew glared as he continued.

"Oh, but of course, you would have taken him to your white village to stand trial. That is your way."

"Three Horns was my friend. We grew up and hunted this land together with Little Wolf. We shared meat over the campfire. He was present when I married Prairie Flower and brought presents when my son was born. He not only saved my life once, he was also my friend." Matthew turned his gaze toward the log. "Douglas Hancock deserved to be judged by Comanche law."

"Yes, the Comanche spirit is still strong in you. I was afraid that the white man's ways had weakened you."

"Being Comanche has nothing to do with your clothes or how you live, Shadow. It doesn't even have much to do with the color of your skin or eyes. It's in your heart. You should know that better than anyone."

Shadow held up a huge hand and laughed. "Yes, I forget sometimes myself. Take care, Manhunter." He clasped him by the shoulder. "May the grass always grow green where your feet stand." He turned to join the others on their walk toward the village.

"Hey, come on. Let's get moving," Cotton said, as they entered the village. Some of the men were already mounted while the others checked saddles and equipment.

"Yes, we'd better go," Matthew said. Al had a sudden urge to dash toward the nearest bush and heave.

Chapter 84

"Well, he was layin' across a log when we came across him, and a bunch of buzzards was having themselves a meal," Cotton said, cradling his coffee mug in his palms.

"Oh, dear God," Alice said, covering her mouth with a linen napkin. Vicky and Susan both grew ashen and dropped their forks in their plates. It was Caroline's eyes that grew wide as she leaned close to the table in order to catch every word.

"I'm sorry, but you asked."

"Poor man," Susan said, shaking her head.

"'Poor man?' He was responsible for killing four people including his own son, and you call him poor?" Dave wrinkled his brow. "If we'd gotten him back here alive, we'd have just had to hang him in a day or two anyway. 'Poor man', huh. Where d'you get off thinking he deserves any mercy?"

"What I meant was...the way he went. Ooooo..." she shuddered.

"How do you think he died?" Alice said.

"Don't rightly know." Cotton shrugged. "I wasn't there when he went. and we didn't find no arrows or anything laying around. To tell the truth, there wasn't anyway to tell if he'd been shot or what might have happened. Could've just fallen off his horse, for all we know." He took a long swig of his coffee.

Matthew took his time buttering his biscuit. He knew Cotton was telling them exactly what he had written in his report. He had sworn the posse to secrecy, and Mike Steel was locked tightly behind bars with the promise of a light sentence for his silence. This was the official end of Douglas Hancock. The whole town was abuzz with excitement as tales of fantasy mingled freely with the truth, and no one disputed their validity. But that was the way it had always been. Tales of war and valor always grew larger than the people involved. He laid his knife on the edge of the plate and munched the biscuit silently as the words of those seated at the table floated around him.

He imagined how the first hunters might have returned to their dwellings with their kills draped over their shoulders and told of the fierceness of their prey - how the stories must have grown. He had seen some crude drawings etched on the wall of a cave once, left there by some ancient people. He was sure they had faced real danger in everything they did. But he was also positive that the stories told around their campfires were gigantic in comparison to what had actually taken place that day. The things that had been written in books and passed around bars and trail camps about his own escapades had little to do with truth. The actual events that took place at the Jamison ranch when Vicky fought with Frank Barnes and his gang had long been forgotten. In their place remained the romantic image of the beautiful woman on the cover of the ten cent novels sold in stores. She stood against overwhelming odds with a blazing six-gun in each hand and a Bible tucked under her arm. While only a smattering of truth was sprinkled between the pages, this was still the Vicky people chose to accept and hold dear to their hearts.

But he was as guilty as everyone else. He had said nothing earlier in the day when Caroline asked about Lowell Ollar.

"He got shot, honey," Cotton said, patting her golden hair.

"I didn't hurt him real bad then?"

"That scratch across his belly? Na, but he deserved every inch of it. You more'n likely saved your mother's life. You probably saved all your lives, to tell the truth. That man was plain crazy."

"I thought I stuck him pretty hard. There was blood on my knife." Her hand shook as she held it up in front of her.

"I shot him, Caroline." Al Meeks squatted in front of her and took her hands. "He was on foot when we caught up with him. I don't know where his horse was at the time. Come to think of it, I don't know where it is right now," he said, glancing toward Dave who shrugged.

"God only knows. Charlie Stewart ran it to death, remember?"

"Oh, yes. Anyway, he had a gun and made it plain he didn't want to go back to jail. So," he lowered his eyes, "I shot him. I was very angry at the time for what he did to Ida, and for what he put you and Mark and your mother through inside the store. I know it wasn't right, and I hope you can forgive me."

"Wasn't right? I don't see how you had any choice in the matter," Smokey said, spitting and wiping his mouth. "I seen it with my own eyes. Lowell already had his iron pulled and was fixin' ta bore young Al when I come up on 'em. But Al whips out his own gun and plugs him right between the eyes." Caroline gasped and gripped Al's shirt sleeve.

"Yep," Smokey continued. "I've seen Cotton and yer daddy pull their irons afore. And I seen Wyatt Earp whip his out down in Dodge City onc't when a young puncher got ram-bung-shoos. But Al here's quicker'n 'em all put together."

That wasn't too damn smart, Smokey, Matthew thought as the crowd gathered around to hear his tale. *Every two-bit gunman in Kansas is going to be looking for him now.*

He'll either get killed or wind up having to kill someone for real next time.

"So, what's going to happen now," Alice said as she started removing empty plates from the table.

"I'll finish filling out my report and give it and the money we recovered to Silas so he can rule the case closed. Then we'll bury the dead and try to pick up where we left off," Cotton said, holding out his cup for Vicky to refill.

"That sounds fine, but there's a few things you men seem to have forgotten." Alice set the stack of empty plates back on the table and leaned close to glare at him.

"I don't think so. But if I have, what is it?"

"What's going to happen to Lillian Hancock and Ida's baby? Neither of them have any family left. They're both orphans, Harvey. Who's going to take care of them? You just can't turn them loose on the prairie to die."

"I believe that's in the process of being taken care of," Matthew said, studying the pattern on the handle of the butter knife. "Jim Larkin's talking it over with his wife right this minute."

"What on earth for?" Vicky said. "Is he thinking of taking them in to live at his ranch?"

"He says Lillian's about the same age as Karan would have been if she were still alive. She even looks something like her with her long black hair. Even wears the same perfume. And," he grabbed for the last biscuit as Alice started to remove the platter, "I think they'll be good for each other. Give him something to love besides his horses."

"Well, I think it's wonderful. When did all this take place?"

"Awhile ago. Before we got back to town." He took a bite.

"Why didn't you tell us, instead of making us worry?" Alice said.

"I didn't know you were worrying." He held his cup out for a refill.

"No, you can choke on that biscuit. It'll serve you right, Matthew Blue," Alice intercepted the coffeepot, "making me worry myself sick over that poor woman and baby. You ought to be ashamed of yourself." She mumbled all the way to the kitchen.

"And what about you, Mr. Meeks? What are you planning to do now that your search is over?" Vicky said.

"I don't know. Go back to my father, I guess. Although I kind of like it here," he said looking around as though the dining room had no walls.

"Noooo, I'll miss you!" Caroline crinkled her brow.

"Don't whine, honey," Vicky said placing a hand on her daughter's arm.

"You're more than welcome to put down roots here in Leon. Folks around here seem to like you enough," Cotton said filling his pipe.

"Yes, but you don't seem to have an ocean or much use for large ships here. That's all my family has ever done, you know."

"Oh I don't know. We do have prairie schooners. I know they're not as big as the ships you're used to, but they seem to get the job done." Matthew got up from the table and paused as everyone stared at him. "Well, the things brought in on the ships back east have to get somewhere don't they? And they get where they're going by wagon or railroad. So, the way I see it, there is a need for some sort of shipping company out here. That is the one thing that Douglas Hancock was telling the truth about." He nodded. "Think about it."

"Knew I kept him 'round him for some reason other than causing me trouble," Cotton said, fishing for a match in his vest pocket.

"Come on." Matthew took Mark by the hand and lead the boy to the front porch, where he instantly began to pester Alice's grey cat who had been sleeping in the sun. The excited discussion drifting through the open window caused him to smile. Opening a shipping company in Leon didn't really make good business sense, seeing as El Dorado was much larger and lay only ten miles or so to the northeast. He took the makings out of his shirt pocket and began rolling a smoke.

There were plenty of wagon trains cutting their tracks across the prairie as it was. And while the railroad ran through Leon, it also had stops in Wichita and Dodge City. Their rails would always bring more items into Leon than they took out. And local farmers and ranchers would always be taking their cattle and goods to other markets. But that was a small price to pay for having the privilege of being able to see the sun rise and set across your own property. He'd been in those larger cities and all he saw was a bunch of buildings and smoky locomotives. Leon might indeed grow into a large city some day, but Matthew hoped and prayed he'd be long gone when that day came. Common sense told him the community was too small to support a large shipping company like the one Albert Meeks owned, but he liked it that way.

Matthew chuckled as he lit his cigarette. Caroline's high-pitched voice carried a life-and-death message as she pleaded with her new friend to move here permanently. She was the one person he could think of who might be able to cause a smart business man like Al Meeks to make a dumb business decision. His own heart had melted a million times as he stared into those big eyes and listened to her pleading. *Damn, I hate to think what she'll be able to do when she's full grown.* He shrugged. *Probably most anything she wants, just like her mother.*

~   ~   ~

The men from El Dorado arrived at their doorstep the following day. "Cleopatra, oh my God, what have the done to you?" Otto Mauerman ran his hand across the skin tacked to the side of the barn.

"Did you have to kill her? Do you have any idea what that animal will cost to replace?" Richard Whiteman waved his arms in the air.

"I didn't kill your lion, my wife did. But you can bet your life I would have if I had the chance. It attacked our daughter, killed three of my best horses, and almost killed our dog."

"I'm sorry, I didn't know. I hope your daughter is alright."

"Yes, she's fine, but it scared the hell out of us."

"Good...that she's alright, I mean. I don't have much money, Mr. Blue, but I'll try to repay you for your horses."

"No, I'd rather that the men who pried the cage open pay for the horses."

"Yes, that does seem fair, doesn't it?"

"I think that can be arranged," Sheriff John Sattler said. "Might be quite fitting at that."

"Tell your man he can have that hide if he wants it." Matthew said. "I think Vicky would rather forget the whole thing. We all would."

Chapter 85

"Matthew?"

"Mmmm?"

"Would you really have shot my leg off?"

"Are you kidding?" He rolled over to stare in her face.

"You were angry. And the way you said it, I thought..." he cut her off by kissing her lightly on the lips.

"Victoria Blue, I thought you knew me better than that. Yes, I was angry. And I'll get angrier if you ever try something like that again. But I love you too much to do anything that would hurt you. The fact is," he grinned and threw the quilt off the bed, "I love your legs too much to shoot them off."

"Matthew Blue, what in the world do you think you're doing?" she said as he began kissing her toes.

"I love your toes. And see how pretty your legs are?" He jerked her nightgown up over her knees and held it as she tried desperately to push it back down. "Both of them. I wouldn't dare hurt either one." He kissed both ankles and began working his way up past her calves.

"Matthew, stop it. The children might hear."

"They're both asleep. Speaking of children," he kissed her stomach, "hello, Luke. How are you this evening?" His breath felt hot as he kissed her soft skin several more times.

"Matthew?" She grabbed his head in both hands. "Come here." Her lips covered his as she pulled him toward her.

~   ~   ~

The sound of horses outside the window caused him to leap from the bed and grab his rifle.

"What is it, Matthew?" Vicky said as he gripped the door latch.

"Nothing, just stay right there." He motioned with his hand. "Shhhhh, Tippy, quiet," he said as the growling dog bristled in the middle of the room. "It's okay." The dog pattered across the floor to poke its nose past his leg as he pulled the door open.

"Manhunter's bed must be warm and filled with joy. It causes him to sleep late." Shadow's pony pranced back and forth in front of the porch. There were two braves and a woman mounted on ponies at the far end of the yard. One of the braves held a rope tied to a small buckskin mare. The sun was just starting to break the morning sky.

"Yes, my bed is warm. What brings Shadow and his friends to my home?" He could feel Vicky and the children crowding in the doorway behind him. Shadow motioned, and the one holding the rope brought the buckskin to the porch.

"For the young Comanche princess." He nodded toward Caroline. "She has white hair and eyes like the sky, but her heart is Comanche. You have taught her well, Manhunter."

"For me?" Caroline bounded past them in her nightgown and bare feet. "Oh, can I Mama?" She looked back pleadingly.

"Yes, you may accept the gift. That is very kind of you, Mr. Shadow." The big man smiled as Vicky gave a small curtsey in her nightgown. "Oh, Caroline, don't," she said, as the girl took the rope from the Indian and tried to leap on the horse's back.

"The pony is gentle like a bird," Shadow said, and motioned for the brave to help her onto the horse, "but it has the heart of a cougar. She will take the princess far from danger when it is needed." Caroline's bare legs gripped the pony's sides as she raced it to the pond and back again. "See?" he said with pride, as Caroline turned the pony in tight circles, first to the left and then back to the right.

"The horse is well trained, Black Shadow. Is it yours?" Matthew said.

"No, the pony belonged to Three Horns. Laughing Brook said he talked of your daughter much and told her how he wanted their children to be like her. He planned to give the horse to her before he died." He motioned again and as the woman trotted her pony toward them in the twilight he could see it was Laughing Brook. She dismounted as Caroline slid off the horse's back to make a dash for the house, only stopping long enough to offer a quick "Thank you" to Shadow as she passed.

"Caroline," Vicky said, grabbing her daughter's arm, "the horse belonged to Three Horns, Laughing Brook's husband." She nodded toward the silent woman.

"Oh, thank you, thank you. I love her." She ran to hug Laughing Brook and disappeared back inside the house.

"Well, it looks like we've lost her for the rest of the day." Vicky glanced toward the door. "I'm sorry for my daughter's rudeness," she said as she took Laughing Brook's hands. The woman smiled and nodded. "But I'm more sorry about you losing your husband." She folded her in her arms and kissed her cheek. "You're welcome to bring your children and live with us. I would love to have you."

"Thank you, but I will stay with my people. Will you come to see me?"

"As often as I can."

"I wish to know you better, my sister." Laughing Brook kissed her cheek before climbing on her horse.

"Oh, I'm sorry, I'm the one being rude. Won't all of you please get down and rest here on the porch? If you'll give me a few minutes to get dressed, I'll fix everyone something to eat."

"That will not be necessary, but thank you," Shadow said. "We must be going." He turned his pony to leave, but turned it back again to face Matthew. "I know we have exchanged harsh words, Manhunter, but you are a true Comanche. You will find our people on the reservation when you choose to see my face again."

"How does White Cloud feel about joining the others on the reservation?" Matthew stepped to the yard.

"It is his counsel that we go. He is tired of seeing our people go hungry and die needlessly like Three Horns. He says if the white people want to chase and kill each other, let them do so, but they should leave the Comanche alone."

"Ride well, Shadow," Matthew said, clasping the man's wrist in a strong grip.

"May the grass grow green under your feet, Manhunter."

Matthew stood silently watching as they disappeared over the small rise opposite the pond. Vicky slipped her arms around his waist and leaned her head against his back. "Does that mean you've made peace with your people?"

"Yeah, I guess so." He turned so he could wrap his arms around her in return. "But I was never really at war with them. I had trouble understanding Shadow until these last few days, but I always liked Three Horns and considered him a friend. He just didn't like white people, and had trouble accepting that I married you." Caroline dashed out the door dressed in her buckskin, and led the pony toward the woodpile where she could climb on his back. "That is, until he met her."

"Caroline, you get off that horse right this minute. You haven't eaten or made you bed," Vicky said, pulling from his grasp.

"I will later Mama." She turned the pony in a complete circle before heading it out past the pond. A lame

Tippy hobbled to the edge of the yard to bark and howl after her.

"Caroline Jamison! You get back here this instant." Vicky's blue eyes flashed as she turned to Matthew. "That girl never listens to anything I say. She hasn't even collected the eggs or done her morning chores. You're going to have to talk to her."

"But I have, dear." He grinned and touched the tip of her nose. "That's why Three Horns liked her so much."

End

About The Author

MAJOR MITCHELL is the author of nine novels and two children's books. He lives with his wife, Judy, in Northern California. Mr. Mitchell is a member of The Western Writers of America and a frequent guest speaker at historical meetings and schools on the West Coast. He has written several songs and recorded a CD of traditional folk music. On rare occasions he takes the stage as a singer.

More about the author, his books and photo gallery may be found at www.majormitchell.net.

Correspondence should be addressed to:
Shalako Press
P.O. Box 371
Oakdale, CA 95361-0371

For your reading pleasure, we invite you to visit our Trading Post bookstore.

Other books by Major Mitchell:

The Doña
Mokelumne Gold
Poverty Flat
Dusty Boots
Joker's Play
Manhunter
Canyon Wind
A Reason To Believe
Charlie Shepherd (children's)
The Witch On Oak Street (children's)

Shalako Press

http://www.shalakopress.com